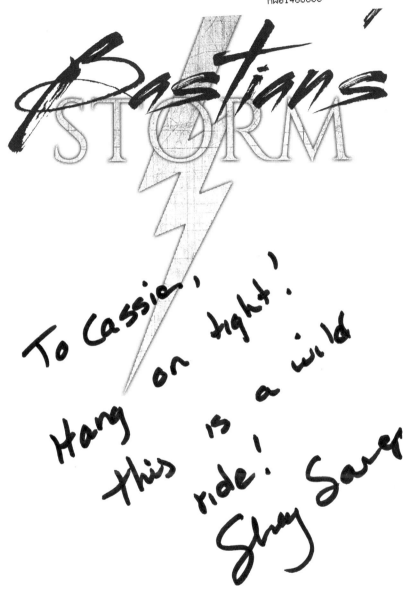

Bastian's STORM

To Cassie,
Hang on tight!
this is a wild
ride!
Shay Savage

Cover Design: Mayhem Cover Creations

Interior Formatting: Mayhem Cover Creations

Editing : Chaya & Tamara

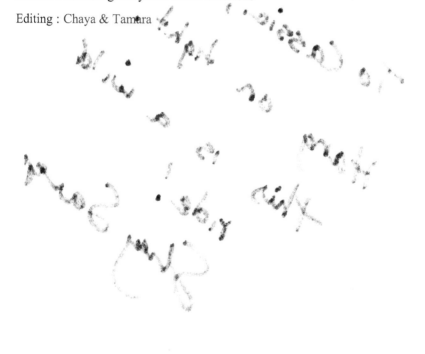

Bastian's Storm

SHAY SAVAGE

DEDICATION

This book is for Sue. You are a true teacher in heart and mind, and I can't begin to list everything I have learned from you. I am eternally grateful for your dedication to my work, friendship, and generous hospitality.

A giant thank you to the wonderful group of people who constantly encourage me, keep me going, and ultimately make sure what everyone reads is quality work: Adam, Candise, Chaya, Heather, Holly, Ian, Jada, Tamara, and of course, everyone on my street team!

Special thanks for all the Surviving Raine fans out there who waited (somewhat) patiently for the continuation of Bastian and Raine's story! You are the reason I write.

TABLE OF CONTENTS

Prologue

I didn't bother to wait until I got outside before I lit my cigarette. The sheer number of people who had shown up for the castaways' welcome home media circus was insane. Maybe I couldn't get trashed like I wanted to, but I still needed some kind of silent *fuck you* to everyone there. Lighting up before I got to the door was all the obnoxiousness I could manage.

Outside, I leaned against the railing surrounding the patio area. I had no idea if I was in a smoking area or not, and I didn't give a shit. There wasn't anyone else out here anyway. They were all inside, monopolizing Raine's attention.

Fuckers.

Somewhere inside my screwed up brain, I knew I was being ridiculous. I didn't care how ludicrous I was, but I still recognized it. When we had been alone on a life raft in the middle of the Caribbean Sea and then on a deserted island together, I'd had her all to myself. Now press people and some asshole congressman who was pursuing the vice presidency next year surrounded her. Sharing wasn't my strongpoint. I'd already shared one woman in my life, and I wasn't going to do that again.

Raine isn't like that.

Logic was irrelevant. Knowing Raine wasn't the same kind of person as Jillian didn't matter when it came to my paranoia. Jillian had taken my trust, used it, and destroyed me with it. She'd taken my unborn child and run away with another man.

I took a long drag off the cigarette and blew smoke up into the air. I watched it dissipate in the warm Miami night and considered just what the fuck I was going to do from here on out. There was no going back to how things were. Raine was so fucking happy being back in civilization again, and though her happiness meant everything to me, all I could think about was the open bar back inside the reception hall and how easily I could sneak in, grab a shot of vodka, and sneak back out to the patio without anyone seeing me. Such is the mindset of a recovering alcoholic.

Was that what I was now?

Was that what defined me?

Fuck if I knew. Raine had made it perfectly clear that it was her or the drink, and the decision was—on some level, at least—a simple one. Vodka was something I desperately, desperately wanted, but I couldn't live without Raine.

A slight scraping sound behind me and to the left brought me from my thoughts. When I turned to look, the cold blue eyes that met mine were unmistakable.

Landon.

Every cell inside my body went on high alert like a decompression alarm in an airplane. All the oxygen seemed to evacuate my lungs, and there weren't any masks in the area to secure around my head.

Inside his gaze, I could practically see the words forming in his mind. I was unfocused. I hadn't heard him approach. I was unaware of my surroundings, vulnerable, and stupid. The scraping sound from his foot was completely intentional. He could have killed me where I stood, buried in my own thoughts.

"Sebastian," he said with a slight raise of his left eyebrow.

All my flight-or-fight impulses went into high gear. I couldn't seem to find any words, didn't have anywhere to run, and was pretty sure I wasn't prepared for a fight against the man who taught me everything I knew about how to kill people. With what little breath I had inside of me, I took another draw on the smoke and tried to look nonchalant.

"Landon," I replied, but my voice choked slightly; the smoke in my lungs got caught, and I started coughing. I nearly doubled over as the unfamiliar, overly-processed tobacco and nicotine—something I was no longer used to having in my body—ravaged my system and left me gasping.

As I recovered, Landon just watched me with a bemused look.

"Motherfucking Marlboros," I growled.

Landon's smirk widened, but he didn't laugh out loud. He never really did.

"You've lost weight," he commented.

There are certainly some people who would have considered his remark a compliment, but I knew exactly what he meant. I wasn't as big as I had been—I'd lost muscle even before being stranded at sea—and his words held a slight tone of challenge: less muscle, less power. He was calling me weak, and I couldn't argue with him.

"Living off fish and seaweed will do that to ya," I said. I was still trying for nonchalant, but I didn't think I was effective. Landon was still looking at me with his half-grin and raised brow. I tried to pull off a shrug, but it wasn't working. I looked back to the cigarette perched between my fingers, but it didn't seem to have any advice for me.

"You finally let someone in," Landon commented.

I moved my eyes quickly to his as he motioned towards the door leading back inside—back to Raine. My chest tightened, and I wondered just how long he had been in the vicinity and what he might have seen and realized.

Since I first opened my mouth and told Raine about my sordid past, I knew I was putting her in danger. At the time, I had been reasonably convinced it didn't matter. I didn't think we'd ever make it back to the mainland and other people again.

But we had.

"What did you tell her?" he asked as he stepped forward and lowered his voice.

"Everything," I heard myself whisper.

Landon nodded slowly. I had only confirmed what he already suspected.

As I held my breath, he moved closer, turned, and leaned against the railing beside me.

"I should probably kill you both," he said with a minute sigh. He turned his head toward me. "You know I don't want to do that."

He couldn't have cared less about Raine—I knew that. What he meant was that he didn't want to end me, not that he *wouldn't* put a bullet in my head, because he totally would, but he didn't *want* to kill me.

Had he talked to Joseph Franks? Did the Seattle mob boss know where I was and what I was doing? He had to; we had been all over the news since we'd been found. They had even included my real name and my connection as a squealer with the crime lord.

"Leave her alone," I said quietly. "Do whatever the fuck you want with me, but don't touch her."

What should have been a threat came out as nothing more than a desperate appeal. I turned toward him, tossed my smoke to the ground, and tried to stand up a little straighter. I had several inches on him in height, but I always felt small in his presence.

"Please," I said. "Please, just…just let her be."

He stared back at me with his ice-blue eyes.

"Not necessarily my decision," he said.

"Have you talked to him?" I asked quickly. I didn't need to name Franks; he was a given.

"Not since you resurfaced," Landon said. "It's only a matter of time."

"I won't say a fucking thing, I swear," I told him. "And she won't either."

Landon tilted his head to one side but didn't comment.

"Please," I said again, "let me have this."

I looked into his eyes, and for a moment, they softened uncharacteristically. In that instant, he was the father I never had and I, the prodigal son. His chest rose and fell slightly as he breathed deep and considered me.

"I tried to keep you out of the light," he said. If I didn't know him better, I could have sworn there was a hint of remorse in his voice. He shook his head slowly. "You had to go and get yourself on the fucking news. Damn, Bastian—how am I supposed to cover that up? You're out in the open, sober, and hooked up with the daughter of Henry Gayle. Do you really think he's going to ignore that?"

"I didn't fucking do it on purpose!" I growled.

"Do you think that matters?" Landon took a step closer to me, his eyes cold again. "Do you think that changes anything? In the eyes of the cops, you're a potential source for more information. In the eyes of Franks, you're a potential threat. You knew that the minute you walked up to the Seattle PD and told them about that night. You told them he'd killed two cops, and since then, I have done everything I possibly could to keep you hidden, to keep you alive."

He shook his head slowly.

"And now you come back like this? With *her*?"

I could practically hear my own heart beating.

"Convince him," I said.

Landon rolled his eyes, and I reached out and grabbed his forearm.

"You can convince anyone of anything," I said. "Tell him I'm not a threat. Tell him I'll behave. I swear to God, Landon-"

"You don't believe in God," Landon interrupted, shaking his arm free of my grip.

"Then I'll swear on whatever the fuck you want," I snarled back. "I'll do anything—just keep him away from her."

Landon stared at me with his stoic and intense eyes.

"He's going to want you to fight," he said. "Prove your loyalty again."

"I can't do that anymore." I shook my head quickly. "Not with her around me."

"You may not have a choice."

"You told me there is always a choice," I reminded him.

"Yeah," he agreed, "live or die. You've managed to weave yourself a noose and wrap it around your own neck."

"There was nothing I could do about that," I insisted. "I didn't even know—not until we were in Venezuela. Whoever went digging for information found what he wanted. It's not like I told anyone my real name; they already knew."

"He might not believe that."

"Convince him." I tried to make my words sound like a command, but we both knew it was a plea. If Landon went to bat for me, I had a chance. If he didn't back me up, I was going to have to grab Raine and get back into hiding as quickly as possible, and I was fairly certain she wouldn't go willingly.

"I'll try to hold him off," Landon said. "I don't know how long that's going to last."

With a sharp breath, I closed my eyes in a moment of relief. When I looked back up, I caught a strange expression in Landon's eyes—one I hadn't seen before. I had no idea what it meant, and he went icy as soon as he realized I was looking at him again.

"I'll keep quiet," I promised. "Not a fucking word. I swear, Landon."

He nodded.

"Bastian?" Raine's voice fluttered from around the other side of the shrubs lining the doors to the building. I turned my head to look at her and then looked back to where Landon had been standing, but he was already gone.

"Right here," I called out.

"What are you doing out here?" she asked.

"Just having a smoke," I said, fully aware that I no longer had one in my hand. I quickly reached into my pocket, pulled out another one, and pointed it toward the doors. "I couldn't take any more of that shit."

"Well, *that shit* is pretty much over now," she informed me. "Congressman Howard is putting us up for the night in the hotel across the street."

"Congressman Howard wants to shove his dick into you," I growled as I shoved the cigarette into my mouth and lit up.

"Oh, he does not!" Raine said, scolding.

I rolled my eyes.

"Did he get you a room adjoining his?" I asked.

I was being a dick, and I didn't care. I had no doubt what that asshole wanted, and what he wanted was mine. Fucker.

Raine just narrowed her eyes at me.

I shrugged and smoked some more. If she didn't want to admit that he wanted in her panties, that was her problem. If he actually tried to touch her, I was going to be his worst fucking nightmare. I could already see it in my head: the fucker leaning in just a little too close, dropping his hand down to cop a feel of her ass, and me coming up from behind and snapping his neck.

Nah, too quick. I'd have to make him suffer.

Raine's voice brought me out of my musings.

"I'm really tired," she said. "Are you going to come with me or let the good congressman walk me to the suite he has arranged?"

I narrowed my eyes and growled.

"So, you're coming then?"

I growled again, tossed the end of my smoke on the ground, and smashed it under my heel.

"Let's go."

Raine smiled and took my arm.

The suite was actually pretty nice. There was a big living area and a separate bedroom with a king-sized bed. Raine collapsed into it without even taking off her clothes, and I crawled in after her. As Landon's little visit resonated in my brain like a bad pop song, I wrapped my arms around her and pulled her into my chest. I looked to the door of the bedroom and listened closely for any sounds outside, but there weren't any. Still, I pulled her closer and tossed one leg over both of hers.

Raine tucked her head into my shoulder and sighed, content.

"I can't believe how good this bed feels," she said sleepily.

"Hot shower in the morning, too," I replied. I couldn't have cared less, but it was one of the things Raine had missed the most when we were stranded on the island. Remembering one of her other complaints, I knocked my head against the pillow a couple of times. "Nice soft pillow, too."

"Hmmm…"

Hearing her so obviously happy filled me with both joy and dread. Closing my eyes, I thought about our nights in the shelter I had built for her, the sound of the waves as they crashed against the shore, and the steady ocean breeze.

I wanted to go back.

"Sorry I was such a jerk tonight," I told her.

"I know you are," she replied simply.

"That guy is an asshole."

"Who?"

"The politician."

"He didn't do anything wrong."

"If he did, I'd fucking rip his arms off," I promised.

"Bastian!" Raine snapped as she looked up at me. "You can't say things like that!"

I rolled my eyes in the most obvious way possible. I could kill him, and she knew it. She'd seen first-hand what I could do when she was threatened.

"We're back in the real world now," she reminded me.

As if I needed the fucking reminder. I knew exactly where we were, and I was pretty sure I hated it. As stupid as it was, I missed the barely-comfortable-enough-to-doze-off floor of the palm frond shelter at the end of the beach.

I tightened my arms, pulling Raine securely against me.

"Bastian?"

A shudder ran through me.

"I don't know how to do this," I whispered against Raine's hair. "I don't know how to be *us* here."

She wrapped an arm around my chest and held me as tightly as I was holding her.

"I love you," I said as my lips pressed to her neck. The sound of my voice echoed everything inside my body—full of fear and dread.

"I love you, too," Raine replied. She moved her hand up to stroke my hair.

"I don't know how to do this," I said again.

"We'll figure it out," Raine assured me. "It's going to take some getting used to—some trial and error—but we're going to be okay."

I wished I could believe her, but Landon's words continued to echo through my head.

Chapter One

Sometimes it just boiled inside of me.

The fucking anger.

It was directed at nothing and everything. It focused on the sights and the people around me because they were the constant reminder of what I had lost. Sometimes it was even directed at the one person who understood and accepted me for the asshole I was.

It made me hate everything and everyone around me even though I knew it didn't really have anything to do with shit on the outside. It was like a hurricane, churning around in my gut, swirling around and around until I needed to slam my fist into something to keep myself from vomiting. The tension would creep up on me; my entire body would tighten and even begin to shake, and there didn't seem to be anything I could do about it except...

Just one fucking drink.

On the other side of the varnished bar top, at least a hundred bottles were lined up in front of me, just barely out of reach. Every one of them seemed to be singing to me, but the ones up on the top shelf on the right called to me the most—Kettle One, Grey Goose, Skye. I wasn't sure why I tortured myself, but I did.

Every fucking day.

"You sure I can't get you something, buddy?" The bartender leaned over and tilted his head to look at me, asking me the same thing he asked me every day. He was a young guy—probably working here to put himself through school or whatever—and had that bright-eyed smile that probably drove the ladies to up the tip percentages on their bar tabs. I didn't meet his gaze; my focus remained behind him.

With a slight shudder, I pushed away from the bar and stood up.

"I'm good," I lied.

Turning quickly on my heel before I changed my mind, I stomped out of the bar and into the Miami evening heat. Raine would be back from class before too long, and I didn't want to risk having her recovering-alcoholic boyfriend smell like a drinking establishment, even if I had managed to make it through another day without actually ordering a drink. If she knew I was hanging out in a bar during the late afternoons, she'd be pissed, and that was a conversation best avoided. Being close to the shit made my palms itch, and I knew if I opened my mouth and ordered one, the strength it would take to stop it from passing my lips would be more than I possessed. I'd give in.

I'd fail.

I still had a little time before Raine returned, so I headed through Pier Park and down to the beach. There weren't a lot of people around, and I was glad of that. I'd had too many confrontations with locals and tourists alike on this particular beach. Though Raine and I had developed something resembling celebrity status after we returned from being lost at sea, I didn't think that was going to keep me out of jail if I attacked another Bermuda-shorts-wearing fuckhead on the beach.

Removing my shoes, I walked barefoot at the edge of the waves. The tide was coming in, and bits of seaweed sloshed against my toes. There were a few dead jellyfish scattered along the tide line, and bits of broken coral sloshed in and out of the waves. If I closed my eyes and ignored the noise of civilization, I could pretend I was back *there* again.

The island.

Alone with Raine.

My paradise.

Mine, but not hers.

The tension returned. The tsunami inside of me was not unlike the one that capsized my schooner last year—the one that led me to being alone with Raine on a raft in the middle of the Caribbean Sea with no hope in sight. She had no one but me to make sure she had water, food, and eventually shelter on an uninhabited island. She only had me to protect and provide for her.

Like a fucking caveman.

I loved it.

On the other hand, Raine liked hot showers, diet variety, and hanging out with her friend Lindsay and Lindsay's boyfriend, Nick. She liked living in a high-rise apartment with air-conditioning and an elevator. She liked shopping at the mall and being able to cook food on an actual stove. She liked being able to go to school to learn about ecology and the conservation of the Everglades. She liked being around people.

I hated it all.

The beach was the only place I felt even remotely comfortable outdoors and then only when it was nearly deserted. It reminded me of being shipwrecked and alone with my Raine, who didn't even want to remain anywhere near the ocean. It took some convincing to get her to agree to stay in Miami—Raine wanted to return to Ohio when we were rescued—but she ultimately let me have my way. She got into the ecology program at the nearby university and discovered her love of the Everglades. I would have preferred a tiny house right up next to the water but settled for a condo in Miami Beach instead.

Raine never went near the beach. She did at first, but she'd end up having nightmares afterward, so she stopped coming down here. She said seeing it from the condo's balcony was plenty for her, and she didn't even go out on the balcony much. She said it was because I was always smoking out there, but I knew it was because she didn't like seeing the ocean waves and listening to the surf.

Everything she loved, I hated. Everything that frightened her, I loved.

How's that for fucked up?

For the most part, we were making it work. Despite the major difference in opinion about the island where we lived alone for weeks, everything was just fine when we were together. Raine was definitely enjoying her studies at the University of Miami, and my nasty moods usually evaporated around her. I couldn't help but kind of wish she would change her mind about living in a remote area next to the water, but I wasn't going to push the issue even if living around all these people wasn't my preference.

I loved her, and loving her was the only thing that kept me sane.

Well, reasonably sane.

I closed my eyes for a second and took a deep breath. The ocean wind brought the scent of brine and sea life to me. When I opened my eyes again, I nearly walked right into a couple on the beach but managed to just brush up against the guy's shoulder as he went by.

"Hey, asshole! Watch where you're going!"

My hands clenched involuntarily as I turned and stared into the eyes of the motherfucker who had just passed me. Dressed in bright blue swim trunks with fucking starfish on them, the guy was maybe in his mid-thirties with light brown hair and bushy eyebrows. The chick in the purple bikini with him couldn't have been more than twenty-five. I wasn't sure if he was trying to impress her or what, and I didn't really care. The slight amount of calm graced to me by the ocean waves was gone, and in its place was the storm of fury I had been trying to dodge all afternoon.

Without a word or a thought, I hauled back and punched him in the chest.

Though I hadn't hit him all that hard, it felt good to have my knuckles connecting to someone's body. Really good. He went down like a fucking ton of bricks despite the pulled punch, and the corners of my mouth turned up.

"Oh my God!" the girl screamed. "What the hell is the matter with you?"

She dropped down on the sand and helped the guy back up to a sitting position as I turned away from the water and headed back up to the street. I could hear both of them yelling for someone to call the cops, but I didn't pay any attention to them, and the few other souls on the beach seemed to just stand in shock and stare as I passed. I made my way quickly to the pavement, yanked on my shoes over my sandy feet, and headed home. It was later than I thought, and I had to jog to the apartment steps to make sure I was home before Raine. I checked over my shoulder a couple of times, but no one seemed to be chasing after me.

Our one-bedroom condo wasn't too big, but it was in a posh area of town and cost as much as my schooner had. It had one bedroom, two balconies, and a decent-sized living area that combined the kitchen, living, and dining area into one big room. It was on the fourth floor of the building, so it didn't take a lot of effort to use the stairs. I hated being on the elevator with other people. They always tried to strike up a conversation, and I was never in the mood for it. After living here for a month, most of them knew exactly who I was, and all those who thought asking me about being lost at sea was a good idea had been proven wrong.

Raine didn't know about most of my encounters with the neighbors, and I was happy to keep her in the dark.

Deceptive?

Yeah, probably, but it could be worse.

The short run from the beach reminded me that I needed to get back into a regular exercise routine. John Paul would be pissed if he knew I wasn't keeping myself in shape, and Landon had made it clear to me the first night we were back that I was losing strength. Maybe some trips to the gym would help me to stop thinking about all the other shit in my life. The condo's fitness center was open twenty-four hours a day, so I could go in the middle of the night to avoid the people. I could do a few miles on a treadmill, hit the dumbbells, and maybe indulge in some squats. I was pretty sure they even had a whirlpool or something I could soak in afterwards.

The only exercise that actually sounded good would be hauling some rocks around to fortify a shelter or foraging the beach for some mussels or crabs, but I was trying hard to convince myself otherwise.

I reached the top of the steps and closed my eyes a moment before inserting the key in the lock and opening the door. I was greeted with neutral colors and the overpriced furniture that came with the place. The luxury condo in front of me was probably a lot of people's dream home, but it wasn't where I wanted to be.

I kicked off my shoes and went out to the balcony off the living room for a cigarette. Being able to buy Marlboros was the only thing I actually liked about living in civilization, but I still sometimes missed rolling my own smokes out of the Indian Tobacco plants I had found on the little island where Raine and I were stranded. I wondered if I could get some of that stuff around here and make my own as I finished the smoke and tossed the butt into a little metal bucket Raine bought for them after the condo association tried to fine me for throwing the damn things off the balcony.

Fuckers.

About ten minutes later, the lock turned again, and my reason for living burst through the door with her hands full of brown paper sacks.

"What's all that shit?" I asked as I took some of the bags from her.

"Dinner," Raine said with a sweet smile. She set two bags on the table while I placed the others on the counter. Raine grabbed some vegetables, beef, and some kind of Asian sauce in a bottle while I put the rest of the groceries in the fridge.

"How was your day?" Raine asked as she chopped zucchini and mushrooms.

"You weren't here," I said, "so it fucking sucked."

Raine looked over her shoulder and smiled at me.

"How do you make that sound so sweet?" she asked.

"Raw talent," I replied with a silly grin.

Raine tossed some of the chopped up food in a big skillet and began telling me about her botany class as she alternated between cooking and setting the table. I probably should have helped, but watching her walk around the kitchen like a domestic goddess turned me on too much to do anything but stare and drool. As far as conversation went, she lost me pretty quickly when she moved into diatoms and how important algae were to an ecosystem. By then she had stopped moving around and swaying her hips, so I snuck out to the balcony for another smoke while she was in mid-sentence.

She must have noticed, because I got quite a glare when I came back in. I offered her a half smile and a wink, but she shook her head at me.

"Rude!" she declared.

I moved up behind her and placed my hands on her hips. I sucked at the place where her neck met her shoulder and heard her sigh. Raine leaned back just enough to put a little pressure against my chest but kept stirring a bunch of vegetables in the frying pan. I moved my lips up close to her ear.

"*Rude am I in my speech, and little blessed with the soft phrase of peace.*"

"What's that from?" Raine asked.

"Othello."

She wriggled a little against me. Every once in a while, that master's degree in English lit was rather handy.

Raine hummed and leaned against me some more, and the closeness of her body reminded me that she had left early this morning. Usually I woke up before her and made sure I claimed her properly before she headed out into a university full of guys but not on Tuesdays when she had an early class. I hadn't been inside of her since last night, which probably explained my overly volatile mood all day.

"Missed you today," I said. I moved my hands around her torso and hugged her against me. I brushed the lower edge of her breast with my thumb.

"I missed you, too," she echoed. "I've got a ton of studying to do tonight, though."

I swallowed, knowing exactly what she meant by that: quick dinner followed by Raine huddled up on the couch in the living room with fifteen books splayed out around her. She'd be so engrossed that I wouldn't get any attention from her at all.

Fuck that.

I grabbed her hips again and pulled her back against me so she could feel exactly what I thought of that idea. I moved my lips back to her throat and trailed kisses from her ear to her shoulder. My cock hardened more as I slid my fingers under her shirt and ran them along the edge of her shorts.

"You're going to make me burn dinner," Raine said as she pushed at my hand. "Maybe tomorrow morning before-"

"Fuck dinner," I snarled. "Turn off the damn stove."

Getting inside of her was far, far more important than food.

"Bastian-"

"Turn it off!"

Reaching farther up under her shirt, I found both of her tits and ran my thumbs over her nipples as I ground into her backside. Raine gasped, and I heard the distinct click of the stove's element being turned off. I wasted no more time. I dropped one hand and lifted Raine up into the air, causing her to squeal and giggle.

My favorite sound in the world.

I didn't give a flying fuck about the dishes and shit already set out on the table in the kitchen. I tore at the button and zipper of her shorts and dropped the top half of Raine in the middle of the place settings. She made a half-assed attempt at moving the plates and silverware out of the way as I pulled open my jeans and leaned over her back.

With my cock in my hand, I rubbed over her slit with the head as her legs dangled over the side of the table. I bent my knees a little to get the right angle and then plunged into her.

"Fuck…yes…"

All the shit from the first part of the day evaporated until there was nothing left except for me, her, and the slight jingling sound of silverware as I rocked into her body. Nothing else mattered.

Small grunts and moans came from Raine as I slid in and out. Reaching up, I pushed her shirt up near her shoulders and rested my hand on her back as the other held her hip for leverage. When I looked down, I could see my cock moving in and out of her with quick jabs. I slowed slightly, reveling in the sight of our bodies meshing together and changing the angle to rub the back side of her clit.

"Oh shit…Bastian…"

"Feel that?" I growled. "Feels so fucking good getting my cock up in you. You like that? Huh?"

"God…yes…please!"

"Please what?" I pulled out until just the head was still in her and then flexed my hips forward until I bottomed out. "You want more of that?"

"Yes! Yes, please!"

I fucking loved it when she begged.

"You're going to make me come," I told her. "All spread out like that. How am I supposed to resist?"

Raine moaned again, and I increased my pace as she moved one hand down to where we were joined. She had to raise her hips a bit to reach, which just gave me a better angle. I grabbed her hand and reached around her waist with the other arm to hold her up a little. Guiding her hand to her clit, I kept my own fingers over hers while she worked herself.

"So fucking beautiful," I whispered. I leaned over her back a bit more and began to thrust in time with the movements of her fingers.

"Ahhh! Bastian!"

"Let it go, baby…come all over my cock."

It didn't take long for her to comply, and as her body tensed around my shaft, I could have sworn we were back there—on our island—lying in the sand with the waves moving over our feet.

"Oh, fuck...yeah..." I grunted. My thighs shook, and I held myself firmly against her as my cock emptied inside her body.

I dropped my head to the middle of her back, panting for a moment. My legs felt like they were going to give out on me, so I couldn't stay connected to her for long. As beautiful as the sight was, she couldn't have been very comfortable splayed out on the table like that, so I pulled out and helped her stand.

"Jesus," Raine muttered as she tried to stand on shaky legs.

I laughed.

"You're so cute when you're freshly fucked," I mused. "Makes me want to do it all over again."

Raine gathered her clothes from the floor, shook her head at me with a big smile, and raced off to the bathroom to clean up. I just used a paper napkin to wipe myself up a bit before yanking my shorts back up and washing my hands. I didn't mind smelling like I just had sex with her, so fuck it.

Raine returned, still flushed and beautiful. She nodded toward the destroyed table display.

"You clean that up."

I smiled, properly chastised and not really caring. I shoved the plates and cups around until they were back in the approximate positions from before our tryst and dropped my ass on one of the chairs to watch Raine finish cooking dinner. After we ate, I sat on the opposite side of the couch and fiddled with a game on my phone while Raine did her studying.

She finally finished and we went to bed. It was late, but I still tried to make up for the quickie in the kitchen by taking her slowly. I rocked into her over and over again until the back of her head was pressed against the pillow and her forehead was covered in sweat.

"Bastian...oh God..."

"So beautiful," I whispered against her ear.

She wrapped her thighs around my hips, and I matched her rhythm until she came apart around me. I followed soon afterward and then held her tight against my chest while she ran her hands over my back.

These were the times I didn't give a shit about where we were. I didn't care that there were hundreds of people living in the same building or thousands of tourists on the beach. Here and now, it was just Raine and I, together.

Peace.

Contentment.

Remembering the random guy I belted on the beach, I couldn't help but feel how much I didn't deserve this shit. Raine was nothing like me in that regard. She was polite, giving, and completely and totally friendly to everyone she came across. If she knew what I had done…

I swallowed hard.

"Tell me the reasons?" I whispered. I looked up at her and felt an odd sense of trepidation. We'd done this before, so I wasn't sure why it made me nervous to ask.

Raine smiled and stroked my cheek. She nodded her head, and I tucked myself into the space between her neck and shoulder to listen. She moved her fingers into my hair and played with the strands by my ear as she spoke.

"I love your strength," she said. She always started with that. "I love the way I feel so safe when you're holding me—like there's nothing in the world that could possibly hurt me as long as you've got me."

"It's true," I said quietly. "I'd never let anything happen to you."

I felt her nod again.

"I love your eyes," she continued, "and the way you look at me sometimes like I'm the only person in the universe. It makes my heart beat faster when you do that. I love the way you want to take care of me all the time. Even when I don't want you to, I know it's because you care about me."

I tightened my grip on her.

"I love that you try so, so hard not to drink. I know it's not easy —it's a daily struggle—but you still endure. You push through it for me. That's part of your strength as well."

My chest rose and fell as I took a deep breath and pressed my lips against her collarbone. I couldn't help but feel a twinge of guilt about my daily trips to the bar, but I still hadn't had a drop since the night my schooner went down.

"Most of all, I love the way you love me," she said. "I love the passion inside of you and how you make me feel like the most desired woman in the world when I'm with you."

"I do love you," I told her.

"I know you do," she replied. She brushed her lips over my forehead. "I love you, too."

I swallowed hard against the tightness in my throat, held her a little closer, and closed my eyes. My mind relaxed along with my body, and I felt her fingers stroking my face as I slipped into slumber.

Smoke burns my eyes. Fifteen people have been slaughtered in front of me, but here I stand, unmoving. Landon holds one of my arms, John Paul the other.

They get to the last one—a cop from one of the smaller districts. I wonder why he's here; it's not his beat. Gunter Darke grabs him and spins him in a circle, and I watch his face change.

Raine takes his place.

I still can't move. I still can't speak.

Gunter pulls her down on her back, and Franks cheers. Four men approach her—a chunky guy, a guy with dreadlocks, one with a buzz-cut, and a guy with a long ponytail.

The uniform worn by the cop is gone, and Dreadlocks tears my T-shirt off of Raine as Buzz-cut and Chunky hold her legs...

I couldn't breathe when I snapped awake. All the muscles in my chest were constricted around my heart and lungs. Sweat ran from my forehead into my eyes, and my limbs shook uncontrollably.

I gripped the edge of Raine's pajamas. I needed her closer to me, but I didn't want to wake her up. I tightened my fingers around the fabric until I could feel my nails in my palms. Pulling her body as closely as I could, I tried to keep myself from shaking, but I wasn't very successful. I did manage to pull air into my lungs, but once I caught my breath, I had to focus on not hyperventilating.

Breathing through my nose, I tried to inhale deeply and let the air out slowly. It just made my chest hurt. I gripped Raine tighter and tucked my head into her shoulder.

Soft fingers caressed the back of my neck.

"Bastian?"

I couldn't answer.

"What's wrong, baby?"

"Nothing," I croaked. The word was utterly ridiculous.

Raine moved her fingers down to my chin and pushed my face to look at her. I did so reluctantly, and as soon as I met her eyes with mine, some of the tension faded, and I could breathe right again.

"Nightmare?"

I nodded.

"Can you tell me about it?"

I shook my head, and Raine nodded in response. She moved one of her arms around my shoulder and the other around my head. She held me against her chest as I tried to regain some semblance of sanity.

Raine knew me so well, it frightened me. Whereas she used to press for more answers, she was now quick with yes-or-no questions I could answer without speaking, and she knew when to give me a little mental space. Eventually I'd tell her what the dream was about, and she knew that.

Still, even when I heard her reasons, sometimes it didn't make the feeling of inadequacy go away. Maybe it was all from the lack of affection during my fucked up childhood, like Raine thought, or maybe it was because the one man who did offer me any kind of parental connection was also the man who taught me how to be a killer—a damn good one.

Maybe it was because I missed being a killer.

"I can't do this," I whispered to Raine as my throat and mouth went dry. "I want a drink so fucking bad."

"I know, baby," she replied, "but you're stronger than that."

I closed my eyes a moment and shook my head vigorously.

"Only on the outside." I met her eyes again. "You have more strength inside than I do."

She moved her fingers into my hair and brushed it away from my sweaty forehead.

"You have more than you know," she said. "You work at it every day, and every day you get stronger on the inside too."

Everything in my head wanted to deny it. I didn't feel strong. I just felt like drinking or fucking.

"I wanna fuck you," I said. I saw the little twinge in her eye at the phrase but couldn't bring myself to regret it.

"Always so crass," she muttered.

I fought with my head for a way to explain.

"When I'm inside you, everything changes," I told her. "It's not about getting my dick wet; it's about being so close to you that I can feel your strength in me. When I feel your arms on my back, and you hold me against you, that's when I feel strong."

Raine's eyes softened and glistened a little. She ran her fingers over my jaw lightly as her eyes moved back and forth between mine. I wasn't sure if she got it or if it made up for me being the crude asshole that I was, and just when I figured I couldn't even make sense to myself, let alone her, she spoke.

"Fuck me, Bastian," Raine said. "Hard."

Without hesitation, I moved to straddle her. Pulling her up by her shoulders, I reached behind her head and pulled her mouth to mine. Our tongues touched with a frantic pace, and I wanted nothing more than to devour her. She gripped the back of my neck, holding my mouth to hers as she returned the kiss with as much passion as I gave her.

I couldn't wait any longer.

Rising up on my knees, I pulled Raine into my lap. She reached down and angled my cock towards her opening, and I lifted her up and then slammed her down on it. She leaned backwards, and I held the small of her back with one hand while the other moved up to caress her breasts.

She moaned, and I thumbed her nipple as she worked herself up and down on my cock. Her skin was so soft on the palm of my hand, and I stroked each breast before reaching back around and grabbing her ass with both hands.

I took over, bringing her up and slamming her back down over and over again until sweat covered both of us. Raine's breath covered the skin of my chest and shoulder as she held my biceps to try to keep her balance.

As if I would ever let her fall.

Our eyes met through a lusty haze, and I had no words for the emotions spreading through my body. There was want and need; there was love, but there was also so much more. Looking at her was like gazing into the eyes of an angel—a guardian angel—one who was sent from heaven just to save my sorry soul.

Raine's cries echoed through the small bedroom, bouncing off the walls and ceiling, and creating the most enticing music to my ears. Laying her back down on the mattress, I grabbed her knee and pulled it up against my hip as I lay over the top of her and continued.

She wrapped her legs around me and dug her heels into my backside. The pressure from her lower embrace was more than enough to increase my pace to a furious pounding. My cock plunged in and out of her with long, hard strokes.

I panted with each penetration and gripped her ass and back as I drove home with each thrust of my hips. I dropped my forehead to her shoulder as my gut began to quiver, and my balls constricted. The tingling continued, built up, and exploded through my cock and into her body as I let out an incoherent cry.

Finally satiated, I slowed and eventually stilled, collapsing on top of her and trying to catch my breath. Raine's legs tightened around my waist, and her arms gripped my shoulders. Pressing my lips to her neck in silent thanks, I rolled us both to our sides.

"You are my world," I whispered against her skin. "I can survive anything as long as I have you with me."

My storm was calmed. At least for now, I closed my eyes and slept without dreams.

Chapter Two

The life raft is behind me, and the rope is wrapped tightly around my wrist. I reach out for the dark hair floating in the water, but I can't quite grasp it. Someone's suitcase floats in front of me, and I shove it out of the way. I can't see her anymore. She's slipped under the waves, and it's so dark, I can't find her...

I woke gasping for air, but the warmth of the tiny body next to mine was enough to remind me where I was. I tightened my fingers around Raine's T-shirt for a moment and tucked my face into her hair to breathe in her scent. It calmed me a little.

Initially.

It wasn't enough.

Not wanting to wake her yet again, I pushed myself out of bed and moved into the living room. I found a pack of cigarettes on the table next to the couch and headed out to the balcony. I smoked two down to the filters before I managed to calm myself enough to get the worst of the images out of my head. Leaning back in the patio chair, I closed my eyes and inhaled the nighttime sea breeze.

It didn't feel right to sit in a chair, so I got off of it and sat on the mat by the door. I leaned forward and wrapped my arms around my knees. With my eyes closed again, I listened to the surf and told myself that none of the fucked up shit in my head was real.

The real part was sleeping in the next room.

Reminding myself that being with her was more important than anything else, I pushed off the balcony floor and went inside. I crawled back into bed and wrapped my arms around my Raine. I held her back against my chest and tossed my leg around her thighs. With her pretty much trapped underneath me, safe from dark waves, I finally relaxed. I didn't get back to sleep at all, but focusing on her body lying beneath mine was enough to get me through the night.

Breakfast, however, was a disaster.

"We're out of milk," Raine announced. "We also need dinner stuff for tonight. I was hoping you would grill out."

"Sure," I said over the rim of my coffee cup. Black coffee, nothing added to it. I tried to forget the way it tasted with half the mug full of Kahlua as I thought about Raine's friends coming to dinner. They were coming from Hollywood for the evening to celebrate Lindsay's success at work, and grilling meant less talking to Nick Sinclair, Lindsay's boyfriend.

"Steak, then?"

"Sure," I said again. I tried not to show how much it pissed me off that our Friday, usually the only night of the week Raine didn't spend on homework, was going to be invaded by those two.

"Can you get to the store today?" Raine asked. "I have a study group after class, and they'll be here around six."

"Will you make a list?" I looked up at her expectantly and found myself completely distracted by the way her hair moved as she turned her head to look at me. She'd blown it dry this morning, and it was perfectly smooth. I wanted to run my hands through it. I wanted to wrap it around my wrist and hold her down on the bed while I rammed…

"Of course."

I blinked a couple of times as I tried to remember what we'd been talking about.

Oh yeah—grocery lists.

"Okay, then," I said. "I'll do it."

There was no way I was going to go shopping without knowing exactly what she wanted—been there, done that. Never again. As it was, there would be something major missing, and I'd have to go back out again, but at least it wouldn't be my fault. Not that I minded going back—a crowded market was somehow better than intimate company in the small condo.

Raine kissed my cheek.

"Thank you," she said with a smile.

"You know, if we were still on the island, I'd already have everything we needed all gathered up," I said. "I'd grill for you every night if you wanted. You could make that chowder out of mussels and crabs that went so well with those little sweet potatoes."

Thinking out loud was rarely a good move for me, but my mouth just continued on its merry little way.

"We could maybe plan a vacation there sometime," I suggested. "You know—just you and me for a couple weeks. Maybe even for your spring break. It would be good to be away from here before all the crazies get to town. Then in the summer, we could go a little longer, a month, even-"

"Bastian." Her tone stopped my words, and the look on her face nearly stopped my heart. "You can't be serious."

I felt a little cold but opened my mouth anyway.

"Why the fuck not?"

"You're talking about going back...back to that same island where we were stranded?"

"Well...yeah."

"That's hardly a...a *vacation*!" she said, her voice rising.

"It's not like we'd be *stuck* there," I argued. "We could fly into St. Maarten and rent a boat. I can sail a small one without help, and I could even teach you how to do it. It wouldn't take long to get there, and we could-"

"No!" Raine snapped. She glared at me for a moment as her chest rose and fell with her breath. "Bastian, I was terrified when we were there! I was attacked by a bunch of human traffickers, and I never knew when some hurricane was going to come through and throw us into the ocean! I hated it! I hate that place!"

I tensed.

"All of it?" I asked quietly. It was a low blow, and I knew it, but I didn't fucking care.

Raine sighed and moved over to where I sat at the island table that separated the kitchen from the living area. Her eyes still held some anger, but she brought her hands up to cup my face and then run into my hair. She sighed again and shook her head as I reached up and gripped the sides of her shirt to hold her closer.

"Of course not," she said. "I wouldn't trade finding you for anything, but we don't have to be there anymore, and just being this close to the ocean is hard enough for me."

"I wouldn't let anything happen to you," I insisted. I tightened my fingers around her T-shirt. "I'd keep you safe, just like I did before."

"Safe from hurricanes?" she asked incredulously. "I know you wouldn't ever let anything happen to me, but some things you just can't control. At least here, there's advance warning and evacuation plans. There are police to deal with the crime."

I rolled my eyes. Yeah, sure—there were police and shit around here, which made me totally superfluous. She didn't *need* me here, which was where a lot of my issues seemed to originate.

"What am I supposed to do around here?" I mumbled. "Just be the fucking errand boy? Got some light bulbs that need changing?"

Raine stilled her fingers on my scalp for a moment then resumed.

"I heard some tourist was attacked on the beach the other day," she said. "Some guy just punched him for no reason. There's plenty around here for you to protect me from."

I couldn't help it; a laugh burst out of me.

"I'm the most dangerous person around here," I said as I looked up into her soft, brown eyes. The anger was gone from them, but the hard determination was still there. Apparently, she forgot who was living with her. "Who is going to protect you from me?"

I shoved myself away from her and out of the kitchen. My cigarettes were on the nightstand in the bedroom, so I grabbed them and opened the balcony door. I heard Raine come up behind me as I leaned on the rail and flicked ash towards the amoeba-shaped pool below.

"Are you going to tell me what's in your head right now?" she asked softly.

I thought about it a minute.

"You don't need me here," I said.

"I do need you," she insisted.

"No," I replied, "you don't."

"Sebastian…" Her voice held warning.

"I know," I said as I raised my hands in surrender, "you love me —I know that. I don't get it, but I know it. You want me—I get that too—but you don't *need* me. Not like you did there."

"I might not need you to find me fresh water or fish, but I still need you."

I really didn't want to fight with her over the fucking semantics. It was obvious we weren't going to come to terms on this one. For a moment, I stayed silent and gathered my thoughts. I didn't want her to leave for school with an argument behind her, so I decided to just drop it. I took one last pull on my smoke, tossed the butt in the bucket, and turned to face her.

"Agree to disagree?" I suggested.

Raine sighed and pursed her lips. I gave her a lopsided grin and held out my arms. She came to me, and I wrapped myself around her, holding her as tightly as I could. She raised her hands to grip the backs of my shoulders and placed her cheek against my chest. Tucking my face into her neck, I reveled in the smell of her hair and the softness of her skin as they calmed me.

"You mean everything to me," she said. "I don't like to see you hurting—you know that—but I can't go back there. I don't ever want to go back there."

I squeezed my eyes shut and tried to ignore the burning behind them.

"I know," I whispered into her hair.

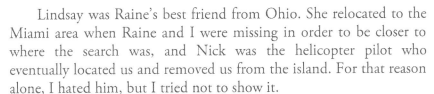

Lindsay was Raine's best friend from Ohio. She relocated to the Miami area when Raine and I were missing in order to be closer to where the search was, and Nick was the helicopter pilot who eventually located us and removed us from the island. For that reason alone, I hated him, but I tried not to show it.

Lindsay came from money, which showed in her demeanor more than Raine ever wanted to admit. Her mother was a judge or something on the state supreme court, and her father was an executive at some corporation. Lindsay didn't flaunt it exactly, but the chick bought fucking everything that caught her eye and then usually tried to get Raine to buy the same thing so they could match.

I didn't get that shit.

"You have to see these shoes I found online!" Lindsay blathered as she dropped an insanely sized designer handbag next to the door and pulled Raine over to the couch. I wondered if there was a pair of Chihuahuas in the bag—they definitely could have fit. Both women leaned over the laptop on the coffee table and pulled up some bargain shoe site. The two of them giggled and pointed at the screen while Nick rolled his eyes.

"Women, huh?" he said with a friendly smile. He placed a large, brown paper sack on the kitchen island and reached out his hand to shake. "How are ya, Sebastian?"

Totally ignoring his hand along with his efforts, I grunted, grabbed my smokes and a lighter, and headed through the sliding glass door. I closed it with a slam behind me.

Out on the balcony, I tried to find it in myself to feel bad about blowing the guy off, but I just couldn't. Every time I looked at him, I heard the whirling blades of the helicopter as it landed on the beach and destroyed my world. I knew Raine and Lindsay wanted us to get along, and Nick certainly tried, but I was an asshole about it all.

I fired up the grill and laid the steaks out on the attached tray. They were nice and thick, so I knew they were going to take a while to cook, which meant more time for talking with Raine's friends.

Fucking fabulous.

I finished my smoke and slid the balcony door open.

"Seriously, Lindsay, what were you thinking?"

Lindsay and Raine were on the near side of the kitchen island with their backs to me, and Lindsay was holding a couple of wine glasses while Nick uncorked a bottle of Merlot at the counter by the sink.

"It's just a bottle of wine," Lindsay was saying. "It's been months. I didn't think it would be a big deal. I want to celebrate my promotion, dammit!"

"He's going to act like a jerk whether we have a drink or not," Nick muttered.

"Stop that!" Lindsay smacked his arm and then turned back to Raine. She placed her hand on Raine's shoulder and leaned closer. "You know he's going to have to learn to be around it, sweetheart. I'm not trying to be insensitive, but you both have to know other people are going to indulge occasionally, and-"

"It's all right," I snapped as I walked in from the living room. "Drink the fucking wine. I don't give a shit."

They all turned toward me with big eyes and fidgety feet.

"Bastian," Raine sighed, "this is your home-"

I barked out a laugh and then shook my head. My home was a long way from here, and I didn't really think a fucking bottle of wine was going to make this place that much worse. With a deep breath, I tried to calm my voice.

"It's all right, babe," I said. I walked up behind her and wrapped my arms around her waist, kissing her neck gently just to prove a point. I wasn't sure what the point was, but I was sure it needed to be proven to someone. "She wants to celebrate or whatever. I'll cope."

And cope I did—hanging on to my fucking iced tea glass like it was a life preserver—for all of about forty minutes.

"Sounds like Raine's doing well in school," Nick said as he slid the balcony door shut and joined me outside.

"Humph," I replied through my nose. I kept my eyes on the grill, hoping he'd get the hint and go back inside. He didn't. Fucker.

"So what are you doing during the day when she's at class?" he asked.

"Jerking off," I replied.

He laughed, but the sound trailed away when I moved my eyes to his.

"I guess it gets pretty boring, huh?" Nick shuffled back and forth on his feet and then leaned against the balcony railing. He took a sip from his wine glass and kept that stupid grin plastered on his face. "So where are you from, Bastian?"

"Chicago."

"The windy city!" he exclaimed, like it was something I didn't already know. "I was there once with my parents and sister when I was a kid. Loved all the museums. We rode that big Ferris wheel at Navy Pier and went to the top of the Sears Tower."

It wasn't worth the effort to correct him and say it wasn't called that anymore, so I didn't say anything. What was it about people's need to tell you about their visits to a place you lived? He wasn't the first to babble about Chicago, but I had seen a lot more of the alleys on the south side of the city than I ever did of the fucking museums.

"I'm from Pennsylvania," he continued. "Pittsburgh, actually. My dad worked for a big container company."

I ignored him.

"Mom was mostly a housewife, but she did a lot in the schools, too. She tutored kids and worked with the PTO—you know, bake sales and all that stuff."

I could feel tension rippling up my back and into my shoulders with every word he spoke. My brain felt as if it were spinning in circles, trying to conjure up an image of a life like the one he had or of the woman who birthed me, but there was nothing to find.

"Do you still have family in Chicago?"

"No." I clenched my teeth and hoped he wouldn't go there.

"So where does your family live now?"

Of course he did.

Fucker.

"I don't have any family," I said.

"Oh, shit…sorry." He scratched at his head and took another drink. "What happened to them?"

"Don't know; don't care," I snapped. I jammed the tongs underneath one of the steaks and tossed it on its other side. "Change the fucking topic."

After a little silence, I hoped he'd go back inside, but my luck just didn't run that way.

"Are you going to get another boat?"

"I never had a boat," I said.

"Oh, uh, I thought that sailboat was yours."

"It was a three-masted schooner," I said, "a ship, not a boat."

"Sorry, I don't know much about boats."

Fuck me.

"So, are you going to get another one?"

"No."

"Why not?"

I let out a long breath and turned to glare at him.

"Because I fucking live here now!" I snarled before I focused my attention on the sizzling meat.

I guess I knew he was only trying to be nice and make conversation or whatever, but I wasn't interested. I didn't have anything to say to him, and I sure as hell wasn't planning to *open up* and give the fucker my life story. It would only get him killed.

Now there's an idea.

I shook my head a little to clear the violent thoughts parading around in it. With my attention on the food, I made it all the way through Nick's attempts at conversation while I flipped steaks. When we went back inside, I made it all the way through Lindsay's incessant babbling about shoes and Raine's sideways glances at me every time someone took a sip of wine.

Raine had completely ignored the glass Lindsay had poured for her and drank water.

That just pissed me off more. I didn't want her to deny herself just because I had a fucking drinking problem. It was *my* issue, not hers.

"How about a toast to the new customer service manager?" Nick said as he held up his glass.

Lindsay squealed a bit. She grabbed the glass Raine was avoiding and placed it her hand. Raine looked at me sideways again, and I rolled my eyes dramatically.

"Just drink the fucking drink, will you?" I snarled. "I really don't give a shit."

Raine cringed a bit and nodded at Lindsay. Nick held up his glass and said something about how proud he was of little Lindsay hitting the big-time of middle management. I sat on one of the stools in the kitchen and fiddled with my lighter.

"Come on, Bastian," Lindsay said, "you have to hold up your glass!"

"It's tea, for fuck's sake," I reminded her.

"You can still toast," Lindsay argued.

I stared at her blankly for a moment, trying to keep all the nasty shit I wanted to say from flying out of my mouth like a swarm of bees from a disturbed hive. All the tension was moving up my legs and into my gut, and I had to swallow to keep the words inside.

"Drop it, baby," Nick said quietly.

"But he can!" Lindsay insisted as she turned toward her boyfriend.

"Please," Raine said as I felt her hand grip my knee as she stepped closer to me, "let's go ahead and eat, okay?"

Awkward silence ensued.

It was better than what happened afterwards.

We all sat around the kitchen island with plates of steak, baked potatoes with little broccoli florets on top of them, and one of those salads with green stuff in it you couldn't actually identify. My fingers tapped repeatedly against my leg as I tried to keep my mouth too full to join in any discussions.

Not that I had anything to add to them.

"So proud of my girl," Nick said with a wide smile. He tossed his arm over Lindsay's shoulders and gave her a stupid-ass grin.

Every word that came out of his mouth I wanted to pound back into his face. It wasn't the words themselves; it was the way he said them. It was the way he beamed at her like she was the center of the fucking universe. She was eating it up, too.

I kind of wanted to puke.

Raine smiled at both of them before tilting her head to look at me. Her smile faltered immediately as she watched me tear into another bite with my fingers clenching the knife so tightly, it probably looked like I was trying to brutalize the cow.

"Only two years at the store, too," he continued.

"Oh for fuck's sake," I muttered, no longer able to keep it inside. "It's a customer service job. She's not on the board of directors."

Half a second of silence before Nick sat up taller and glared at me.

"What the fuck is your problem?" Nick finally snapped.

I glared right back.

"Let's see where to start." I tapped my finger on my chin. "Oh yeah—you're a dickhead."

"Bastian!"

I slammed my hand down on the table and stood up.

"This is fucking pointless!" I yelled. "I can't sit around here and pretend all this is just fine and dandy, Raine! It's bullshit!"

I wasn't really sure exactly what was bullshit, but I was pretty confident that there was bullshit about the room. I didn't like it. In fact, I couldn't fucking tolerate it another second.

"Jesus, Bastian…" Lindsay's face crinkled up as if she'd just seen some poor girl on the beach in Wal-Mart flip-flops. "Calm down already."

I curled my fingers into a fist, my nails digging into my palms. I wasn't going to hit her—I wouldn't actually do that—but the desire was certainly there. I was pretty sure if I did, Nick would come to her rescue at that point. Pummeling him was a very attractive idea, and I found myself actually considering making a move on her just to get the opportunity to hit him.

I glanced in Raine's direction, and all those thoughts left my head. She'd never fucking forgive me if I did something like that, and the only thing that could possibly relieve some of the tension I felt was knowing once these two idiots were gone, I'd take Raine to bed and forget about this whole evening.

It occurred to me that I might have already blown that opportunity.

"Fuck this," I muttered as I stood up and grabbed my jacket from the hook on the wall.

"Bastian, where are you going?" Raine asked.

"Getting the fuck out of here."

Raine pushed away from the table and started to walk over to me, but Nick, who was closer to the door, beat her to it. He stepped around me and blocked me from getting from the doorway to the elevator.

"Come on, man," he said with his hands up in some kind of stupid-ass surrender motion. "It's all good. No reason for you to go."

"Get the fuck out of my way!" I yelled. I shoved Nick aside and grabbed the handle of the door. I wasn't about to wait around for the elevator, so I slammed both hands onto the metal bar on the door to the stairs and started down them, skipping two steps at a time until I reached the bottom. About halfway down, the sound of Raine yelling after me had diminished enough to be forgotten.

Every muscle in my body was painfully tight. I tried to keep my mental focus on getting the fuck out of the general area and not on going back upstairs to punch that asshole in the face. If Raine hadn't been there, there was no doubt in my mind that I would have beaten the shit out of him, and it was only her presence that kept me from going back up there.

I needed a major distraction, and thankfully, there was something on the lower level that was good at capturing my attention.

Inside the underground parking garage were two spaces for our vehicles. One contained Raine's Subaru, which she had driven from Ohio prior to going on the cruise that landed us both on a life raft. Next to it was the only thing I had bought since we arrived in Miami —a Honda CBR600RR.

My motorcycle.

I flipped my leg over it, started it up, and threw it into gear. A few moments later, I was doing ninety on the MacArthur Causeway, heading to I-95. I didn't know where I was going, just that I wanted to get as far away from that condo as quickly as I could. Driving as if there were a bunch of fast-moving zombies from World War Z on my tail, I slipped between cars and trucks as I headed west, reached the interstate, and sped northward.

The wind on my face drew water from my eyes, but I reveled in the feeling, the unhindered freedom the bike gave me. It wasn't as good as the schooner on the sea because of the traffic I had to buzz around, but it was a decent substitute. The air still smelled like salt this close to the ocean, and I could nearly taste the sea on my tongue.

I didn't keep track of the time I spent just speeding up the highway. At some point I took an exit, turned around, and headed back toward Miami Beach. I didn't get that far though, choosing instead to get off the interstate and head through some back streets. I zipped through some neighborhoods with unkempt lawns and boarded-up windows then past some strip malls with half the stores closed up. There weren't a lot of people around, and those that were looked like they'd rather be somewhere else.

I finally pulled the bike over, dropped the kickstand, and put my head in my hands. I leaned over the handlebars and took several deep breaths before I sat back and looked around.

I hadn't been to this area of town before, and it looked shady, to say the least. It definitely looked like the kind of area tourists avoided because they were more likely to get mugged than offered a drink with an umbrella in it. It immediately reminded me of living on the streets of Chicago before Landon found me and hauled me out to Seattle to start training.

Training.

I snorted to myself.

I'd learned how to kill and how to avoid being killed so I could fight and win in death-match battles to amuse the stupidly rich and powerful people of organized crime all over the world. I'd earned an insane amount of money for taking the lives of others in the most brutal ways possible. It had never bothered me in the slightest.

Why should it have? It wasn't like those who came up against me didn't know what they were getting into. At the level I played, all of them had been in tournaments, and none of them came out with clean fingernails. There was blood on the hands of everyone I killed.

If I hadn't done it, one of the other fighters would have. It was only a matter of time. Very few tournament players ever actually retired—most of them just got beat. John Paul and I were two of the very few who actually gave it up and went on to something else, though the circumstances made it more of a necessity than a choice.

You didn't testify against the mega-super crime boss for torture and murder without having to go into hiding. It wasn't like Franks was going to offer me my job back after that. Landon had to cut his losses, give me a new identity, and send me on my way with John Paul looking out for me as I dived further and further into a perpetual bottle of vodka.

Thinking about training with Landon made me realize I wasn't exactly following what I had been told to do—watch my surroundings and always know what dangers might be lurking. In a neighborhood like this one, I needed to pay attention. I straightened up and took a good look around me, wondering which of the idiots around here might have thought I was a good target for pickpocketing.

The idea of someone coming after me and stealing my wallet was kind of intriguing. Maybe that was exactly what I needed—a good fight in a shitty neighborhood where the police wouldn't show up until I was long, long gone.

I tossed my leg over the bike and started meandering down the street. A few dodgy people walked by, but I must not have looked like a viable target to them. After walking up and down a few alleys, I came across a hole-in-the-wall bar with a decent amount of noise coming from it.

There was a guy standing by the door, giving everyone who approached the bouncer-vibe. He checked IDs, turned a few people away, and then leaned back against the frame of the entrance to smoke. When I approached, his eyes lit up.

"Hey, are you the dude they're waiting for?"

Slightly startled, I debated lying to him and saying yes, but lying in this kind of circumstance was a little too risky. For all I knew, he was waiting for the boss-man's boyfriend.

"Don't think so," I replied. "Why?"

"Oh," he said as his forehead crinkled a bit, "that's a shame. You look like a good match."

"Match for what?" I asked.

He crooked his thumb and motioned inside.

"Just a little friendly competition," he said with a sly smile. "You wanna watch? They've been letting anyone stupid enough to give it a try into the cage tonight since the other dude hasn't shown up."

I shrugged but couldn't help feeling a little excited. I brushed passed the dude to get a look inside and found myself in a warehouse with a makeshift bar off to one side, a bunch of tall tables and chairs around, and hundreds of people yelping and hollering at the center of the place. Surrounded by a ring of chain link, a large platform housed two guys in shorts who danced around each other, punching and kicking as everyone cheered and handed wads of cash back and forth.

Cage fighting.

This place obviously wasn't UFC regulated or anything. The referee was a chick in a black-and-white striped bikini, for Christ's sake. There was one dude in orange trunks who obviously had some MMA experience and was decently big and another one who was obviously a drunken college idiot who knew what the inside of a gym smelled like, but that was about it. The green trunks he was wearing didn't even fit him right and were probably borrowed from the bar.

College-boy was getting hammered.

I handed the cover charge over to the bouncer and made my way to the side of the cage to watch the beating. My fingers twitched as I ran them over the edge of the chain-link fencing, and I felt my heart rate increase. I'd never been in a cage fight, but this was similar enough to the street fighting I did as a kid. Everything around me felt familiar.

A couple of hard lefts to the face and a quick kick to the side made college-boy drop to his knees. Orange-trunks jumped on his back and immediately began slamming the kid's head against the mat. Stunned, the poor guy could barely smack his hand against the other dude's shoulder to tap out.

The winner began to jump around the cage, smacking his hands on the chain-link and yelling at the audience. I watched him closely —the way he moved, where his eyes went, and how his feet touched the floor—while college-boy was handed over to his buddies and another dude walked into the cage and looked out at the patrons.

"Who's next?" he shouted.

I had to bite down on my lip to keep from volunteering.

There was no fucking way Raine would approve of any of this shit. She wouldn't like it, not at all. She wouldn't like the idea of me fighting, getting hit, or hitting another guy. It was entirely possible she would give me shit just for walking into the damn bar, and she would probably be right, but knowing how Raine would react to the whole situation wasn't what made me stop.

I was going to do this shit—no doubt. I just wanted to see the dude fight again before I made myself known.

My interest was piqued. At least for now, I was going to watch.

Chapter Three

The announcer called the dude in the orange shorts "Brutal Brutus," which I thought sounded absolutely ridiculous, but it did seem to fit. He didn't waste any time going after the next guy who walked into the cage with him. This one was a little older than college-boy, who was nursing a bloody and probably broken nose over by the bar. The new opponent was a muscular guy with biceps about as big as mine, but he also sported a lot of gut and very little hair.

Brutal Brutus wasn't impressed with Muscles. He avoided the guy's lame attempts at a left hook with ease. As big as he was, Muscles obviously didn't have much fighting experience, and he went down quickly. The short fight still gave me enough opportunity to observe Brutus's fighting style.

He favored his right way too much, and it left him unbalanced. He also stuck to very basic patterns that left little to the imagination. Right-right-left, right-right-left. He was predictable, which made him vulnerable.

"Does anyone else dare to face Brutal Brutus?" The MC-slash-announcer walked around the ring, pointing his finger at the audience. "There's a hundred dollars to anyone who can stay up for three minutes, five hundred if you can take him down!"

I didn't give a shit about the money, but I approached the edge of the ring and caught the MC's eye.

"Looks like we have a challenge!" he announced, and the crowd began to cheer.

One of the bouncers led me back to a small room that served as a locker room but looked like it was supposed to be a large custodial closet. The smell was nearly enough to make me gag, but I breathed through my mouth and went inside. The bouncer dude pointed out a shelf with a few pairs of shorts on it, and I grabbed blue ones. He politely stood facing the door and away from me as I removed my shirt, dropped my jeans, and pulled on the trunks.

"Ya ready?" he asked.

"Just about," I said. I rolled each shoulder around, stretched my arms and chest a bit, and then nodded to him.

The bouncer brought me back out to the edge of the cage and opened the chain door. As I stepped into it, the MC leaned toward me.

"What are ya?" he asked. "Six-three? Six-four?"

"Six-three," I replied.

"Weight?"

"About two-twenty."

"What's your name?"

I paused for a moment.

"Daniel," I said.

"Got it!" The announcer cracked his knuckles as he looked me over a bit more.

"Here we go again, everyone!" he called out. "Next into the cage is Dangerous Daniel!"

I rolled my eyes. The chick in the referee bikini took my hand by the wrist and held it over her head as the MC went over my stats.

"He's six feet three inches tall, and weighs in at two hundred and twenty pounds of solid muscle! Ladies, keep your eyes on this one!"

I glanced out over the audience and listened to the hollering coming from the women in the bar. A warm tingle went up my spine as the familiarity of the situation relaxed me and I focused my attention on what was to come.

Looking over at Brutus, I gripped my hands into fists and took a deep breath as the chick referee pushed a mouthguard between my teeth.

This was where I belonged.

Brutus walked up, danced on the balls of his feet, and waited patiently for me to make the first move. Knowing he would start with his right, I moved into his space to give him what would appear to be a clear shot. The slight grin on his face told me he had fallen for it before he took his first swing.

I dodged to the right, ducking and slamming my fist into his kidney as I went past him. He grabbed at his side for a second but recovered quickly and came at me again, his eyes narrowed. He swung again, missed again, and lost his footing briefly.

When he regained his composure, he took a step back and watched me carefully. He had realized I wasn't going down easily and was going to take his time now. Assuming he thought I would go with another ploy, I went straight at him, diving against his body and punching him rapidly in the gut and side.

He returned the favor though his blows weren't very hard from that angle. His arm twisted around mine, and he brought his free hand up high before slamming it into my temple.

The blow sent me down and backward, but I didn't fall. In fact, it just pissed me off. I leapt forward, diving at his body and sending us both to the ground. We rolled, both of us punching at each other's sides until we hit the edge of the cage. My head bounced against the chain link, and Brutus pushed away from me, standing again.

I followed suit, jumped up, and readied myself. I watched him closely as he danced from left to right, then came at me with his predictable pattern. I dodged right, turned swiftly, and locked one of my legs behind his. I grabbed his shoulder and pulled his back to my chest.

With one leg wrapped around his torso, I threw him to the mat. I tightened my arm around his neck, wrapped my other arm around his head, and slammed his face into the ground twice. I pulled one arm back and elbowed him in the shoulder as hard as I could. He continued to struggle under me, trying to get his arms under him enough to push me off, but his efforts were wasted.

I turned my head to the side and spit out the mouth guard.

"You gonna tap out, or should I go ahead and kill you?" I snarled.

I felt the pressure of his Adam's apple under my forearm, but he couldn't actually swallow as I flexed against his throat. His hand flew out, and he slammed it three times against the mat.

I paused just a little longer than I needed to before tossing him to the ground. He lay there gasping as everyone in the bar started to cheer, and the post-violence high swept over me.

I was elated. With wide eyes and what probably looked like a crazed smile, I looked over the crowd and felt my heart pounding in my chest. I could feel blood—hot and sticky—on my knuckles. The crowd continued to scream as the chick in the referee-styled bikini held my arm up as high as she could. She looked up at me with raised eyebrows.

"Nice job," she said with a smile and a wink. "I don't think Brutus is going to forget that anytime soon."

"He better fucking not," I replied, wriggling my eyebrows at her, "or I might have to come back and remind him."

She laughed. As she released my wrist, she ran her hand up to my shoulder and squeezed it a little before she wrapped her arm through mine.

"All right, folks," the announcer said as he waved his hands at the crowd, "that's it for tonight! More fights next week! Don't miss 'em!"

The bouncer who had taken me to the locker room knelt down next to Battered Brutus and hauled him out of the cage while the referee chick escorted me through the screaming patrons. They reached out to me, patted me on the back, and yelled out various forms of congratulations as we made our way to the locker room so I could get dressed.

When I came out, the ref was still there and still dressed in nothing but the skimpy bikini. She was all smiles as she took my arm again and led me over to the bar. She handed me an envelope full of cash, which I didn't bother to count. The guy standing behind the bar with an empty beer glass in his hand reached out to give me a high-five.

"Buy you a drink?" the referee asked. She leaned against the counter, which hiked up her boobs to put them more on display than they already had been, and motioned to the bartender.

For a moment, I almost accepted her offer out of habit.

"Nah, I'm good." I shook my head and looked out at the people milling around. Most of them were looking at me with bright eyes, and many were leaning in to talk to their friends with hushed voices and nodding in my direction.

"You sure?" Referee chick tilted her head and smiled up at me.

"Yeah, pretty sure," I gave her a half smile back.

I should have picked up on her vibe right away, but I was still in the zone from the fight and I wasn't thinking straight.

"I'm Andi," she informed me as she leaned forward again.

"Daniel," I said.

"I heard that…*Dangerous Daniel.*" She giggled. "I think it suits you."

"Sometimes." I smirked back at her.

She pushed off the bar and took a step closer.

"I like dangerous guys," she said as she placed her hands on my chest. Her eyes followed the movements of her fingers as she took inventory of my pecs and shoulders through my shirt.

"Doesn't seem very smart," I observed. I took a half step back, feeling a little uncomfortable. As my violence-induced haze began to fade, I realized she was coming on to me.

It was a strange feeling. A chick hadn't hit on me since Raine and I had returned from our little exile. When I'd been living on my ship, I'd usually been the instigator of any contact with the opposite sex. Still, as long ago as it had been, it felt familiar.

Not just familiar, but *right.*

This was what was supposed to happen after a fight. Fight, win, sex. That was the natural order. As if it were ingrained somewhere deep inside of me, my body began to react to the situation.

I was instantly hard.

Andi's hands were running from my chest to my abs, and she was standing close enough for me to feel the heat from her body all around me. She reached around and placed her hands at the small of my back as she pressed her body against me. There was no doubt she could feel how affected I was—my dick was right up against her stomach.

Then panic set in.

What the fuck was I thinking? This wasn't a normal tournament fight, and I wasn't a single guy. I had Raine back at our condo, probably freaking out, wondering where the fuck I was, and my dick was reacting to some random chick in a bar.

I grabbed her wrists and pushed them down.

"Sorry," I said with a shrug, "I really ought to go."

"It's not that late," Andi said. She twisted her wrists in my hands and looked up at me with a twinkle in her eye. "I don't live too far from here."

"Maybe another time," I said quietly. A lump in my throat formed, and I had to swallow hard to get past it. I took a step back and dropped her hands. "Thanks for the offer."

I turned and got the fuck out of there.

Back at my bike, I sat down and tried to regain a little composure. I closed my eyes tightly and took a few calming breaths. My stomach was churning, and I felt like I was going to puke. I'd let that girl run her hands all over me, and I hadn't even been thinking about Raine at all.

You didn't do anything wrong.

No, I didn't, but damn if my dick didn't want to.

I slammed my foot against the kickstand and started up the bike with a roar. It was nearly three in the morning, and I kept the motorcycle at the speed limit through the streets, down the highway, and back over to Miami Beach.

I needed the time to think, but it didn't help that much.

I was still sweating as I headed up the stairs. I wanted to blame it on the humidity, but I knew that wasn't it. I had no idea what I was going to walk into when I got up to the condo. Were Nick and Lindsay still going to be there? Would Raine be waiting up for me, pissed off and ready for a fight?

A mental image of her sitting at the kitchen island smoking my cigarettes and drinking scotch came to mind. It was a ridiculous notion, but the vision wouldn't go away as I quietly slid the key into the deadbolt and opened the door.

The living area was empty. There was one dim light still on above the stove, but that was it. The whole place was quiet.

Was she even here?

I swallowed hard. My skin began to crawl at the thought that she might have left. I tiptoed to the bedroom, terrified of finding the room empty. The space beyond was dark, and the door was partially closed. I pushed it the rest of the way open.

I could see Raine on the bed, lying down and breathing steadily, her shape clearly outlined by the light slipping through the blinds. A breath escaped from my lungs, and my shoulders dropped in relief. She didn't move as I carefully and quietly slipped off my T-shirt and jeans and ditched them in a pile by the laundry hamper.

Slipping into bed as silently as I could, I shoved my legs in under the sheet. Raine didn't stir as I maneuvered myself behind her and snaked my arm around her waist. I relaxed against her, let out a long breath, and closed my eyes. For a moment, I thought I was home free.

"You going to tell me where you've been?"

Ah, shit.

I opened my eyes though I couldn't really see much in the dim light from the balcony door. My throat seized up on me, and it took me a second to find my voice. I tensed my fingers around the fabric of her shirt and gripped it tightly, like I was afraid she'd try to get away from me if I wasn't holding on.

"Just took the bike out for a ride," I claimed. I swallowed a couple of times and licked my lips.

"For seven hours?" Raine rolled over and looked into my eyes. Even in the dim light, I could still see the shine in her beautiful, red-rimmed brown eyes. She'd been crying, and I felt like a total asshole.

I kept my grip on her shirt as if I could keep all of this from happening just by holding on tightly enough.

"I just needed to…to get away for a bit." I looked down her bare arm and dropped my head against her shoulder. I rubbed my forehead against her skin and felt myself relax further when she didn't push me away. "Those people were driving me bat-shit."

"Those people," Raine snarled, "are my friends!"

Yeah, there I went again—making shit worse by opening my big fat mouth.

"I didn't mean it like that…I mean…ah, fuck it!" I started to push away from her, but my arm got wrapped up in the sheet and held me back. Maybe it was because my fingers wouldn't initially loosen from her shirt—whatever. I fought with it for a second, finally freeing myself, and sat up.

Raine sat up beside me, glaring.

"Well, what did you mean, then?" she asked.

I had meant exactly what I said, but I wasn't about to admit that. There was no way I was going to come out and say I hated them being in the condo at all, even if they did keep their mouths shut, which of course they didn't. She was already pissed off at me enough, and I had to figure out a way to make it better, not worse.

"I just…I don't like people."

Raine stared at me for a moment.

"Why?" she asked.

My mind began to race. I wasn't really sure how to answer the question. I never considered myself a people person, but I never really thought about the reason for that. It was just the way it was.

"I just…don't."

Apparently, Raine wasn't going to let me off the hook and prodded me to give her a better answer.

Tensing, I tried to come up with a decent answer that didn't make me sound like an ass, but I couldn't think of anything. As I struggled inside to come up with the perfect words, the turmoil inside of me increased and eventually overflowed. Closing my eyes tightly, I opened my mouth and let shit run out of it.

"Because I don't have anything to say to them!" I blurted. I covered my face with one hand and slammed the back of my head ineffectually into the pillow. It didn't help.

"What does that mean?" Raine's voice was soft as she propped herself on one elbow to look down at me. A small amount of my tension ebbed.

"When people are around, they end up asking me questions," I said as I shoved myself off the pillow and sat up. I wrapped my arms around my legs and put my chin on my knees. "I don't have any answers for them. I don't have anything to say."

"Will you give me an example?" Raine asked, her tone going soft.

"What the fuck am I supposed to say?" My voice rose in pitch as my throat constricted. My gut churned as if a little tornado were forming inside of it. "What am I supposed to talk about? About how I was such a fucked up kid that my own parents dumped me? Should I tell them about how every foster home I was ever in kicked me out? How about my time in juvie? There's a fun topic. Or the best question of all—'what do you do for a living?' How am I supposed to answer that? Oh, you know, I made a shit-ton of money killing people, but I'm retired now."

Raine's face scrunched up, and she squished her lips together. She let out a long sigh through her nose before opening her arms and pulling me back down to the pillows.

"I never thought about it that way," she admitted. "I can see where that would be difficult. You are right—the kinds of things people usually ask would be difficult for you to answer."

With a shudder, my body relaxed, and the whirlwind inside dissipated. I wrapped my arms around her and held her against my chest in silent appreciation of her understanding.

"But, Bastian," Raine continued, "even though you might not be able to answer the questions people ask, that doesn't mean you get to blow up at them and storm out, leaving me to try to explain and defend you. You can't do that."

Well, yeah, obviously I could. I had in the past, and I'd probably do it again in the future.

"You think I should just stick around and tell them to fuck off instead?"

"No," Rain said with a loud sigh. "There are other options, you know."

I took a deep breath as the anger inside me began to bubble again at the thought. There was one option I had considered but didn't take.

"I didn't think you'd appreciate me hitting him," I said.

"You're right," Raine replied. I could hear the tension rising in her voice again.

"It's better if I just leave," I rationalized.

"Maybe for you," Raine agreed, "but what kind of questions and comments do you think I get when you do something like that?"

I hadn't thought about it. Once I left, everything that happened afterward had never really concerned me before. I wondered what Lindsay and Nick had to say after I took off and how Raine responded.

"I spend enough time trying to get them to understand you," she said. "When you do something like that, I can't defend your actions. It just gives them more justification when they start telling me I ought to get rid of you."

I secured my grip on her clothing as a wave of panic crashed over me. It was just one more thing my selfish ass hadn't considered. Of course Lindsay would be telling her to dump me, and Nick would be right behind her. They probably had another guy already picked out as a better suitor for Raine, and he probably hadn't killed anyone lately.

"What did they say?" I growled. She had known Lindsay since

they were kids. Raine was bound to listen to whatever advice Lindsay had to offer. The thought kick-started my paranoia.

"It doesn't matter," Raine said. "I'm not going anywhere, Bastian."

I relaxed slightly, but the idea of Raine with someone else continued to terrify me.

"That doesn't stop them from saying I should, though. When you behave like that, it makes it a lot harder to explain to them why I love you."

The tension inside me began to build again, and I fought against the desire to tell her all the reasons she shouldn't have anything to do with me. Her friends were probably right, but I felt like I was looking out over the proverbial cliff, and if I opened my mouth to say what I was thinking, I was going to fall.

"I'm sorry," I whispered instead.

Raine moved her hand up into my hair and held my head against her shoulder. Closing my eyes, I tried to understand the shit that was going through my head, but as usual, I couldn't make anything of it. My brain just didn't work right, which I realized was the problem.

"I know there's something seriously wrong with me inside," I said quietly. "I can't deny it."

"Bastian-"

"Let me finish," I said quickly. If I didn't get it out now, I never would. "This isn't about not being worthy of you or whatever—there's more to it than that. There is something wrong with me, and don't tell me you don't know that."

I paused, but she didn't interject.

"I don't know that I can control those…those urges. There's a need inside of me to lash out. It's so fucking deep, and I can't explain it; I just know it's there. As far back as I can remember, it's always been there."

"Sometimes you do okay," Raine said. "You do all right when John Paul is around."

"That's different. He doesn't ask those kinds of questions."

"So you feel comfortable around him."

"Yeah, I guess so. Most of the time."

"Why is that?" she asked.

Well, fuck if I knew. It just was.

"He's…he's always been there for me."

"And what? You don't think Lindsay and Nick care?"

"They care about you, not me."

"That's not fair," she said. "They've both tried to get along with you. You aren't very receptive."

"It's fake," I said. "They do it for you, not me. It's kinda hard to take their shit seriously when it's all an act."

"How do you know that?"

"I can just tell, okay?" I snapped. "It's like knowing when a chick is faking an orgasm; if she's not clenching down on my cock, she's not coming."

And just like that, I was back to being a dick again.

"Being crude and obnoxious doesn't help," Raine growled. "It's just me here now, so why don't you stop the shit?"

Raine almost never cussed, so it usually caught my attention when she did. Recognizing it didn't even change my behavior though. When push came to shove, it was always the same for me— get the fuck out. I shoved myself off of the bed and away from her, grabbed my smokes, and went to the balcony.

Raine followed.

"You can't just walk away from the conversation," she informed me.

"I dunno," I said, still in pissy-mode, "I've done it before."

I knew I was being a jerk, but I also thought if I came right out and told her that I'd love to send Nick flying off this balcony, she would like that even less. I wanted to say or do something to make it all right again, but as usual, I was clueless.

I turned toward her, and the small light near the top of the balcony door shone over my face, making me squint. Raine narrowed her eyes, and she took a step closer to me. Her fingers brushed over my cheekbone, and though I tried not to, I flinched as she touched the bruise on my face. Her eyes went wide.

"What happened to you?"

"It's nothing," I said.

She straightened up and leaned forward to get a better look at me. With her hand on the side of my face, she tilted my head into the light and glared a bit.

"What happened?"

"Just a little tiff," I said with a shrug. "Seriously, it's no big deal."

"You got in a fight? With who?"

"Just some dude," I shrugged again. "I went riding, stopped for a bit to walk it off, and then ran into a guy who wasn't all that pleasant. It's all good—he got it worse than he gave."

"Is that really all you have to say about it?"

I took a slight step back but was stopped by the balcony door. I looked off into the distance and watched the waves slipping back and forth over the beach.

"I guess I'll take that as a yes," Raine mumbled.

"Pretty much," I replied. I looked back to her. "I'm fine."

"If you say so."

"Don't be pissed."

"It's kind of late for that," Raine sighed. "I just don't know what to make of you sometimes."

"I'm a dick," I said. "You already know this."

"Not usually." Raine reached up and ran her fingers through her hair. I tried not to get distracted by the way the dark strands lay against her neck and shoulder. "When you are, I usually understand why, but not with this. I don't understand why you don't realize Nick is trying to be your friend, and I don't understand why you react to it by going out and beating up someone else."

"He was asking for it," I said quietly.

"Nick or the guy you beat up?"

I wasn't really sure myself, so I went back to the ever-present and noncommittal shrug.

"You're really trying my patience," she said.

I looked back at her, realizing how angry she still was. I didn't know what I was supposed to do or say—all this relationship shit was a mystery to me. I never said the right shit, and I certainly didn't do the right shit. I was probably the worst match for my gentle Raine as I could possibly be, and that just made me want to cling to her, so I did.

I stepped forward and wrapped my arms around her. I pulled her close to me and kissed her gently on the forehead.

"I'm sorry," I said.

"For what?" she asked.

"Everything I do wrong," I replied. "I'm a shitty boyfriend, you know that."

She took a deep breath and blew the air across my shoulder as she laid her head against my chest. Her arms came up around my neck.

"You are my hero," Raine said. "You've always been that to me. My savoir, and despite your flaws, I still love you. I just wish you'd tell me what was going on in your head in a way I could understand."

"My head is fucked up," I told her. "I don't know how much of that is fixable, babe."

I leaned back a little and looked down into her eyes.

"Seriously," I said. More tension flowed through my body as I tried to choose the right words. "If…if your father was still alive, do you really think he'd approve of you being with me?"

I felt Raine tense in my arms. Bringing up her father might not have been the wisest thing to do, but it was the best way to get my point across. After all, I was right there when he was tortured and murdered, and I didn't do a damn thing to stop it from happening.

I hadn't known Raine then and had no idea who her father was other than being a small-town cop in the wrong part of the big city at the wrong time. Why he was there I didn't know, only that once he was discovered, Landon's crime boss, Joseph Franks, wasn't about to let him live. Everyone in the area who was considered a threat to Franks and his organization was rounded up, brutally tortured, and eventually executed.

I had watched it all, unable to intervene.

I shifted my eyes back to Raine's face and observed her far-away expression. Tightening my arms around her, I pressed my lips to her shoulder. I hadn't meant to upset her by bringing up her deceased father, but I needed to make the point.

"He wouldn't want you dating me," I said.

Raine flicked the tip of her tongue over her lips.

"I don't know," she said softly. "He wouldn't like what you used to do, obviously, but neither do I. I think if he got to know you—really know you—I think he might have been okay with it."

I snorted through my nose at the ridiculousness of her statement.

"I mean it," Raine said. "I don't know if I can honestly say he would have liked you or wanted to hang out with you on the weekends, but I think if he saw how you are with me, I think he'd understand."

"You're crazy," I muttered. "What exactly do you think he would see? Me snapping at you for no fucking reason? Running out on you when I get pissed off? What do you think he'd like more—the chain smoking or the bike?"

I laughed dryly.

Raine turned to look at me. She stared into my eyes, and I watched her expression go from annoyance at my harshness to something softer. She reached out and ran her finger from my elbow up to my shoulder.

"Sebastian," Raine whispered, "when you look at me, I can *feel* how much you love me. Sometimes it's a little overwhelming—like a tidal wave—and it can make me feel like I've been turned inside out. I can feel it in my skin and in the pit of my stomach. When you look at me like that, I can feel your love for me in my soul. When you wrap your arms around me at night, I can feel your desire for me, and I don't think there is any woman alive who has ever felt more wanted than I do when you're close to me."

She touched the side if my face.

"Dad would have seen that in you, too."

Her point was made. At least for now, I wouldn't argue with her.

Chapter Four

"Lilliana," John Paul said as he slid into the booth seat across from me. He had to duck his head a bit to keep from hitting the low-hanging lamp poised above the middle of the table.

"What the fuck does that mean?"

"It's her name," he said.

"Whose name?"

"The chick I was banging last night."

John Paul was my one and only true friend. We'd both fought for Landon in the tournaments, and when I had to go into hiding, John Paul came with me. Now that I was beached in the south of Florida, he'd taken up residence in North Miami Beach, which wasn't too far from our condo, and we tried to meet up regularly.

I rolled my eyes and sucked the straw in my glass of iced tea while John Paul ordered a beer and a pile of nachos.

"Since when do you eat that shit?" I asked.

"I worked it all off already," he claimed. "She was fucking phenomenal. *Luscious Lilliana.* She's got one of those nice, round asses you just want to squeeze and bite. I hate how skinny most of the chicks around here are. I need a woman with some meat on her bones."

"Like that bro-hemoth you dated in Seattle?"

"Stacey?" John Paul leaned back in his seat. "She was a beast."

"Yeah, exactly," I replied as I remembered the dark-skinned woman who was all muscle and no tits. She wasn't *that* tall, but you couldn't tell it by her attitude. John Paul had dated her for a couple of months, which was probably a record for him. "She took more steroids than half the guys we worked out with."

"Ah, you're just pissed she could squat more than you could."

"She fucking could not!"

"She did that one day."

"Fluke," I waved my hand dismissively. "I was off one day, and you started all that bullshit just to fuck with me."

John Paul laughed and adjusted his black cowboy hat as he leaned over the table and looked more closely at me. His eyes narrowed slightly as his lips smashed together.

"You look like shit, ya know."

"Fuck you," I replied.

"Just sayin'." He leaned back again and started drumming his fingers on the table. He watched me for a minute as the server deposited a huge plate of nachos with all the extras in the center of the table. "So what's up with you?"

"Meh." I shrugged. "Been fighting with Raine a bit."

"Trouble in paradise?"

His choice of words vibrated in my ears and sent unwelcomed tingles down my back. In paradise there hadn't been any trouble.

All right, that was total bullshit, but it was the sort of trouble I could handle. Raine had been attacked by a bunch of shit-bag human traffickers who promptly died by my hand. Aside from that, there had been bad storms and my ever-present grumpiness. I'd always been moody, and Raine had to put up with my shitty attitude on a regular basis while we were stranded, but now it was worse. I still had a shitty attitude, but here I also had five thousand extraneous variables to set me off instead of just the fucked up shit inside my head. I had no idea how Raine put up with me at all.

"I'm an asshole," I said with a shrug.

"No shit! Really?" John Paul placed his hand in the center of his chest and made his mouth into a big "O" before he started laughing. "Is she tired of your crap?"

"I dunno," I said. "Probably."

"So what did you do?"

I shrugged again. I didn't really want to get into it, but I also couldn't stop thinking about the whole situation. Maybe it would be better to tell him everything.

"Lindsay and Nick came over for dinner," I finally said. "That dude pisses me off. I was a dick, Raine got mad, and I left."

"Sounds like you handled that superbly."

"You can shove your sarcasm up your ass, you know."

"You going to argue the point?"

I wasn't, but I also wasn't going to justify the remark with a response. I was still thinking about what I had revealed to Raine and —quite frankly—to myself. I didn't like talking to people because I didn't have anything to say.

"It's not them, really," I said. "I know it's me. I just…don't have any purpose here, ya know?"

"What kind of purpose?"

"In Raine's life," I said. "She needed me there, and she doesn't need me here. I just…exist beside her without anything to do."

"Get a job," he suggested.

"Yeah, right," I snorted. "Doing what? With what resume? I've got a master's degree I've never used and no employment history I can actually put on paper. What should I apply for? Parking attendant or McDonald's? Oh wait…all the parking around here is automated. There's also probably some hippie health group around here trying to make fast food illegal."

"Bouncer?"

"You trying to get me back on the booze?" I glared at him, challenging. I wasn't about to admit I made a trip to a bar almost every day. He didn't need to know that shit.

John Paul tossed his hands up in the air in acknowledgement. He sat back for a moment and took a long swig of his beer before speaking again.

"Raine's pretty into you," he said. "I don't think she's looking to have you around just to bust up any dickhead that comes close to her. For some fucked-up reason, she likes you."

He stared at me for a while.

"You want to go back there, don't you?"

I nodded. There wasn't any need to clarify where *there* was.

"She won't have anything to do with it."

I nodded again.

"Yeah, you're fucked."

"Thanks a lot."

John Paul just grinned and scratched the dark beard on his chin. I grabbed a handful of nachos and shoved them in my face, effectively ending the conversation.

"You been going to that gym in your building?" John Paul asked.

I stared down at my glass and didn't answer.

"Yeah, I didn't think so," he snickered. "You're getting soft, motherfucker. Get yourself in there before I beat the shit out of you."

"Whatever." I flipped him off. I knew he was right, but I wasn't going to admit it.

"Seriously, bro," he said as he leaned forward again. "Hit the weights. Five days a week, just like we used to."

"Why?" I looked back up into his eyes, and they flickered away from me.

"Because," he said as he lowered his voice and looked back at my face, "you may not be in the wilds of your island paradise anymore, but that doesn't mean there isn't shit she needs to be protected from here. They know where you are, and they know what she knows. It's only Landon's reputation that's keeping them from busting down your door and taking you both out. You go soft, forget your training, and you just might miss something."

I felt my chest clench at his words. They were far too true to be ignored, and I suddenly felt like a complete moron. I had been slacking off, not just at the gym but with everything. I was so unaware of what was going on around me, I had even managed to walk into a dude on the beach. No one from Franks' organization would be as obvious as a guy on the beach—those people would be sneaky bastards, not tournament fighters but real hit men.

We polished off the nachos. John Paul finished his beer, and we parted ways. I hopped back onto my bike and sped back down I-95 to Miami Beach. With John Paul's words still in my head, I changed my clothes and headed up to the gym for a good workout.

He was right; it had been a while. I couldn't do as much on the weights as I used to, and I needed to fix that shit. I finished my sets and headed back to our floor by running the stairs. I was a little out of breath and decided my endurance was also a little lacking. I'd have to hit the beach early in the morning and run again. I'd start keeping track of distance and time.

And so my fitness craze began.

I hit the beach every morning and was pretty pleased with how well I was progressing. I started going really early before there were any tourists on the beach and before Raine even headed off to her classes. My routine runs on the beach became cathartic. The pounding of my feet in the sand, the call of gulls, the scurrying of sandpipers, and the chill of the early morning waves across my shoes were relaxing. At the hour I began, the sun wouldn't have quite risen over the horizon, and the beach would be all but empty.

One weekend morning, as the sun broke over the sea in brilliant red and purple, I reached my halfway point and turned to head back south. There were a handful of early risers looking for seashells left from the high tide, a couple other joggers, and some fishermen around. I dodged the fishing poles jutting out over the water and the tractor smoothing out the high tide line and slowed to a fast walk.

There was a guy sitting at the edge of the water, dark Ray-Bans concealing his eyes, but his head was angled in my direction. Just as I veered away from the shore, he spoke.

"Good morning for a run."

I narrowed my eyes a little. Who wears sunglasses this early in the morning? Then again, the whole Miami fashion scene didn't make any fucking sense to me, so for all I knew, it was normal. I looked him over, appraising the tattoos on his decently muscled arms and chest. He wasn't my size but obviously spent more than the occasional day at the gym. Around his neck was a long chain with a pair of dog tags hanging from it. Across his chest were the words "God forgives I don't" in scripted black ink.

"It's South Beach," I replied. "It's always a good morning for a run."

He shrugged.

"Guess so," he said. "I'm not from around here, so I typically hit the gym. Too cold for outside running."

He tapped his sunglasses up with one finger, and I could see a bullet tattooed on the inside of his wrist. It was one of those brothers-in-arms symbols, marking him military. There were more words on the inside of his right arm and down his left side, but I couldn't make them out.

The guy was looking at me and appraising me as much as I was appraising him, maybe even more so. I tensed, suddenly anxious. I wasn't sure if he was spoiling for a fight or actually checking me out in some other way, but I didn't like it—not at all.

"Who the fuck are you?" I asked.

He smirked.

"Well," he said slowly, "I'm not the pheasant plucker."

I narrowed my eyes and looked him over again. I thought about his words, and determined the guy must be high or something.

"What the fuck is that supposed to mean?"

"It's a tongue twister," he said. "Haven't you ever done tongue twisters?"

I glared, and he laughed.

"I'm not the pheasant plucker," he said again and much faster, "I'm the pheasant plucker's son. I'm only plucking pheasants 'til the pheasant plucker comes."

He stood up, adjusted the sunglasses again, and gave me another half smirk.

"Here's the catch," he added. He briefly pointed his finger at me like a gun. "You're the pheasant."

One more smirk flew at me before he turned and walked away. I stood there at the edge of the water with a sense of dread and just watched him walk off. By the time I had collected myself enough to run up the beach with the intention of beating an explanation out of him, he had disappeared.

A week went by, but I didn't see him again. Thoughts of the strange encounter became a faint memory. My routine continued. I still went to Bar Crudo most days, but I didn't feel as much of an urge to order something. I usually left feeling pretty good, and I even called John Paul to tell him his advice had helped. Raine seemed really happy I'd found something to occupy my time, and I was a little less irritable.

I'd even found a dude named Zack at the gym in the condo building who didn't totally piss me off. He was a big guy like me and spotted me a few times for bench presses.

"Thanks, bro," I said as he helped me rack the bar. "See ya tomorrow."

"No problem," Zack replied.

I took the stairs from the top floor gym down to the fourth floor. I caught my breath at the landing outside our condo and then proceeded to the door. As soon as I opened it, I paused.

The hairs on the back of my neck stood up, and I held my breath. My fingers tensed reflexively, and my body went on alert.

Nothing was out of place. Everything was exactly how I had left it a couple hours ago. There wasn't anything missing, moved to the side, or disturbed in any way. There weren't any abnormal smells in the condo, and the balcony door was closed and locked from the inside. I still knew it, though.

Someone had been in here.

I felt my skin crawl, and I continued to hold my breath as my eyes scanned the room to find...nothing. I let the air out of my lungs and took a few steps inside. I stealthily made my way through every room, but the only evidence of an intrusion was the tingling in my spine and the raw, gut instinct that came from spending years watching my back to stay alive.

Maybe John Paul was fucking with me.

I knew he wasn't though. Not only was it not his style, he also knew such actions could get him killed before I would realized he was the intruder. John Paul wouldn't break into my apartment because he wouldn't have a reason to do so. He also had no skills when it came to breaking and entering.

I shook my head to try to get the tension out of my body, but it didn't work well. I wondered if I was just on edge because of what John Paul had said, but I dismissed the idea immediately. I would be the first person to admit I had the occasional attack of paranoia, but this didn't feel the same—not at all. My fingers were twitching, clutching slightly, as if they'd like to wrap themselves around a shot glass about now.

Fucking fabulous.

A noise at the door caused me to startle, and God knows what Raine saw in my eyes when she opened the door, but her expression went from a smile to wide-eyed fear in a split second.

"What is it?" she asked quickly. "Bastian? What's wrong?"

I shook my head.

"Nothing," I lied. "Just in my head, I guess. You surprised me."

Her eyes narrowed into a "don't give me that shit" glare.

Unable to voice what was going on in my head, I turned without a word and headed to the bathroom. I even shut the door to pee though I didn't usually bother. Too much time in the wild made me kind of oblivious to someone watching me take a piss.

She hammered on the door.

"I'm not buying that!" she called. "Tell me what happened!"

"Can't hear you, babe!" I called back as I flushed and turned on the water at the sink.

"Open the door!"

"What's that?"

"Bastian!"

"Huh? What?" I yelled. "Can't hear ya over the water!"

This went on for a few minutes while I left the water running, shaved, and brushed my teeth. When she finally seemed to give up, I turned off the water and waited another minute before I opened the door. I could hear her in the kitchen, so I went through the bedroom to go out on the balcony to smoke.

Raine obviously wasn't happy when I came back inside, but I had calmed down enough to put my happy face back on and deny anything was wrong. I only had to put up with a few glares and some snippy remarks about what we were having for dinner. That suited me just fine because it meant I could be just a little bit pissy in return and claim it was because she was grumpy.

Yeah, we guys can have our mind games, too.

Raine dove right into her studies while I did the dishes. I could hear her clacking away on her laptop as I placed clean silverware in the drawer as quietly as possible. When I finished, I stood behind the kitchen island for a few minutes and watched the back of her head as she worked. Her shoulders were stiff and squared, and she didn't turn to look at me when I came to sit in the chair across from the couch.

Clearly I wasn't getting anything but the silent treatment tonight, so I cut my losses and went to bed early. Raine continued to ignore me when she finally came into the bedroom. She changed into a set of pale blue short pajamas instead of one of my T-shirts and climbed into bed without a word.

I couldn't tell her. It would only scare her, and I was paranoid enough for the both of us.

Even with her not speaking to me, I still reached out and wrapped an arm around her waist. Raine remained stiff and turned away from me but didn't push my hand away. I couldn't handle it if she did that, which she knew very well. At least I hadn't pissed her off so much she refused to come to bed. That would have killed me.

Despite the inner turmoil, my dick immediately noticed the close proximity of the only pussy he cared about and started making himself a little more impressive. I had to shift my hips back a bit because I was certain my cock shoving into her side wasn't going to go over well at all.

I lay my head on the edge of her pillow and watched her. I wanted to tell her I loved her, but my throat was dry, and the words wouldn't form. Outside, a sudden storm blew up from the east and slammed drops of rain against the balcony doors. I closed my eyes and eventually dozed off, but the nightmares came immediately.

After a few hours of restlessness, I gave up.

With a cigarette in one hand and a lighter in the other, I sat at the table and looked out the glass door of the balcony toward the ocean. The flame rose up and lit the tip of the smoke, and I inhaled in a long, slow motion before blowing smoke out into the room.

Raine would be pissed—well, even more pissed—when she found out I had been smoking inside, but it was pouring outside, and I wasn't going to get soaked. I'd light a fucking candle or something to cover up the smell though I knew it wouldn't work.

I couldn't get the thoughts out of my head. Someone had been here. I couldn't explain why I knew it, but I did, and it was scaring the shit out of me. All my senses were on hyper-alert, and they sent waves of tension through my muscles until I could barely hold my cigarette.

I kept remembering the cage fight I was in, and the idea of doing that again was extremely attractive. It wasn't something I could explain to Raine. She wouldn't get it, and I was a hundred percent sure she wouldn't approve one iota. I never did tell her where I had been or what I had been doing, but I had been gone a long time. I couldn't get away with that again.

What if I wasn't gone so long?

The bar really wasn't that far away—I'd spent a lot of time just cruising around before I had stopped. I could easily get there in a few minutes, pound some dude, and be back within an hour. Raine would never know.

I looked up at the clock. It was only a few minutes after midnight, which meant the bar was still open and probably still running fights. I could get there in ten minutes, maybe sooner.

A plan formed in my head: I could get up quietly, scrawl out a little note saying I'd be back soon just so she wouldn't worry if she did wake up, and silently let myself out of the apartment. I couldn't ride the bike in the storm, but I could take Raine's Subaru and keep to a reasonable speed all the way to the bar, walk in, beat the shit out of the guy in the cage, and make my way back home.

I'd feel good when it was done. Not completely right again, but good.

Raine would be here alone. Whoever came into the condo could come back again.

All thoughts of leaving her alone vanished. With the window barely cracked open, I chain-smoked the rest of the night. As the storm passed and the sunrise over the ocean began to light up the balcony window, I found a bottle of Febreze and sprayed it around the kitchen.

If Raine noticed, she didn't say anything.

———⊶••⦿•⊷———

I was on guard the whole next day though it probably didn't make any difference. With my paranoia still at its highest, I considered following Raine to her classes. I knew she'd be seriously pissed if she caught me hanging around the campus. Still, if whoever had been inside the condo had been looking for her, she was vulnerable whenever she was away from me.

I made a mental list of who might have been inside the condo. The most obvious answer was one of Franks' men, maybe even one sent to kill us both. As likely an idea as it seemed, I didn't think it was right. John Paul was still in close contact with Landon, and he would know if Franks had ordered a hit on me. Landon would have given me some kind of warning; I was sure of that.

Wasn't I?

The only other person I could think of was Landon himself, but like John Paul, it wasn't his style. If he wanted something from me, he'd just come out and demand it.

So who, then?

I had no idea. As I watched Raine walk out the door, I couldn't stand the idea of her going to class alone, and I ended up following the bus on my bike. I hung out around her classrooms all day, trying to keep myself to the shadows. Thankfully, it was Wednesday, and she didn't have any evening labs.

She almost caught me when she headed to the university cafeteria for lunch, but I managed to duck behind a tree before she could see me. It was a good thing, too—I was fairly sure that conversation wouldn't have been a civil one. By three in the afternoon, she was back on the bus and heading home. I sped past and beat her back to the condo.

We ate and she talked about her day. I smiled a lot without saying anything. Every time she asked me what was up, I changed the subject. When we went to bed, I held her against me but couldn't get past my own head enough to even fuck her.

"Are you going to tell me what's bothering you?"

"I'm good," I lied. "Maybe I'm coming down with something. It's fucking spring break all over the damn beach. I probably caught something from a tourist."

She wasn't buying it, but she dropped her line of questioning.

At three in the morning, I couldn't sleep.

Again.

The dream that had awakened me played back through my head.

We are on the beach, and the helicopter has landed just a few hundred yards away. Raine's stomach is rounded, and she places her hands over the top of it as she looks down and smiles. She waves at me as she gets in the front seat of the helicopter, and it starts to rise up and away from me. I raise my hand to wave back, but she's already gone.

My breath caught in my throat, and Raine stirred, opening her eyes slightly.

"What's wrong?" she asked immediately.

I let my eyes drift to hers and shrugged one shoulder.

"Nothing," I muttered.

"Bad dream?"

She knew me way too well.

"Yeah, I guess."

"Are you going to tell me about it?"

I didn't want to. Talking about it was like living it over again. I also didn't want her to know how much being back in civilization where people could find us easily scared the shit out of me. I also knew her patience was going to wear out, and eventually I would have to tell her. Telling her about the dream would be far less complicated than telling her I thought someone was stalking us.

Might as well get it over with.

"We were on the island," I said quietly. Images of the beach and our little shelter near the line of palm trees invaded my head and made my chest ache. "The helicopter was there, and you were getting on it."

I paused for too long, and Raine pressed me for more.

"I wasn't going with you," I finally said.

"Why not?" Raine asked as she moved to prop herself up on one elbow and look at me.

I shrugged again.

"You didn't want me to."

"Bastian…"

"It's just a fucking dream," I snapped. "You asked."

Raine tilted her head to get a better look at me in the dim light of the room. She reached out and ran her fingers over my jaw as she stared intently into my eyes.

"There's more to it, isn't there?" she said.

Too fucking intuitive.

I looked away from her, let out a long breath, and stared at the balcony door. When I didn't answer, she poked me in the arm.

"Tell me."

I let out a long, overdramatic sigh.

"You were pregnant," I told her.

This time, the long pause was hers. She gripped my jaw and narrowed her eyes at me.

"I'm not *her*, Bastian."

Jillian.

She was the woman who conned me into fucking her bareback so she could take my child away to be raised by some other guy. The woman I thought I loved had only used me to get what she wanted— to get what that guy couldn't give her.

"I know that."

"I'm not going to leave you," Raine continued. "Besides, you can't get me pregnant, remember?"

I'd made sure something like that could never happen to me again.

"Vasectomies are not exactly something a guy forgets."

I dropped back to the pillows, pulled her down against me, and closed my eyes.

The conversation was over. At least for now, I'd try to keep my paranoia to a minimum.

Chapter Five

The next day, I got a lot of answers, but they definitely made everything worse, not better.

I'd shaken up my routine quite a bit. I'd added both morning and afternoon workouts at the gym and still spent my early mornings running on the beach. The workouts were filling up a decent amount of time when Raine wasn't around and kept me from spending quite as much time at Bar Crudo in the late afternoons when Raine was still in class.

Sitting in a small coffee shop off the beach, I finished off my espresso and checked my watch. The bar would open soon, and I wanted to be there before there was any kind of crowd around. There were already way too many people on the beach, especially for a weekday.

I tossed a few bills down on the table and started walking through the palm trees to the street. I didn't get far before someone called out to me.

"It's been a while."

A shiver moved through me, and no amount of Miami heat could have kept it from chilling me to the bone. That voice—though it had been a long time since I heard it—was enough to send me into a near panic even without the added stress of an unknown intruder at my condo.

It can't be a coincidence.

"Landon." I turned as I spoke the name and found my former mentor leaning against the wall behind me. Though I had a couple inches on him, I always felt like I was looking straight into his eyes. Usually I had to look down on other guys, which was a feeling I enjoyed, but Landon seemed like the exception.

In many ways.

He made for a damn imposing figure: blond, blue-eyed, strong jawed, and probably everything Hitler would have looked for in his youth brigade if Landon hadn't been approaching his forties. He wasn't as big as I was in the shoulders and chest, but anyone who looked at him knew he spent more than just a couple hours a week in the gym. He had the stoic military bearing of his SEAL training though he'd retired many years ago.

He'd beaten the shit out of me in the past, especially in the beginning when I was learning from him. He could still take me down, a fact we both knew quite well, and he was bound to do it again sometime. John Paul said it was his fucked-up way of showing he cared, and I had to agree with the assessment. As terrifying as he was, Landon was the only father-figure I'd ever had in my life.

Raine hated him. I could tell that from the way her face would scrunch up like she just stepped in dog shit anytime I mentioned him. She thought he made me a monster, but I knew better.

Landon Stark made me, no doubt about it, but not into a monster. He took me off the streets where I was destined to end up either dead or in prison at some point and turned me into who I was, for better or worse.

He saved my fucking life.

"How are you, Sebastian?"

I swallowed hard.

"Been worse," I stated. My heart was racing, and I had the feeling he could hear it. Hell, he could probably see my carotid beating in my throat; Landon never missed a detail.

"I can attest to that," Landon replied simply. "You're still off the booze."

The remark alone made me want to bury myself in a bottle or two. At least he hadn't caught me walking into the bar. If he had waited another minute or two to make himself known, he would have discovered my intended destination.

"Yeah, almost a year now," I said. I shoved my cigarette into my mouth and inhaled deeply as I tried to center myself and get my shit together. "What are you doing here?"

"Checking up on you," he said.

Landon was never one for hiding his intentions. When I thought about it, I realized after all this time that it *was* plausible. He might be here only to check up on me, but I doubted it.

So why was he here?

There were too many answers to that question, and I didn't like the sound of any of them. Having him show up so soon after someone had been in my apartment raised my hackles. I braced myself as I wondered just what this meeting was going to entail.

"Well, I'm good," I said. "Consider the check complete."

"Good, are you?" he said. He nodded back toward the door to Bar Crudo, which was just across the street from where we walked down the sidewalk. "Hanging out in a bar every day? Cage fighting? Really, Sebastian?"

He wouldn't have had to have been in the area long to know I went to the same bar almost daily. However, my single escapade to the part of town with the cage fighting venue had been a month ago, which meant Landon had either been in Miami that long or had someone in the area keeping tabs on me. John Paul hadn't mentioned it, so he probably didn't know. I wasn't sure if I should consider that a good sign or not.

"It's good for quick cash," I said with a shrug. I wasn't going to be able to dismiss it so easily, though. Not with Landon. Aside from Raine, there was no one who knew me better.

He just raised an eyebrow, and I shrugged again.

"It was a good stress reliever," I added. "I only went there once."

"You're getting back in shape," he noted.

"Yeah, I've been hitting the gym a lot," I said.

"Good," he said quietly. "You're going to need it."

I felt my heart sink into my stomach.

"We need to talk," Landon said. "Let's go."

I followed him up Ocean Drive and past the park. We stopped at a little café called The Local House. Landon was silent as the server brought out fresh bread with marinara sauce. He took our orders with a practiced smile and served us iced coffee in little Mason jars, and Landon ordered salmon for both of us.

"What's going on?" I asked when the server disappeared inside.

"I've got some news that concerns you," Landon said flatly. He reached into his pocket and dropped a photograph on the table in front of me.

I dropped my eyes to the picture, and as soon as I saw what was on it, I grabbed it up and held it closer to me and out of the vision of anyone who might have walked by.

It was a body.

Actually, two bodies—a man and a woman.

"Jillian," I heard myself whisper. She was curled up in a near fetal position, and there was an obvious bullet hole at her right temple. A few feet from her was the man she ran off with when she left me. He was on the floor in a similar position.

"Mrs. Koe and her husband, Ian Koe, were found in their Italian home last week," Landon told me. "The police are investigating, of course, but they haven't found anything."

I moved my eyes away from the picture and to Landon's face. Instinct told me everything—their blood was on his hands. He'd killed them, or at least had them killed, but why?

My breathing stopped. My heart might have stopped, too. All I could do was stare at the picture—the picture of a woman I hated. A woman I might have killed myself if given the opportunity, but I hadn't seen her since she ran off with the other person in the photograph. I'd tried to stop her, but Landon intervened. He would have killed me before he let me go after her.

She's dead.

"Apparently, there's a child left behind."

I flashed my eyes up to his. Of course there was a child. *My* child.

"Child?" It was the only word I managed to choke out.

"A little boy, six years old."

I clamped my eyes shut. It was too much at once, and my brain was overwhelmed. Images of Jillian and me when we were together shuffled through my mind like pictures from one of those ancient toy movie projectors run with a hand-crank—all black and white and choppy. A flash from the diamond ring I had bought for her the day she left blinded me from the inside.

I opened my eyes and looked back at Landon. I wanted to speak.

I wanted to ask him a thousand questions, but I couldn't form a single one.

He leaned forward.

"Let's get to the point, shall we?" he said quietly. "He's alive. He's safe. And he's all yours for just one little favor."

"Favor?" I could barely hear myself speak.

"One little fight, you and five others. Half of them have never ever done a real tournament before, so it'll be a piece of cake, assuming you really are back in shape. Three weeks of a little catch-up training, a few days up north for the tournament, and you walk away with the instant family you've always wanted."

I looked in his eyes and considered his words. I was about to deny it—there was no way I wanted a family—but before I could even consider the words, I knew they were wrong. It was exactly what I wanted. It would replace the family I had never known, and I could make my own shit childhood seem less crappy if I could give a kid the life I never had.

I'll never be able to give Raine a child.

The server dropped off our entrees and refilled our drinks. He asked if there was anything else we needed, but a glare from Landon sent him scurrying away with a towel over his arm.

"Why this fight?" I asked, pulling myself from my thoughts. "Why now?"

Landon sighed and sat back.

"There's war in Chicago," he said as he forked a chunk of his fish. "The Greco family and the Moretti family have been fighting over heroin and caviar for a while now. Last year, the Russians moved in and stirred things up even more. There were a couple of confrontations, and people were killed on both sides. Now they're in the process of reclaiming territory. Franks is losing money over the whole situation, so he's come up with a solution."

"A tournament," I said.

"Exactly." Landon leaned his elbows on the table and took a drink from the Mason jar. "Franks wants control of the caviar—it's becoming more and more lucrative—and this was his way of getting both that control and ending the wars. Warring families hurt business around the globe."

"What if I win?"

"What if?" Landon echoed. There was a challenge in his voice.

"*When* I win," I corrected, "what does Franks get out of it?"

"He'll get oversight of all the caviar business in Seattle, New York, LA, and Chicago," Landon said. "The feuding between the Italians stops, which is good for business in general, and the Russians get their asses out of Chicago altogether and act as Franks' supplier overseas."

As I processed this information, my mind cleared a little. Though we hadn't had such a conversation in many years, it was familiar territory.

"Who's in from New York and LA?"

"Grant Chambers," he said. "He's big in the arms trade in New York. There's also Maria Hill in LA, who's been having problems with the heroin business since the war broke out."

"Don't know her," I said. "I remember Chambers."

"She's not been involved in the tournaments before," Landon confirmed, "but she's pissed off enough at Greco and Moretti to get involved. Most of her business has been with Latin America—coke and the like. She also hates the Russians and wants them out of the picture."

"So three from Chicago, one from LA, one from New York, and me. Six players."

"Small game," Landon said with a nod. "And only one who is of any concern."

"Who is that?"

"Moretti's man," Landon said. "I'll let you do your own research, and you can tell me what you think."

"You are assuming I'm going to agree to this," I said. Even as I gave voice to my observation, I knew he wouldn't be here if there was any choice involved.

"You are."

There was one question I couldn't stop myself from asking.

"What if I refuse?"

"Well, who knows what will happen to the kid?" Landon asked with a slight shrug. "He's technically Franks' nephew or whatever, so he could end up living with him. Then again, maybe Franks doesn't want a kid. Maybe he'll get rid of him, foster care or whatever."

I swallowed hard as the muscles in my arms tightened.

Not my kid. No fucking way will that happen to my kid.

"I know for a fact that he'd get rid of you and your little piece of

Ohio-born tail."

I knew the threat was coming; I didn't really have to ask. Hearing it still sent my mind spinning. Most of me didn't care if Franks decided to have me killed, and Landon knew that. Threatening Raine, though—that was a whole other thing. Threatening a child I didn't even know shouldn't have mattered to me, but it did.

A lot.

I guess I wasn't a heartless bastard after all.

The server dropped off the bill when Landon indicated we didn't want to entertain the idea of dessert. I hadn't managed to eat my meal, anyway. Landon leaned back in his chair, handed a stack of cash to the server, and looked across the table at me.

"Well?" he said simply.

"You say that like I'm being given some kind of choice," I spat back at him.

"You aren't," Landon acknowledged, "but I like to give you the illusion."

"Thanks a lot," I mumbled with a low growl.

"You have every reason to win," he said. "You'll get the kid you wanted, and you'll have the girl. I'll also make sure you're never asked to do anything like this again. I'll get you set up far away—some place all of you can live and be happy together. You'll have everything you ever wanted, and no more fighting, but you have to do this one last time."

"One last time," I repeated.

Closing my eyes for a moment, I tried to come up with any way to get out of this, but my mind drew a blank. Landon wasn't one to skip any details, and he wouldn't have approached me until there were no options left. It was probably why Jillian and her husband were dead—just so he could be sure he had more leverage over me than just Raine, as if threatening her wouldn't have been enough.

Maybe it wouldn't have been. Knowing they could hurt Raine would have given me time to get her and take off. We'd be on the run, but I could have still protected her. I would have tried, at least, but with my kid out there somewhere, orphaned? Landon had played me perfectly.

"One week from today," Landon informed me, "we'll all meet. You, me, Franks, the other bosses, and the competition will be at a location south of Miami. I'll send you all their names so you can check them out ahead of time. John Paul is going to beef up your training a little now, but as soon as we're done with the pow-wow, you come with me for real training."

"Why can't John Paul do it?" I asked.

"Because Franks wants *you*," Landon said simply.

"He's hoping I'm going to lose?"

"No, he's counting on you to win. Despite what you did in the past, you've never come close to being beaten in the fights. He needs you. Why do you think he let you live?"

I leaned my head back and stared up at the fans attached to the ceiling. I didn't have a choice; I knew that. My mind didn't know what to focus on first—the idea that I was going to fight again, the threat against Raine, or the fact that I had a son out there somewhere.

"Where is he?" I asked quietly. "Where's my kid?"

"Still in Italy," Landon replied.

"He's safe?"

"For now."

"What's his name?"

Landon stared at me coldly for a moment.

"Alexander," he finally said. "I believe he's typically called *Alex*."

Alex. The name floated around in my head for a bit. I put the dates together and realized he'd be in the first grade by now.

"I have another appointment," Landon said as he stood up. "I'll be in touch with your training schedule."

"What do I tell Raine?" I asked.

"I really don't give a shit." Landon walked by me without another word.

I watched him walk off, turn the corner, and head up the street before I made my own way back toward South Pointe Drive. My fake calm dissolved immediately as I headed away from Landon and down the street—straight to the door of Bar Crudo. The more my mind raced, the more desperate I became.

There's no way out of it.

I was going to have to fight—no question about it. Landon didn't make idle threats, and if I refused, Raine would pay the price. God knows what would happen to Alex.

I was dizzy as I sat on one of the tall barstools, grateful for the high back. I leaned against it, but the dizziness turned to nausea, so I leaned forward again with my head spinning. With my eyes closed, I took several deep breaths, but I couldn't stop my hands from shaking.

I have a son.

Holy fuck, a son.

The bartender approached. It was the same guy who was always there during the week in the early evenings. A deeply tanned couple sucked martinis through straws and made googly eyes at one another. There was only one other person down at the end of the bar. He was also tan with tattoos running up one arm and a pair of Ray Bans balanced on the back of his neck. He had a glass of something caramel colored perched between his fingertips. I probably would have recognized him if my mind hadn't been in such a state.

I stared down at my hands on the bar as they twitched and shook.

"Can I get you something?" the bartender asked.

I shook my head but didn't look at him. I twisted my fingers around themselves on the counter top and stared at nothing.

My throat was dry. I swallowed over and over again, but it didn't help. Everything inside of me came crashing down over my body, sending a shudder through every muscle. I squeezed my eyes shut, but that didn't help what was going on inside my head. I opened my eyes to find myself staring at the row of bottles on the shelf.

I can't deal with this.

The couple who had been sitting to my left got up and wrapped their arms around each other as they sauntered out. The guy at the end ordered another scotch. When the bartender came back to my side of the bar, he wiped down the counter and grabbed a tip that had been left nearby. He stopped in front of me and again asked if there was anything I wanted.

"Vodka," I heard myself say. "A…a shot of vodka."

"Sure thing," the bartender responded, obviously surprised. I couldn't blame him for that, though—I'd been coming in here for months without ordering anything.

I motioned with one hand up to the top shelf of the bar.

"The good stuff," I said quietly.

"You got it."

He placed the shot glass in front of me, and the clear liquid sloshed slightly for a moment before settling. I ran my finger around the edge of the glass before wrapping my hand around it.

Another tournament.

A fight to the death.

Winning meant protecting Raine and being united with my son.

I have a son.

Fuck me.

I gripped the little glass. It was quite a bit bigger than a single ounce shot and filled nearly to the top. I swallowed past the lump in my throat. I tried another deep breath, but it came out in a shuddering gasp.

It will calm me down, I told myself.

Raine's voice rose above all the other turmoil in my brain.

"I can't be with that man, Bastian."

She wouldn't like this. Understatement of the fucking century. I started to release the glass, but I didn't quite manage to get my fingers off of it. The tips remained as if they were glued there.

She doesn't have to know…just one.

My vision blurred. I couldn't swallow anymore—my throat was too dry.

"You aren't that person anymore, Bastian." Raine's voice echoed through my head again.

"I'm not so sure about that, baby," I whispered to myself. "I might have to be him again—just for a little while."

I focused on the glass again, steeling myself against the desire to bring it to my lips. The muscles up my arm flexed automatically, and I tightened my fingers around the glass again.

It felt good.

Natural.

Squeezing my eyes shut, I lifted my hand and brought the glass up closer to my face. Tilting it back and draining it seemed like the easiest thing in the world to do, while setting it back down was impossible.

If I do this, it's done. I can't go back.

It's only one drink…it's not like I'd be instantly back to the same old me again.

She'll hate me for it.

I need to calm down, or I won't be able to figure this out.

Just one.

I stopped thinking, tossed it back, and felt the burn as it slid down my throat. I dropped the empty glass back down on the top of the bar as the liquid coated my insides.

Can't go back now.

"Another," I said.

The bartender refilled the glass.

What the fuck am I doing?

<hr />

The exit from Bar Crudo loomed in front of me as I stumbled toward it. I wasn't sure exactly how a glass door could look so fuzzy, but it did. I glanced at my watch and realized I didn't have much time before Raine would be returning from class. I had to get back to the condo.

"Sweetheart, you look like you could use a little help."

I flicked my eyes in the direction of the effeminate voice to see a tall, African American man with bleached-blond hair. Upon closer inspection, I realized he wasn't all that tall; he was just wearing ridiculously high platform shoes, which were mostly covered by his long, billowing skirt. Maybe it was a swimsuit cover up; I wasn't sure. I blinked a few times and wondered if he was wearing a woman's style bikini underneath.

He waved his arms around, nearly spilling the contents of his designer purse all over the ground, and called to another dude in a flowing, green-flowered robe of some kind. He had a tattoo on his arm that read "Don't Judge," and his eyebrows had thin vertical lines shaved into them. He checked for traffic before he walked across the street with his arms held out wide.

"Oh may *gawd*!" the second guy called out.

I laughed at the spectacle, which made me dizzy, which made me laugh more.

"You found quite a little chunk here, didn't ya, sweetie?"

"I don't think he's doin' too well, babe."

I wondered what he meant but then realized I couldn't quite stand up straight. I had to get home before Raine got there, and all the humor of the situation left me.

"Well, we should help him out!"

"You mean 'help yourself!'"

They both started waving their arms around and squealing at

each other in the most stereotypical way and didn't seem to notice as I backed away and turned, fumbling over my feet a little as I made my way toward our building.

Only a couple of blocks…

Looking up the street, it seemed like a lot farther. I concentrated on that whole "one foot in front of the other" thing until I realized I had passed the entrance and was standing in front of the gelato place on the corner. Gelato sounded really good, so I went inside and tried to focus on the various flavors offered. I couldn't seem to choose, and a bunch of tourists walked in and started placing their orders, occupying the woman behind the counter.

With my head still swimming, I forced myself back outside and made my way to the entrance of the condo building, swiped my keycard, and pushed open the security door. The elevators were on my right, and the door to the stairs was on my left. I veered left out of habit, went up three steps, fell down, and then used the banister to pull myself back up.

Just need to get inside…

I reached the second floor and decided I wasn't going to make it up two more flights. I fumbled at the door handle a couple of times before getting it to open, then careened into the wall next to the elevator button. Somehow, I managed to get it to light up, and the elevator door opened.

There was a couple inside, probably in their late forties, dressed to the nines like they were heading to some dinner party. They took a step away from me as I entered and tried to find the number four on the key panel. Once I pushed it, I leaned against the wall of the elevator and kept my eyes to the ground.

"Are you all right, sir?" the man in the suit asked.

I laughed.

"Gonna have to kill a few people," I slurred. "After that, all should be good."

The woman's eyes went wide as she grabbed the man's arm and whispered something to him. He pulled her to his side and stepped back to press them both into the corner of the elevator.

The door to the elevator opened, and I found myself just outside the condo. I had to lean heavily against the door as I tried to fish my key out of my pocket. Once it was between my fingers, getting it into the lock and turned was a whole other problem. Eventually I managed to make it work and gave myself a mental shove to get through the door. I turned to close it by throwing my hand out and slapping it, which hurt a bit but got the job done. I looked down to my palm and began to laugh again.

Then I fell backwards and landed on my ass.

Deciding it was as good a place as any, I lay backwards and watched the room spin around me. There was that niggling bit in the back of my head that told me I needed to pull my shit together before Raine came home, but it wasn't loud enough to cover up the ringing in my ears.

Fuck, I didn't like this part.

I wasn't completely sure how many shots I had done, but I didn't think it was enough to have such a profound effect on me. So many months of sobriety must have driven down my tolerance quite a bit.

Raine will be home soon.

"Shit." I pushed myself up with my arms and leaned back on my elbows for a second. I rolled, or maybe fell, over on my side and tried to get my bearings enough to stand. It didn't work, so I crawled a little way across the living area until I realized I didn't actually have a destination in mind.

"She can't see me like this."

I took a deep breath and tried to regain some concentration, but all I could focus on was my alcohol breath.

"Gotta brush my teeth."

At least now I had a plan.

Though I made it to the bathroom, the toothpaste and toothbrush just weren't interested in cooperating with each other. I ended up spurting fluoridated gunk all over the sink then rubbing the toothbrush around in it, or at least trying to. Once I brought the brush up to my face, I realized I had missed.

"Fuck it."

I dropped the brush in the sink and stumbled to the kitchen. I pulled open a couple of drawers, looking for gum but came up empty-handed.

"Better to smell like smoke," I announced to the room. My cigarettes were still in my pocket, so at least it didn't take any effort to find them. I made my way to the balcony, slid down the wall until I was firmly planted on my ass, and lit up.

I chain smoked for a few minutes until I was pretty sure there wasn't any other stench on me but that. Of course, the brief amount of time that had passed had done nothing to sober me up, and everything around me was still spinning a bit.

It was brief, wasn't it? How long had I been sitting here?

I shook my head to try to clear it, which was a big mistake. I tried to count the cigarette butts that lay between my feet to judge how long I'd been there, but those little fuckers were less cooperative than the toothpaste had been. Staring at them nauseated me. I took a long breath through my nose and let it out my mouth as I stared at a single cigarette butt that had made it into the bucket and tried to add it to the count. Focusing on a small object helped to slow the circling motion of the world around me.

I heard the door open.

My hand started shaking a bit as I pushed myself back onto my feet and straightened the edge of my shirt. I just needed to keep myself focused long enough to say I wasn't feeling well and go lie down.

I can do this. I can fake this. Done it plenty of times before.

I turned, checked my breathing, and opened the balcony door to see Raine placing her book bag down by the coffee table and turning to smile at me.

Her smile faded immediately.

"Bastian?"

I bumped into the kitchen island and winced as my hip jarred against it.

"Hey, babe," I said…or maybe I slurred it.

"What's wrong?" Raine asked as she narrowed her eyes.

"I'm ferfectly pine," I said with a serious nod. At least, I hoped it looked serious—that was the goal. I took a couple of unsteady steps toward her.

"You're *what?*"

I stopped and thought about what I had just said. It had made sense, hadn't it? I tried to repeat the words in my head but found I had forgotten what I had said. With wandering eyes, I finally found Raine, still standing in the middle of the living room and staring at me. I smiled and walked toward her.

Well, I tried to.

Instead, I lurched off to the side a bit and had to catch my balance. A chuckle escaped from me, but when I looked at Raine, she didn't seem amused.

"Oh shit, it's not funny, is it?" I snickered. I didn't intend to snicker; it just came out that way.

"Oh my God," she murmured. "Bastian, you're drunk."

Shit.

Our exchange from the airport bar where I almost took a shot ran through my head. We had just returned to civilization, and I'd gone from blissful isolation to being surrounded by crowds demanding Raine's attention. At the first opportunity, I found a place that would serve me vodka.

"Bastian…don't do this."

"Do what?" I barked out a laugh. "Drink? I'm a fucking alcoholic, Raine. I told you that the first fucking day. That hasn't fucking changed just because I didn't have any alcohol available. I never stopped wanting it. Never. You know this shit."

"You aren't that person anymore, Bastian. I meant that. I wouldn't be with someone like that. I couldn't be with someone who I thought would hit me again."

"I love you," Raine said softly, her hand still on my arm, "but when you drink, you become someone else. I can't be with that man, Bastian."

"I won't be."

She took a couple of steps backwards, and I knew—I just *knew*—she was going to leave. My mouth dropped open, but I couldn't form any words at first. I couldn't move, either. It was as if my central nervous system was trying to fire every neuron inside of it at once, and each and every one of them failed to respond.

Can't let this happen…just can't…For fuck's sake, Stark, get your shit together.

"Don't," I whispered as I shook my head. "Please don't."

Even through my drunken haze, I could see it all in her face—the confusion, the sorrow, the anger. Her face seemed to fall as her shoulders slumped. I could see the tears forming in her eyes as she backed away again.

"No…no, Raine…" I reached out for her, but toppled forward and down onto my knees. My head pulsed and my eyes couldn't focus well, but I could still see her in front of me. Reaching out and crawling forward, I found her thigh with my hand.

With my chest tightening around my heart and lungs, I grabbed for her and pulled her closer until my head was against her stomach.

"Don't leave!" I begged. "Please, baby. I'm sorry…I didn't mean to…please, please, God, Raine—don't go!"

I clung to her.

Raine.

My lifeline.

The sails of my ship.

The only calm for my storm.

My only reason to exist in this fucked up world.

"Don't leave me!" I sobbed against her. If she pushed me away, if she turned around and left me, I wouldn't survive. No tournament game would matter. No orphaned child would matter. I couldn't do any of it without her.

When I felt her hand cradle the back of my head, I almost dropped the rest of the way to the floor. If I hadn't been clutching her so tightly, I probably would have. Tears burned as I clenched my eyes shut, and I was sure Raine's shirt was getting soaked with them. I didn't care. None of that mattered. The only thing that mattered was holding on to her.

"Don't go," I pleaded again.

"I'm not going," she said quietly. "I'm right here, Bastian. I'm not going anywhere."

"I'm sorry," I cried. Raine said something under her breath, but I couldn't hear it through my own sobbing. Her hand ran through the hair on the back of my head as she sunk down to her knees and held my head against her shoulder.

We stayed like that for a long time, kneeling on the floor and holding on to each other. I wrapped my arms underneath hers and up around her shoulders, trying to keep her as close to me as possible. Even though she said she wouldn't leave, I was afraid she could change her mind at any moment.

The dizziness of overindulgence wrapped itself around my head. My nose was stuffed up, and I couldn't breathe properly. A moment later, my stomach joined the party.

Fuck.

"Gonna be sick," I muttered as I pushed away from her. I blundered my way into the bathroom just in time to fall against the toilet and start puking. My stomach heaved and my hands shook. My back arched as my body tried to eliminate all the shit I had put into it. I could hardly hold myself up when I was done, but Raine was right there with her hand on my shoulder, offering me a glass of water.

I rinsed my mouth and spat into the toilet before reaching up to flush it.

"What the hell happened with the toothpaste?" Raine mumbled quietly.

I glanced up to see her picking my toothbrush off of the floor and wiping the paste out of the sink. She carefully distributed a little onto the brush and knelt beside me.

"Do you think you're done?" she asked.

I thought about it for a second before nodding.

"Do you need help with this?" She held up the brush, and I shook my head. "I'll be in the bedroom when you're finished."

My head was a little clearer as I leaned against the sink and cleaned myself up. I brushed my teeth, splashed water all over my face, and looked at myself in the mirror. My normally blue eyes looked almost purple with all the bloodshot lines running through them. I was pale, and my hair was a mess. I tried to calm it with my fingers before I put everything away as best I could and headed to the bedroom.

I looked at Raine where she sat up on her side of the bed. She had the blankets pulled back on my side, so I crawled in beside her, reaching out tentatively. I was relieved and a little surprised when she accepted my embrace and pulled me close to her.

"What happened, Bastian?"

"I ordered a drink," I whispered.

"Where?"

"Bar Crudo."

"The place down the block?"

"Yes," I said. "I go there every day."

"You go to that bar *every day*?"

I nodded.

"And…and what?" her voice broke. "You usually just sober up before I get home?"

"No!" I looked up to her, pleading. "I never have before—I swear. I'm there every day, but I never order anything. This was the first time. Please believe me, Raine—this was the only time. I didn't mean to…it just…it just *happened*."

Raine's lips mashed together as she stared at me.

"I don't know if I should believe you or not," she said.

"I swear," I repeated. "I never drank anything there or at that other place."

"What other place?"

Shit.

I really wasn't handling this well. I was just sober enough after puking to know how much worse I was making it.

"There was one other bar I went to," I admitted. "That night I got pissed and left you with Lindsay and Nick."

"That's why you were gone so long," she surmised.

"Yeah," I admitted, "but I didn't drink anything, not a drop."

She nodded her head slowly. I wasn't sure if she believed me or not, but when she started stroking the back of my head, I decided not to care right at the moment. I tucked my head into her shoulder. She smelled so nice, and her hands were warm on my head. I felt my dick getting hard from the proximity of her body, and I pulled her a little closer.

"My cock still wants you," I said.

"I kind of doubt you are up for that right now," Raine replied tersely.

"It's up for it," I countered. "Anytime I'm near you."

"I've noticed that."

I debated if I should confess about the cage fighting but decided against it. She might have forgotten about me coming home battered, and I didn't want to make an already painful situation worse by adding additional transgressions. I thought affirmation was a better idea.

"All I ever want is you," I proclaimed. "Even when that other girl touched me, I just thought about you and came back home."

Raine tensed.

"What girl?" she asked. Her voice was hard and flat. Her hand cupped my cheek, and she turned my head to face her. Raine's eyes were dark, and I realized what I had just said.

Ah, fuck.

Bad affirmation.

"What girl?" she demanded.

"At the other bar," I whispered.

"What other bar?"

"Um…" I stammered. "Over in Hialeah."

Raine continued to stare at me.

"I didn't touch her," I said. "She touched me, but I left."

"What do you mean, she *touched* you?"

A whole new typhoon of panic swirled around me as I tried to figure out how to tell her what had happened without bringing up the fighting. Thinking about the fighting made me realize she still knew nothing about my talk with Landon and about what I was going to have to do. I was still too intoxicated to make any sense, and I knew if I opened my mouth, all the wrong shit was going to come out of it.

"Bastian, tell me what the hell you are talking about!"

"I can't," I said. "Not right now…please? I have to tell you, but I can't right now."

"I have no idea what you're talking about!" She started to push away from me, but I clung on.

"There's shit I gotta do—for you…for him…" I babbled, not even completely sure I knew what I was saying. "I gotta do it, Raine. I don't want to, but I have to."

"I don't understand!" Raine insisted.

I knew I wasn't explaining myself well; there just wasn't anything else I could say. I was too fucked up to tell her I had to fight again, and every word out of my mouth was the wrong one. Anything I said could and would be held against me and with good reason.

I reverted to the single phrase that couldn't get me into more trouble.

"I'm sorry, I'm sorry…" I mumbled against her neck over and over again.

"Why, Bastian?" she asked. "Why did you do this now? If you've been going to that place every day, why did you take a drink today?"

I squeezed my eyes closed, gripped her tightly against me, and took a deep breath.

"I have a son," I whispered.

My declaration was made. At least for now, we'd leave it at that.

Chapter Six

At some point in the middle of the night, I woke and hobbled over to the bathroom. I was still a little drunk and thought I might be sick again. I crouched down and leaned against the tub as I stared into the toilet water.

I'd fucked up, big time. I had no idea what Raine was going to do in the morning, but I knew it wasn't going to be a barrel of laughs for me. She said she wasn't leaving, but did she just mean tonight or at all? Was there any room in her for forgiveness when she had already told me she wouldn't put up with me drinking again?

I had to convince her it was a one-time deal.

It was, wasn't it?

As fucked up as it was, I already wanted another drink. It was the only coping mechanism I knew when shit got too deep for me to handle. Knowing my son was out there alone in the world definitely fell into that category.

Raine and I both knew I had a kid out there somewhere, but somehow hearing that it was a son, a son who was now orphaned like I had been, made it all hit home a lot harder. When I told Raine about him last night, she had agreed to wait until morning before we talked about the subject anymore. She knew I was in no shape for any kind of rational discussion, and I had passed out soon afterward.

I dragged myself from the bathroom floor and went out on the balcony. It was dark and cool outside, and the only sound in the air was from the surf far below. I lit my cigarette and smoked half of it before tossing it into the metal bucket. I also picked up the ones I had missed before and tried to sweep the ash over the side with my hand.

If I was going to start serious training again, I was going to have to cut back on the smoking. At least Raine would appreciate that. It was one topic she and Landon would agree upon wholeheartedly.

Probably the only one.

I still didn't know who had been in our condo, and I was probably going to have to tell her about that as well. Now that I had talked to Landon, the possible suspects had increased by five—representatives from the five crime families I'd be battling against in the tournament. Any one of them could be scoping me out. Their bosses probably wouldn't let them kill me before the tournament started because there were rules against that, but they wouldn't have any problem with removing Raine from the situation in hopes of throwing me off my game.

It would probably work, too.

There was the added problem of what to do after the tournament was over. What would keep Landon or Franks from calling on me again? They would always be able to hold threats of Raine and my son over my head, and there wasn't a whole lot I could do to stop them. I couldn't even manage to get Franks to end up in jail when he'd ordered the deaths of sixteen people, including Raine's father. There was no way I could go to the cops with information about tournament games without landing myself in prison for life, so that wasn't an option either. I'd learned the hard way that informing on organized crime wasn't a wise option.

I couldn't cope with this shit. Even if everything went down exactly how it needed to, and I came out a winner, it wouldn't be over. Franks and his organization would always be able to make me play again. That fact didn't change the situation. I was going to have to do this. I was going to have to fight for my family.

My family.

For all I knew, Raine wouldn't want anything to do with it. Assuming she did forgive my recent transgression, that didn't mean she was going to want to help me raise a kid that wasn't hers, and I couldn't give her one of her own. Maybe she didn't even want a kid.

No, that wasn't true. I'd seen it in her eyes before whenever my vasectomy had come up. It was a great way to have sex without pregnancy risk, but now that I was with Raine, other options with less permanent effects would have been preferable.

Assuming Raine doesn't think better of it and ditch me as soon as she wakes up.

One hurdle at a time. I had to make sure she wasn't going to tell me to get lost as soon as she got out of bed. Despite my inclination to cut back, I chain smoked for the rest of the night and came up with ways I could try to apologize.

In the morning, I started by making her breakfast.

My head was pounding, and despite four large glasses of water to wash down pain relievers, the usual hangover remedy wasn't doing anything for me. The smell of the food made me want to get sick again. I was woozy, and nothing sounded better than just passing out on the couch with the TV playing some movie I'd seen a hundred times before. I felt like total shit.

Totally deserved *shit.*

"You're up early."

I startled a little before glancing over my shoulder to find Raine in her bathrobe, watching me. I smiled half a smile and motioned toward the cooking bacon.

"I figured I at least owed you breakfast."

She raised her eyebrows and sat down at the kitchen table as I poured her coffee and brought the flavored creamer she liked out of the fridge. She blew across the top of the cup before taking a sip.

"How are you feeling?" she asked.

I just shrugged.

"That bad, huh?"

"Been worse." As soon as the words were out of my mouth, I knew they were wrong.

Note to self—say as little as possible today.

Instead of talking, I spoke with actions. I served up eggs, bacon, and toast to go with her coffee. I gathered up all the fruit in the condo and made a little fruit tray for her. I even squeezed fucking orange juice though just the pressure from pushing down on the juicing tool increased the tension in my muscles, and my head pounded harder.

I really wanted to pass out, but when I checked the clock, it was still an hour before Raine would need to head to class.

One hour. I can last that long.

The hour came and went. I cleaned up the remaining mess in the bathroom so Raine could take a shower, but after she got dressed, she sat on the couch and stared at me.

"It's getting late," I said.

"I'm not going to classes today."

"You're not?"

"No," she said as she sat back against the throw pillow. "I think we have a little talking to do, don't you?"

Fuck me.

I looked away and rubbed at my eyes. It did nothing for the throbbing in my head, but I hoped I would look pathetic enough to get a bit of pity.

"I'm not sure I'm up for it," I said.

"I'm not giving you an option," Raine retorted.

Fuck me twice.

"Fuck, Raine," I groaned.

Oh there ya go, drop a few f-bombs on her. That's bound to help.

She kept glaring.

So much for pity.

"I can't do this." I dropped my hand from my head and sat down on the opposite side of the couch. "I feel like shit, and everything I say is going to come out wrong."

"You deserve to feel like shit," she said. "I'll keep it in mind while you explain yourself."

I leaned forward with my elbows on my knees and my head in my hands. I stayed that way until she cleared her throat and plopped her bare feet up on the coffee table.

I obviously wasn't getting out of this, so I went for delay tactics instead.

"Can I run first?" I asked quietly as I looked back at her. "Clear my head a little?"

She glared at me. I thought I might have heard an actual growl.

"It really would help," I pleaded. I was trying for something between pathetic and desperate, but I wasn't sure if I could pull it off. Mostly I just needed some time to think about what I was going to say.

"Fine," she snapped. "Be back in an hour."

I nodded, got dressed, and took off for the beach.

It was later than my usual run, and there were already a few people milling about the sand. The skies were grey, so I had that going for me; at least the sun wasn't making my headache worse. The pounding of my shoes against the sand wasn't helping, but I trudged on.

As the clouds began to thicken, the sky turned a darker shade of grey. Each step along the beach reverberated through my legs and up into my torso and shoulders, keeping time with my throbbing temples. It should have been relaxing and cathartic, but it wasn't. I wanted each step to take me farther away from the decision I had to make, but I knew it only brought me closer. Even as the huge condo buildings of Miami Beach fell behind me, I knew I couldn't escape what I had to do.

What was I going to tell Raine?

Sandpipers pointed their beaks at me as they tried to scamper out of my way. I crushed shells under my shoes and dodged washed-up jellyfish as I ran. A Cuban dude with a metal detector walked along the beach just above the tideline with his blue jacket blowing around in the wind. He smiled and said good morning to me, and I ignored him.

It started raining.

Within minutes, I was drenched.

I didn't care. I just kept pounding the sand with my feet and dodging whatever shit the tide brought in with the waves. If I kept my head down so I couldn't really see the buildings off to one side or the few people wandering around, I could almost believe I was back on the island.

Except I was wearing a pair of pricey running shoes.

I stopped, ripped the shoes and socks off my feet, and tossed them to the sand up the beach. Maybe someone would steal them, but it wouldn't matter much to me. I kept on running down the edge of the shore in my bare feet until I couldn't run anymore. I slowed, walked a bit, and then dropped to the sand and stared out over the water.

My kid is out there.

My son.

I have a fucking son.

The initial shock I had felt over hearing of Jillian's death had worn off, and all I could think about was him—Alex. My son. My fucking six-year-old son. Landon didn't have a picture of him, just the name. I had no idea what he looked like. Did he have my color hair? Her eyes? Did he even know about me? Even if he did, would he want anything to do with me? He'd miss his mother and the man who had at least played the father role in his life so far, and he might very well hate me for all of it. If he didn't know, well…I didn't know how I was supposed to explain it to him.

I didn't know how to explain the process of getting him to Raine either.

She's going to fucking freak out.

As much as I had told her about my past and the people in it, she wasn't going to understand that there was no way I could avoid the tournament. She'd want us to run, and I'd have to convince her there was no place to hide. If we did run, I'd never find my son.

This was so screwed up, I realized all the shit I had already seen in my life was a goddamn birthday cake with fucking whippy icing compared to this clusterfuck. The freaking sprinkles on top were Landon's voice popping into my head.

"*When all odds are against you, and there's no way out, you can't lose your focus. That's the time you have to find that point inside of yourself—the one that knows there is no such word as defeat—and fucking tie yourself to it, you hear me? If you don't, you're lost.*"

Strangely enough, the words calmed me. I breathed deeply and leaned my arms across my knees.

I needed to put it all in perspective. I needed to find that focal point inside of myself and cling to it. Once I had my focus, I'd be able to complete the tasks necessary to get all of us out of this mess.

First things first: I got drunk.

Raine was pissed, and I was going to have to explain how it happened. I had the option of glossing over it for the really nasty shit that would follow in hopes that she kind of forgot the whole night I spent off my rocker, but I was pretty sure her short-term memory was better than that. The only other option was promising it wouldn't happen again and apologizing profusely.

At least I was good at that. With a partial plan in my head, I stood and brushed sand from my ass before heading back in the other direction at a slow jog.

Assuming Raine didn't pack a bag and head for the door at that point, it brought me to the next item—my son. She knew about him from our time on the raft together. When you're in a situation you don't think you'll survive, there's no point in hiding anything from each other. I'd told her every sordid detail about my life, the pregnancy of my former girlfriend included. I'd also promptly forgotten about the whole topic because thinking about it fucking hurt.

It was all a lot more real now, and sweeping it under the rug wasn't an option any longer. I had to deal with it. There was only one way I could face it, and that was with Raine by my side. If she wasn't there for me, there would be no point in any of the rest of it. If she was there for me, I knew she'd also be there for my son.

And now for the big one: I had to fight in another tournament.

Strangely enough, the fight itself wasn't my biggest concern. On one level, I knew it would be dangerous—it always was—but it wasn't the fear of losing my life that caused my concern. No, my worry was what would happen after the battle was over. When I was standing over the last dead body, what would Franks demand next in exchange for Raine and Alex's safety?

Anything and everything, because he was a cold-hearted motherfucker.

I wasn't sure if Landon really believed what he had told me or not, but I knew Franks wasn't going to let me off so easily. I'd testified against him, and there was no forgiving that. He would always use it against me, always hold a grudge. He would want more when the time came, and he'd always know exactly what to hold over my head to get it. There was only one way to stop that cycle.

I'm going to have to kill Joseph Franks.

It wouldn't be an easy task. A guy like that is never without his personal security. Even if I managed to do it, which was a long shot, there would be one other person who couldn't allow it to happen without punishment—Landon Stark.

I'd have to kill Landon, too.

My steps faltered at the thought. Though there had been plenty of times I'd wished him dead, and more than one occasion when I seriously considered killing him myself, this was completely different. Despite everything that had happened in the past and everything that was happening now, I didn't hold any anger toward him. I knew he was only doing what he was told to do. It was part of the life, and he was just as buried in it as I was.

Does Franks have something on Landon?

I had no idea. As far as I knew, Landon had no family, no ties, nothing at all to hold over his head except his loyalty to Franks' organization and his dedication to the fighters he trained.

Back to the more immediate issue: explaining all of this to Raine. She wasn't just going to be pissed off; she was going to shit kittens over the whole idea. She knew about the kind of people I had been associated with from her father's days as a cop, but she'd never been immersed in it. Raine prided herself on being a good, upstanding citizen. She hated what I had done in the past. It's not like she was the kind of girl who would have married into the mafia for any reason. She was with me under the pretense that I was no longer involved in any of that shit.

But I was. I am. On some level, I always would be.

There was no getting out of it once you were in unless it was in a coffin or tossed in a convenient body of water. Around here, they even had the added bonus of gators to clean up the mess. I had never discussed any of this with Raine because it simply hadn't come up. I wasn't expecting my retirement from the games to be subject to recall.

Pretty fucking naïve.

There was only one way to make her understand, and that was to tell her everything. It was going to scare her half to death, and I didn't want to do it, but if she didn't realize all our lives were on the line, she was going to fight me the whole way, and I couldn't have that.

If I was going to keep us all alive, I needed her to have my back. I needed to know she would be there with me, even if she didn't like it, all the way through to the very end. With her on my side, I'd make it.

I shook the raindrops out of my hair and looked at the watch on my wrist. I had about twenty minutes to get back, and I was going to have to run faster to avoid being late. Adding tardiness to Raine's list of my screwups would be bad. I raced along the shore, grabbed my shoes and socks when I got to them, and made it back to the condo just in time.

In my head, I told myself I could do this. One more fight. One more fight would get me my son—the only child I would ever have.

All of that was much easier than explaining to Raine everything that was happening.

Focus. One thing at a time.

I took a deep breath and opened the door.

Raine was still there on the couch, looking like she hadn't moved since I left. She glanced over to me, picked the remote up off the arm of the couch, and flipped off the TV.

"You ready now?" she asked.

She'd been crying. I could hear it in her voice, and it threw me off my game immediately. I just wanted to wrap her up in my arms and tell her everything was going to be just fine, but that was a bigger load of bullshit than I could have pulled off.

"Yeah," I said. "I guess so."

"You have a lot of explaining to do," Raine said. "Where are you going to start?"

"Are you going to leave?" I asked. I swallowed hard as I braced myself for her answer. If she decided she was going to leave, everything else was moot.

"That depends a little on what you say next," Raine said as she crossed her arms. "I'm pissed at you, Sebastian Stark. I can't deny that. I don't think I've ever seen anyone that wasted, and I have no idea what to think about your finding out you have a son."

"You knew I had one out there somewhere."

"But you never knew anything about him," she said. "You didn't even know if it was a boy or a girl before, and you never talked about him at all. Obviously, something changed. Did you see that woman?"

I shook my head. I had seen her, kind of, but I knew that wasn't what she meant. The picture of Jillian with her brains blown out scurried around in my head until I pushed it away.

Raine raised an eyebrow at me, and I looked at the floor for a moment to gather myself before I sat on the couch. She turned toward me and tucked one leg underneath her. After a moment of silence, it became clear that I was supposed to start.

"I got drunk," I said quietly.

"That much was blindingly obvious."

I nodded and went with what I knew.

"I'm sorry," I said. "It's not going to happen again. I just...I just slipped."

"Into a bottle of booze?" Raine uncrossed her arms and leaned back against the arm of the couch with her elbows. I shrugged in response. She stared at me a long moment before sighing. Her expression softened. "Please just tell me what happened. How did you find out about your son?"

Might as well get it over with.

"I saw Landon yesterday," I told her.

"Here?" Raine's eyes widened. "He's in Miami?"

"Yeah," I said. "I think he's been here for a while."

"Where did you see him?"

"We went to lunch at that place up Ocean Drive," I said. "The one attached to a hotel."

"You went to *lunch* with him?" Raine gasped.

I could just see the mental images in her head of Landon and me sipping fruity drinks at some beachside café. It was almost enough to make me laugh but not quite.

"He didn't really give me an option."

"Why didn't you just walk away?"

My arms tensed and I gritted my teeth, which did nothing for my headache. This was the part I didn't know how to approach. I wasn't sure I could explain what it meant to be tied to someone the way I was tied to him.

"I've told you about him before," I reminded her. "He's not the kind of person who lets you just walk away from a conversation he intends to have with you. He asks; I answer. That's how it works. He had shit to tell me, so he told me over food."

"And he chooses *now* to tell you about your son? He had to have known about him before now."

"He did," I nodded. "It's just…well, circumstances have changed."

I took a minute to figure out how to continue, and Raine gave me the time. I turned to sit with my hands clasped together on my thigh. I twisted my fingers around themselves, wrapped them around my knee as some lame-ass support mechanism, and licked my lips before I went on.

"You know all about Jillian," I started. "You know she got pregnant and then left with another guy. Well, they got married and were apparently raising my kid in Italy. Last week…"

I trailed off. I didn't even know how to tell her this much. How was I going to get everything out? This was going to take a lot of talking if I kept stopping, though, and I had to get through it, convince her, and get prepared to fight. I couldn't waste any time beating around the bush or whatever, so I just blurted it out.

"Well, they're dead, and now he doesn't have anyone."

Raine bit down on her lower lip, and her forehead creased.

"What happened to them?"

"They were shot," I said. I cleared my throat. "Murdered."

She sat up a little straighter, and I could see both shock and sorrow in her eyes.

"Do they know who did it?"

It was just like Raine to be concerned about people she'd never met. Even if everything she knew about them was bad, she'd still be sorry something had happened to them.

"They'll never know," I said. "That's usually part of being involved in the kind of business Jillian's family runs. She's related to Franks, so she grew up in it. She probably wasn't expecting it to hit her like that, but the risk is always there."

Raine eyed me.

"You know, don't you?" she said. "You know who killed them."

I took in a long breath and rubbed at my eyes. Apparently, I took too long to answer.

"Bastian?" Raine's voice went soft, and I could hear the fear in her tone. "Did you…did you do it?"

"What?" I looked back to her quickly. "Fuck—no! Shit, Raine, when would I have gone to Italy?"

She scrunched up her face and glanced away before speaking so softly I could hardly hear her.

"You could have…had someone else do it."

"Well, I didn't!" As much as I might have hated Jillian, I wouldn't have done something like that. The idea that Raine thought I was capable of taking out a contract on my ex pissed me off. "For fuck's sake, Raine!"

I shook my head and let out an exasperated sigh.

"Well, who then?" she asked.

"I have my theories," I admitted. "It doesn't matter. What matters is, they're dead, and now Franks is holding my kid for ransom, basically."

"He wants money?" Raine said, confused. "I would think he'd have plenty of that."

"He'd always take more money," I said with a humorless laugh, "but no, he's not asking for any money from me."

Raine's face went pale.

"What does he want?" she said so quietly that again, I could barely make out the words.

She already knows.

I looked down at my hands on my leg. The words wouldn't come at first even though they were right there in my head. As soon as they were said, I wouldn't be able to take them back again. When I looked back at her, I could see she had herself braced for whatever impact the statement I was going to lay on her would have, so I went with it.

"He wants me to compete again," I said. "He wants me to fight in another tournament."

Her eyes flew open.

"He wants...he wants...he wants *what*?" She pushed back with her heels against the cushion and pulled her legs up to her chest. Her mouth stayed open like she was going to say something else, but no words came out. Her face said it all. Whatever she had been expecting, this wasn't it.

Okay, so maybe I misjudged that one.

"I have to fight in one more tournament," I repeated. "Just the one, and then he'll give me my kid."

"You mean...you mean like...like killing people?"

Ah shit, this was going to go even worse than I thought. It wasn't that I expected her to take any of it well, but she was flipping out.

"No," Raine said. Her eyes widened again. "No, Bastian! You can't do that! You can't do one of those...those *death matches* again!"

She stood up and took a step closer to me. With her fists balled up on her hips, she glared down at me.

"No way, Bastian!" she yelled at me. "If you decide to fight again, that's it. We're through, drunk or not! I can't be with someone who would do something like that again!"

The focal point I had managed to find disintegrated. Tingles of dread crawled over my skin as her words sank in. Maybe she'd forgive a single misstep when it came to drinking, but this was too much for her. The idea of me killing again wasn't something she would be able to handle, and she'd run.

I couldn't do this without her. If she left, I was dead.

If she left, *she* was dead, too.

My greatest fear was actualized. At least for now, I was going to speak without thought.

Chapter Seven

"I don't have a fucking choice, Raine!" I bellowed. "It's not like I'm itching to kill people off! If I wanted to do that, there are plenty of people in this fucking building I'd like to see dead!"

Well, shit. I knew I was going to fuck this up, but part of me thought she would guess as to the nature of my meeting with Landon. None of his words had really surprised me. They weren't expected, but as soon as they were out of his mouth, I had accepted them.

"Don't say things like that!" she yelled back at me.

"Well, it's fucking true!" I had already lost the focus I had managed to collect on the beach. I was full of adrenaline at this point, and I was resigned to make it all worse with my stupid mouth.

I should have stuck with the profuse apologies.

"Some of them fucking deserve it!"

"For the love of God, Bastian!" she cried. "You aren't like that anymore!"

"I might not act on it," I growled, "but that doesn't stop me from feeling it. I can only control so much!"

Every word out of my mouth was compounding the situation and speeding up the hurricane rotation inside my head. It was already bad, but if you want to make the worst of a bad situation, I'm the guy to invite.

"Apparently, you can't." She glared at me. "So did Landon get you drunk after telling you all this? Is that why you were trashed when I got home?"

"No, he didn't," I said. My anger faded slightly as sheepishness seeped in. It would have been nice, in retrospect, to have been able to blame it on Landon. I should have thought about that before I said anything. She probably would have believed it, too. "I did that on my own, after he left."

"Jesus," she muttered. She put her face in her hands and dropped back to the edge of the couch. "You can't do this. Not again."

"I have to."

"No."

"Goddammit, Raine!" I snapped. "If I don't fight, they're just going to walk in here and kill us both! What do you think is going to happen to my kid then, huh? If they decide to let him live, he'll end up a fucking crime boss someday!"

"They can't just walk in here," Raine argued. "We're in a secure building. There's a guard downstairs!"

"Seriously?" I snarled. "Do you seriously think you can sit up here and be safe from people like that? Are you that fucking stupid?"

I regretted the word immediately, but I couldn't take it back.

Open mouth, insert entire leg. Throw a hipbone and maybe an arm in there, too.

"Is that really what you think of me?"

"Fuck...no, of course not," I grumbled as I tried to backpedal, "but when you say shit like that...well, it's just not how it works. They can do whatever they want. That's kind of the point. Besides, one of them has already been here."

"What do you mean? Who's been here?"

Ah shit. That wasn't supposed to come out.

I tried to brush it off, but she wasn't having any of that. I finally told her about the other day when I had the feeling someone had been there. Seeing the fear in her eyes centered me, calmed me, and I remembered how much focus I was going to have to maintain for any of this to come out well in the end.

If I lost focus, I was going to lose her.

"I don't know who," I told her, "but considering what Landon said, any doubts I had are gone. It could have been anyone from

Franks' group or even one of the other tournament players from the other mob organizations."

"You really mean it," Raine said. She wrapped her arms around herself and curled up into the corner of the couch as if that would somehow protect her from what was going on. "You're really going to do this."

I shoved myself off the couch and onto the floor. I knelt in front of her and placed my hands over her thighs. I hated seeing her so frightened, and though I needed her to understand there wasn't a choice, I also needed her to know she was safe as long as she was with me and I followed every order they gave me.

"I have to do it," I said for the hundredth time. "I don't want to, baby—I have to. Nothing fucking matters more to me than you, and I'm not risking you."

Her eyes grew wider as she stared at me.

"We could run away," she suggested.

I didn't have to respond. I could tell she didn't believe it even as she said it. She was grasping—trying to find something to hold on to, something I might not have considered already, but there was nothing. I shook my head slowly.

"There's nowhere to run."

"There has to be another way."

"There's no other way, baby. I have to keep you safe, and if that means I have to fight, then I'm going to fight. I've done it plenty of times before. It'll be simple."

"Wait until you actually complete the task before you evaluate its simplicity," Raine muttered.

"What?"

She shook her head.

"Something I heard from a professor." She wouldn't look at me, and strangely enough, I knew why.

Raine had never lied to me before, not about anything. Still, I knew she was covering something up. I rose up on my knees to look her straight in the face.

"Where did you really hear it?" I questioned.

Raine bit down on her lip and fiddled with her fingers before answering.

"A group meeting," she admitted.

"What kind of group?"

With a tightened jaw, she finally looked into my eyes.

"It's a support group for people living with alcoholics," she said. "I don't have a study group on Tuesday nights; I go to that group instead."

She'd been telling me she was at a study group every week for the last couple of months and had apparently been lying to me about it the whole time. The revelation had taken me aback to the point where I didn't know what to think, let alone respond.

What had she heard at this group? Was this organization trying to help people get away from people like me or how to live with us?

Pressure built up inside of me again.

"So, what?" I asked. "They tell you how to deal with people like me? Help you get away from me?"

"No," she said. "I mean, yes, they sometimes talk about that, but that's not why I went. I just thought they could help me understand you better."

"Did it help?"

"Honestly, no," she said. "I was hoping that it would, but it really hasn't. It's mostly people trying to one-up each other on who has had the roughest life. There were a few helpful things, and some really nice people, but no. Dealing with you is rather...unique."

I let out a short laugh.

"I bet. You mean I'm a bigger asshole than the other alcoholics?"

"No," she said, "you've got a better reason for it."

I thought about that for a minute. Maybe I did have a good reason, and maybe I didn't. Considering all the crazy shit in my past, she could probably top a big-ass cake with my stories, except she couldn't tell anything to anyone.

She did realize that, didn't she?

"You...you didn't actually *tell* anyone..." I trailed off.

"No," Raine confirmed, "of course not."

Thank fucking God.

As I thought about it, I realized what a shit position I put her in. At least those other people had a place where they could vent—a place to explain what was happening with their lives, but Raine had nothing. She couldn't tell people about me at all, which meant she had no one to confide in. Lindsay didn't even know about all the shit in the past. Sure, she knew what had been revealed on television, but that iceberg could take out a fleet of Titanics.

I'm such a shit.

I stared at her as she went on.

"Knowing your reasons doesn't mean I condone what you did," Raine said. "I'm still mad about you getting drunk. I understand, though. I'm kind of wanting a drink myself right now."

"I know," I said with a nod. I was actually a little relieved to be back on the topic of drinking, considering everything else that still had to be said. "It's not like I'm happy about it or anything—I feel like a total shithead. I don't know what else to say about it. I fucked up. I won't do it again. I can't do it again."

"Why not?"

My chest tightened.

"You'll leave me," I said. I felt pressure behind my eyes to go along with the tightness inside my chest. "I could tell when I saw you last night. If…if you did that, well, I'd still fight, but I'd probably lose. There wouldn't be a fucking point to winning."

"What about your son?"

I thought about my words for a second before responding, but all the revelations I had at the beach were still clear in my mind.

"It wouldn't matter anymore," I admitted. "I already knew he was out there. I already knew he was in that family. Without you, nothing else would matter to me anymore, not even him."

"I don't know how I feel about that," she said quietly. "You should care about him."

"I do," I said. "Fuck, he's the main reason I got drunk. I haven't even seen a picture or anything, but I couldn't stop thinking about him. That and the whole tournament thing…I just couldn't deal with it all."

"And now you can?"

"No," I admitted. I tried to compose myself again. "But when I saw your face last night…shit."

I could feel myself putting up shields, trying to protect that inner core deep inside of me that knew I should let her go; she'd be better off. This whole situation was further proof being around me was dangerous and ultimately not in her best interest. I'd said it many times, and though she assured me over and over that I was worthy, it was still easy to forget.

Focus.

"I know I can't do that again," I said. "Fuck, I thought you were going to leave. I was so fucking sure of it."

The pressure that had been building throughout the conversation reached a threshold, and I lost it. I launched myself at her, no longer able to tolerate any distance between us. Raine gasped as I grabbed her and pulled her against me.

"I can't lose you!"

"I'm right here," she said. She moved her arms around me and returned my embrace.

"I'm sorry…I won't ever do it again," I promised. "I'll get us through this. I'll keep you safe—I swear!"

"Oh, Bastian," she said.

Raine pressed her lips to my forehead, and I turned quickly to capture them with my own. It was just a brief kiss, and as soon as we parted, I looked into her eyes.

"I can't be without you, Raine," I said. "I love you so fucking much, the thought tears me up. It makes me want to destroy everything in here, because if you left, every fucking thing in here would remind me of you. None of it would matter anymore because you are my fucking world."

"I'm not going," she said. She brought her hand up to my face and stroked my cheek. "I'm still here. I'm not happy about what happened, but I'm not leaving you. I love you, Bastian. That hasn't changed."

"I didn't fuck it up?" I asked, needy asshole that I was. I needed to hear her say it again.

"You did mess up," she said, "but I understand why you did it. Everyone's allowed to make a single mistake. To be totally honest, I was pretty surprised you made it this long."

I wondered if that's what her support group had said—that I was probably going to drink again and that it was just a matter of time. I wanted to be pissed about it, but the evidence was on their side.

"One time," I said quietly. "Never again."

"I can put up with this one mistake," she confirmed. "That doesn't mean I'm going to tolerate this happening repeatedly."

"We're okay?" Damn my need for reassurance, but I had to hear it. I had to hear it again and again because there was still the child deep inside of me that knew—just knew—he wasn't wanted. Not by her, not by anyone else, and not under any circumstances. No matter how perfect the man-child tried to be, no one would ever want him.

"I love you," she said again. "We're fine."

The tension inside of me snapped. I brought her face back to mine and fought with myself to be gentle. I wanted to hold her so tightly that she could never get away from me. I wanted to possess her completely and know that she was mine and mine alone.

Instantly, I needed her. I needed her if I was ever going to get through any of this fucked-up mess called my life. She was my salvation, and I had to feel the physical affirmation of her forgiveness.

I kissed her slowly at first, but as everything that was piled up in my head threatened to resurface, I expelled the energy into her. I traced her lips with my tongue, grabbed at her bottom lip with my teeth, and pressed her body against the couch. Her hands came up under my arms and gripped my lower back through my shirt as she groaned into my mouth.

"I fucking need you," I growled. "Now."

Raine gripped the bottom of my shirt with her fingers and pulled it up over my head in response. I grabbed at my belt and struggled to pull it open as she removed her tank top and unhooked her bra. As soon as I saw her tits, my belt was forgotten. I went for her nipples and sucked one of them into my mouth and circled the other with my hand. I brushed over her nipple with my thumb as Raine moaned softly.

With my shorts only partially undone, my cock pressed painfully against the zipper, trying to get free but failing. I was too busy wanting to touch every part of her, stroke her skin, and attack her mouth with mine to even care. I managed to kick my shoes off as I shifted her so she was lying lengthwise on the couch and went back to her nipples.

Raine moved her hands down my back, sliding them lower until she reached my ass. She grabbed it with both hands and pulled my hardened cock against her leg. She pressed her thigh up against me and groaned.

"I want you," she said. She took my face in her hands and pressed her mouth to mine. "Please—take me to bed."

No argument there.

I lifted her from the couch, my cock still only partially freed from my shorts, and carried her bridal-style into the bedroom. I tossed Raine on the end of the bed, grabbed at the yoga pants still covering her legs, and ripped them off of her. I grasped her ankles as I crawled onto the bed and then maneuvered them over my shoulders as I looked up at her.

All else was forgotten for the sake of the moment, the need for her, the lust. The raw desire to watch her come undone due to my actions overwhelmed all thoughts of the turmoil ahead of us.

Her mouth opened slightly, and her eyes darkened as I moved in. I pressed my open mouth to the inside of her right thigh as I slid my hand up the left one. I didn't go too close—not yet. I loved to watch her squirm.

And squirm she did.

"Please...Bastian..."

"Please what?" I teased as I kissed up her thigh, getting closer and closer without ever hitting the mark. I kissed up over her pubic bone and then over to the other side. "You want something?"

"Ughhh..."

I snickered, kissed the very edge of where her leg met her core, and then hummed against her skin.

"You want a kiss, baby?" I purred. "You want to feel my tongue all over your clit? 'Cause I'll give it to you."

"Yes...please!"

"You want it here?" I pressed my lips off to one side and then the other. "Or maybe here?"

I missed the mark every time, and she started trying to twist her hips to where she wanted my mouth, but I held her in place.

"No you don't," I scolded playfully. "I don't think you're ready yet."

"I am...I am..."

"Not yet..."

Using the back of my fingernail, I scraped the skin of the inside of her thigh, right up to the very peak. I followed the motion with open-mouthed kisses as she continued to twist below me. I could smell how much she wanted it, and my cock throbbed where it lay trapped between me and the mattress, begging for attention, but I wasn't going to give into that just yet.

Her first.

Always.

Finally, when she really didn't seem able to stand any more, I slipped my tongue right against her hole and licked from bottom to top. She lurched, almost sat straight up, and then dropped back to the bed.

I couldn't help but smile.

I circled her clit with my tongue as I brought my hand around into position. Tracing lightly, I explored her with my fingers as I used my tongue against her apex. She shuddered, and I felt her hands against my head, trying to pull me forward for more friction.

This time, I relented.

"You are going to come so hard, people on the beach are gonna hear you," I promised.

I could see her chest rise and fall with her breaths, but she didn't say anything in response. Her eyes said it all—dark, hooded, and full of desire.

I slid a finger inside of her, pulled back, and then inserted two. Moving them in and out of her slowly, I went to work with my tongue. I circled, licked, and hummed against her clit as I used my fingers to curl up and press inside her body.

Raine's thighs pressed against the side of my head, and she dug her fingers into my scalp in the most fantastic way as I pressed harder with my tongue. My lips closed around her, and I sucked hard as she started screaming my name.

Beautiful fucking music.

Releasing her legs from my shoulders, I reached down and pushed my shorts and boxers the rest of the way off as I crawled up over her. Finally free of my clothes, I kissed up the center of her body and between her tits until I reached her neck. I sucked gently at her skin as I positioned myself and thrust forward.

My cock found its sanctuary, and the sensation rocketed through my entire body. I felt as if I had been hit with a sledgehammer. It wasn't the physical feeling of joining with her that struck me, but the sudden, intense realization of where my true focus resided.

Inside of her.

Find the focal point and tie yourself to it.

I'd always thought of Landon's words as meaning something inside of myself, and maybe at one point it had been, but that had shifted. Like everything else in my life, it all changed when Raine became a part of it. She made me a person who could be loved and forgiven. She made me the kind of man I might have been if I hadn't been so fucked up early on in life. She took me for who I was—flaws and all—and made me better with nothing more than her acceptance of me.

She was life.

There was nothing —absolutely nothing—I wouldn't do to keep her safe. I'd kill anyone, destroy any organization, and fight a fucking mountain if that's what it would take to keep her with me, safe and happy. I'd never touch another drink again. I'd be nice to her friends, and I'd give her the fucking world if that's what she wanted.

Her body encompassed my cock, and her very being encompassed my soul. I cried out, not in pain or even in orgasm, but from an epiphany. It was an ecstasy beyond any true comprehension, but it was more real to me than any feeling I had ever experienced.

Beyond love, beyond life.

I moved slowly in the beginning with a gentle rocking as her hands found my back and gripped my skin. She looked up at me, and inside her eyes, I found everything I would ever need. She ran her hand up to the back of my head and pulled me to her, capturing my mouth and kissing me deeply.

Sliding in and out of her, faster and faster, the bed shifted under the motion and the headboard slammed into the wall. The rhythmic thumping only caused me to thrust harder, reveling in the sound as it mixed with her cries.

"Oh…God…Bastian!" Raine brought her legs up around my ass, clenching me to her and pulling me further in. Her head was pressed back against the pillow, and she squeezed her eyes shut as incomprehensible sounds flowed from her mouth.

She was the most beautiful sight I had ever seen, and the vision spurred me on.

The headboard slammed into the wall over and over again, drowning out Raine's cries. I didn't let up even as I felt her release, and she dropped against the mattress. I kept at it, and sweat started running between my shoulder blades.

My back arched as I shoved into her and held there, unloading inside of her and crying out at the ceiling. I felt her legs tighten around my hips as she held our bodies together for a final few second before I collapsed on top of her.

Best workout all week.

My body gave one last shudder as I lay on top of her, breathing heavily and trying to keep my heart from bursting through my chest. Raine was shaking, and for a moment I thought it was because of another orgasm, but then I realized she was crying.

"Raine?" I pushed up with my arms until I could look down at her. Tears ran down her face, and she brought up her hand to wipe them away before she reached up and pulled me against her, tucking her forehead against my body.

"I don't know how to deal with this!" Raine sobbed against my chest. "What are we going to do?"

I wrapped my arms around her and rolled so I wasn't crushing her. I got her up on top of me and stroked her hair away from her face.

"Shhh," I said. "It's all right, baby. I'm going to make it all right. I swear I will."

"You don't know that!" she cried. "You can't know that! You could die...oh my God, Bastian, they could kill you!"

I closed my eyes and squeezed her tighter.

"Not gonna happen," I said. "I don't want to do it. You know I don't, but I *can*, and I will. I'll win this tournament. No one's going to take me down."

I hoped I sounded convincing.

"You don't know that," she said again. "Bastian, you can't promise that!"

I untwisted my arms from around her and took her face in my hands, forcing her to look at me.

"I *can*," I told her as I stared into her deep, brown eyes. "I *can* fucking promise you that! I'm going to do this, and I'm going to fucking win. I never lose, Raine—*never*. I did it for the fucking money before. Do you really think I won't win when it's you and my kid on the line? No one will fucking touch me. No one. I'll wipe them out in the first day, you hear me?"

Tears fell to her cheeks again, but she nodded.

"You understand me?" I asked.

"Yes," she whispered. "Bastian..."

"Shhh." I released her face and embraced her again. I kissed the top of her head as I held her, and she clung to my shoulders. Her audible cries stopped, but I could still feel her tears on my skin.

"If anything happens to you," she said, "if you get hurt, or... or..."

"I'm going to be fine," I repeated.

"Not if something happens to you," she argued. "I'd die."

"Nothing will happen to me," I said. "Not you, either."

She let out a long breath, and the air tickled my skin. I felt her relax against me, and I tilted my head to kiss her gently on the side of her face.

"I've got you," I whispered against her cheek.

Eventually her breathing evened out, and I knew she had fallen asleep on me, emotionally exhausted. I closed my eyes and tried to figure out how I was going to make good on my promise to her. I had meant every word of it, but I also knew this would be like no other tournament I had fought before. It wasn't money or my reputation on the line—it was Raine and my son. She was my world, and now, so was my son. I wanted him to be a part of it, too.

Alex.

I had to win. There was no question about it. I couldn't even entertain the possibility of another outcome. To win, I was going to have to know exactly what I was up against. I had to know each and every one of my opponents, what they were capable of, their weaknesses, and exactly what I needed to do to defeat every last one of them.

I needed to do some research.

The decision was made. At least for now, I had to prepare myself to fight.

Chapter Eight

I woke early in my usual position: my arms wrapped tightly around Raine with my body partially on top of hers. I had one leg tossed over both of hers as well, and her head was tucked securely against my shoulder. There were fading thoughts of dreams in my head, but I couldn't remember their nature.

Looking down on Raine's face, the anger, fear, and passion from the night before had transformed to an unusual sense of peace.

Pushing a little strand of hair off her forehead, I stared at her closed eyes and thought about her list of reasons she loved me. She always listed my strength first. I planned to keep her safe through my physical strength and my skills as a fighter, but I knew I needed more. I needed the strength of mind to overcome what was happening.

I needed to plan, which wasn't exactly my strong point. I usually acted more impulsively, responding to the situation as it unfolded as opposed to setting the stage to ensure the outcome I chose. Offing a major crime lord wasn't going to be something that happened without a precise plan, and I knew that. I was going to have to devise a way to give me access to Franks long enough to kill him and get myself back out alive.

Raine would have to be kept in the dark about all of it. There was no way I was going to let her in on my plan to kill Franks. I didn't want her to be even more worried than she already was, and I was afraid of giving her too much information about what was going to happen. She already knew enough, and she hated what the inescapable future held. My Raine valued people's lives in a way I wasn't accustomed to, and she wouldn't like the idea of me taking any additional lives to ensure the continued safety of her and my son.

I still wasn't sure what to do about Landon, but that was secondary. I would prefer to find some way out of it all without having to kill him, but I wasn't sure if that was going to be possible. Ultimately, he was still the father I never had.

I'm a father.

Every time I thought about Alex, I tried to create some kind of picture in my head of what he might look like. I wondered if he looked like I did at the same age, and that reminded me that I didn't even have a picture of myself from when I was a kid.

Raine stirred a little, and as I glanced back at her, I wondered how it would sound if she added "you're a good father" to my list of positive traits. The thought warmed me, and I held her a little closer as her eyes fluttered open.

Like most mornings when there wasn't an immediate need to get out of bed, we spent time just looking at each other. I pushed her hair away from her face and stroked her cheek softly, and Raine smiled up at me, closed her eyes to my touch, and sighed.

"You're beautiful," I said quietly.

"I doubt that," Raine snickered. "I'm always a mess in the morning."

I had to correct her.

"A beautiful mess."

Raine smiled. I was about to kiss her, but my phone buzzed with a text from John Paul.

Wakey wakey! Eggs and fuckin bakey!

I rolled my eyes.

"Who is that?" Raine asked.

"JP," I said. "I have to get up."

I took a quick shower. When I was done, I found fresh coffee waiting for me in the kitchen. Raine had her own cup in her hand, and she held onto it tightly without drinking.

"What happens now?" Raine asked. The tension in her voice was plain.

"I'm going to train with JP," I said. "That will be for the next few days. After that, Landon said three weeks of training."

"Where will you go for that?"

"I don't know for sure," I said. "Landon's being in Miami makes me wonder if the tournament will take place somewhere around here, which would mean we stay close—in the same atmosphere. It's best to train in the type of environment where you're going to fight."

"Where will I be?" Raine asked quietly.

Fuck. So much for my planning skills.

"I haven't gotten that far," I admitted. "I'll talk to John Paul."

"I could stay with Nick and Lindsay," Raine suggested.

"No," I said. "They can't protect you."

"We could go on a trip or something," she said. "Stay out of the way?"

I shook my head.

"I want to know exactly where you are," I replied. "If you're not where I expect you to be, I won't know if you're safe or not."

I was teetering on scaring her, which I didn't want to do, but I wasn't going to let her far from my sight if it could be helped. I moved closer and wrapped my arms around her. Raine placed her head on my shoulder and sighed.

"I hate this," she whispered.

"I know," I said. "I hate it, too. This time next month it will all be over, and you, me and Alex…well, we have to figure that part out."

A thought occurred to me, and I leaned back and placed my palm on her cheek.

"I need you to help me figure that shit out," I said. "I need you to get whatever the hell we're gonna need with a kid around. I don't know anything about that shit."

"You think I do?"

I think you need to focus on something that isn't about me killing people.

"I think you have a better chance of understanding it than I do. If you can put up with my childish ass, you can probably deal with a six-year-old as well."

Raine gave me a tight lipped smile as another text from John Paul told me to come and meet him at the front door.

"I'll be gone a while," I told Raine, "just to the gym upstairs. Keep your phone close, and don't open the fucking door for anyone, even if you think you know who it is."

"Okay," she said as she bit down on her lip.

"I've got you," I said again, and she nodded.

I kissed her softly before we parted, and I went downstairs to meet John Paul at the entrance to our building. We headed up to the gym and started working out.

"Funny how old patterns fall back into place," John Paul remarked as he watched me do leg presses on the machine. "It's just like old times, isn't it?"

"You knew about this the other day, didn't you?" I accused.

"Maybe," John Paul said as he winked at me. "Couldn't say anything, but glad you took my advice anyway."

"I thought it was an order," I muttered. I pushed out another set of leg presses and then switched to dumbbells.

I kept it up until sweat was pouring off of me, and every muscle in my body ached. I was glad I had been spending some time at the gym lately because John Paul was ruthless on the weight training. I could keep up, but only barely.

I wasn't about to let him know that, though.

So I pushed myself as much as humanly possible. It was territory I knew—push beyond your limits and never stop, never let go. I ached, I sweated, and I burned through sets like a maniac just to show John Paul that I could.

He knew exactly what I was doing.

"Is that all you got?" John Paul snorted. "You're a wuss."

"Fuck you," I said as I slammed the weights down to the floor. "I don't see you pushing out this many reps."

"Not my training, bro."

I extended my middle finger toward him as I completed another set of curls. At least I hadn't lost much strength in my biceps, but I'd neglected leg workouts, and even I had to admit my gut was a little flabby from lack of ab work. I never should have let myself go so much. Now that Raine had to count on my strength, I wasn't at my best.

I had to rectify that.

I also had to make sure she was safe even when I wasn't around.

"I need Raine protected," I said to John Paul as I shifted my weight on the bench and switched arms. "I want someone I trust around her all the time when I'm not."

"Not sure who that would be," John Paul said. "Is there anyone you trust?"

"You," I said simply.

"You want me looking after your chick?"

"Who else?"

John Paul scratched his arm, looked up at the ceiling, and considered for a moment.

"Can I fuck her?"

I stood up, dropped the dumbbell to the floor, and punched him in the face.

He stumbled backward from the blow but righted himself quickly as he laughed and rubbed at his chin.

"I guess that's a no."

"Fucking right it's a no," I said as I glared at him. "Don't you fucking touch her."

"Duly noted." He laughed again.

We finished our session, and John Paul came with me back to the condo. Raine had her school books spread out on the couch and coffee table, but I could tell she wasn't getting any actual work done. I sat down beside her and tossed my arm over her shoulder, pulling her close, as John Paul helped himself to a bottle of water.

"Ugh!" Raine groaned as she placed her hands on my chest and pushed me away. "You stink."

"You should have smelled him back in the day of booze and whores," John Paul said.

Like I really needed him to bring that shit up.

"Don't make me fucking beat you in front of her," I snapped. "I bet I can find some other meathead around here to train with me."

"Won't be as pretty as I am," John Paul said. He emptied the water bottle and tossed it into the bin. "I'm out. See you bright and early tomorrow."

———— ⬥ ————

I trained with John Paul for four days—weights, endurance, and hand-to-hand fighting. I was sore, bruised, and tired on the fifth day when he came to the door and told me we weren't training that morning.

"Meeting time," he said simply.

We met Landon a few blocks away in a hotel room. He looked uncharacteristically tired and a little on edge. We sat down at a small, round table and waited for him to start.

"Your competition," Landon said. He pushed a folder to me across the table, and I opened it. There were five sets of documents inside with names and pictures. "Study them. See what you can learn about them, and make sure you know how to take each and every one of them out."

I scanned the documents, stopping immediately when I saw a familiar face.

Fuck me.

Even without the sunglasses, I recognized the picture as the dude on the beach with the ridiculous, fucking tongue twister, only now it didn't seem so ridiculous. Now I saw it as the threat it clearly represented.

"You're the pheasant."

Evan Arden. He was listed as Rinaldo Moretti's key hit man. The picture showed him at a shooting range with a high caliber rifle in his hands.

"I believe I may have mentioned that he's your primary concern."

"I've met him," I said quietly.

Landon eyed me.

"When?"

"A couple weeks ago," I said. "He talked to me on the beach when I was out for a run."

"Recon is a specialty of his," Landon said. "He's probably been on a rooftop with his sniper rifle pointed at you already."

"He's a sniper?" John Paul said.

"Former Marine," Landon informed us. "One of the best shooters they've ever seen. I knew of him through my military contacts before he got himself involved with Rinaldo Moretti. He's taken out hundreds of Moretti's enemies over the years, but he disappeared shortly after the war broke out."

"Seems like a weird time to take off," John Paul remarked.

"I couldn't get a lot of detail," Landon said, "but I got the idea he might have been at the crux of the issue that started this war in the first place."

"You think he had sights on me but didn't shoot me?"

"Arden knows the rules." Landon stood up and walked over to the window to look out at the ocean. "Taking out a player once the tournament has been announced would inflame the war, not end it. He's military, and following orders is in his blood. He's also probably the next in line to run that organization if something happened to Moretti. Moretti's only other options are his daughter Luisa, who might very well do it, or an illegitimate son he barely recognizes. Ending the feud is in Arden's best interest."

"But Arden hasn't been involved in the war recently?" John Paul asked.

"Not at all," Landon said. "He doesn't even appear to be residing in the Chicago area. Probably has a place outside the country—no one seems to know for sure where he's been, not even Moretti himself. Obviously he has a way to contact him though, or he wouldn't be here."

John Paul looked over to me with concern in his eyes.

"Tomorrow we meet with everyone," Landon told us. "All six family heads and your competition will be there, Bastian. The others aren't much of a worry, but I want you up close and personal with Arden before you have to take him on. Figure him out. Fuck with his head, if you can—I understand he's a pretty hard nut to crack."

"Yeah, I can see that."

"He was a POW in the Middle East. It fucked with his head, which is why he was discharged shortly after he was recovered from a camp in Afghanistan. There's video out there—go watch it. Use it against him."

"Will do." I picked up the folder full of information and stood. John Paul followed suit, and he drove me back to the condo where Raine was still trying to study.

"Good workout?" Raine asked. She looked me over, and it was obvious I hadn't been at the gym.

"I learned a lot," I responded vaguely. She didn't press for more, and I wondered if she just didn't want to know.

"We have to move," she said suddenly.

"What? Why?"

"We can't fit us and a kid in this condo," she said, "and I don't like the public schools here. We need to move somewhere where Alex can get a good education, and we can get a place that will have enough room for him."

As I looked around the apartment, I didn't have much of an argument. She was right; there wasn't enough room for another person in here even though we did have an extra bedroom.

"A house, maybe?" I said.

"I think that would be nice," Raine agreed. "Someplace with a yard where he can be outside and play. I don't want to worry about traffic."

"Here in Miami?"

"Not in the city," she said.

I knew what she really meant—not too close to the beach. I didn't like it, but considering everything else, I wasn't going to press the issue. She had my back on this, and I'd sacrifice whatever it took to make it work for all of us. Maybe I'd manage to convince her that Alex would benefit from living near the beach.

I went over to the couch and knelt beside her. I looked up into her face and captured her eyes with mine.

"Anything you want," I told her. "Anywhere you want. I just want us all together when this is over."

For once, I really meant it.

She bent over and placed her lips on mine.

"I love you," she said.

"Right back at ya, babe." I smiled and kissed her back.

I followed John Paul to his car after I made sure Raine was good for the day. I had no idea how long this meeting was going to last or where we were even going. John Paul drove south for some time, and as we reached Homestead and the unending fields of squash filled with migrant workers in wide-brimmed hats, we turned down a gravel road and headed toward a large barn out in the middle of fucking nowhere.

I'd spent the night studying all the documentation Landon had given me. I'd even found a video of a news release about Lieutenant Evan Arden and his capture in the Middle East. It included footage of a man being executed right beside him. I hadn't studied the others as closely, but I was prepared to meet them all and get a better idea of their weaknesses. For the most part, the rest didn't concern me.

As we got out of John Paul's truck, I looked up to see ultralight planes and a few gliders up in the sky. Far across a field of yellow crook-necked squash, I could see a small airfield. Other than that, there was nothing and no one to be seen except for two menacing guys standing by the large double doors of the barn. John Paul's boots kicked up dusty gravel as we approached, and the guards checked us both for weapons before they opened the doors to allow us inside.

I wasn't sure what I was expecting, but there were a lot of people in there. They formed six small groups around the mostly open area. I checked each group, silently naming the associated crime lords and their tournament participants.

Gavino Greco from Chicago was the closest to the door. Towering over him was a massive guy sporting hundreds of tattoos. There was enough ink showing on him that I wondered if even his dick was decorated. Aside from his face, he was covered in them. I remembered from the documents Landon had given me that he was called Hunter, and he wasn't going to be easy to take down in a melee fight though he was mostly a bow-hunting fanatic. Of all the other fighters, he had the most tournament experience, with or without weapons.

The next group was also from Chicago. Since the start of the war and the fall of the last boss in Chicago, the organization had nearly failed completely. It was now run by two guys from Azerbaijan— Sergi Dytalov and Igor Severinov. They were unimpressive figures physically, but they had the most at stake in this little game, and they watched me carefully with calculating eyes as I walked in.

Their representative in the game was nearby, slouched in a chair and glaring at his own hands. His dark hair hung in his face a little, and the look on his face was anything but calm and collected. Erik Dytalov was into knives, according to the information I had on him, especially Busse and Kunai knives. A distant cousin of one of the new bosses, but not Russian born, he'd survived in the games for a couple years before he backed off and eventually quit playing. He hadn't played for a while now, and I wondered just what he had been doing for the last few years instead of fighting.

To my right was Grant Chamber from the New York mob. There was a woman beside him I was pretty sure I recognized though I hadn't figured it out from her picture. She was tall, dark-skinned, and had enough muscle on her to make you look twice, no doubt about it. As I looked at her in person, I realized I'd met her before.

"JP?"

"Yeah?" he responded quietly.

"Isn't that the chick you dated in Seattle? Stacey?"

"Yeah," he said, "I know. She goes by Reaper now. She's been playing in the games for about a year."

Obviously, he wasn't surprised to see her here. He didn't look at me, and I wasn't sure if he cared or not that I was going to be killing her in a couple of weeks. If it mattered to him, he didn't show it.

On the other side of the New York group was an imposing-looking woman with short hair and flashing eyes. I assumed through the process of elimination that it must be Maria Hill—the woman who ran the operations in Los Angeles. The tall African-American guy with her was Tyrone Chimes, an expert in knife combat and a good shot as well. He'd also been in the games for the last year or so.

In the very back, there was a tall, bald man with sausage-like arms and a bit of a gut. He made an imposing figure with two gigantic body guards on either side of him.

Joseph Franks.

I hadn't seen him since the trial where I testified against him and Gunter Darke. Gunter had been convicted and killed in prison shortly afterwards. Franks, however, had gotten off scot-free even though I'd told the jury he ordered the deaths of everyone in the room. He just had that kind of pull, in and out of the system.

John Paul led the way as we walked toward Franks and his group.

"Sebastian," Franks said in a cool voice as we approached, "it's been a while."

I nodded, took his outstretched hand, and took in a deep breath.

"Mister Franks," I said. We shook, dropped hands, and looked at each other for a moment.

With guys like Franks, it was all about ego. Everything centered around who was the farthest up his ass at any given time. I'd done the unthinkable and dared to cross him.

For the first time, I considered that I may have been duped. He might have just lured me here to kill me, but as soon as the thought occurred to me, I knew it wasn't true. If he wanted me dead, he'd just put a price on my head, and it would eventually be collected by someone. He wouldn't have any need to go through an elaborate plot or involve all these people if my death was his goal.

He narrowed his eyes and leaned close to me.

"You were a bad boy, Mister Stark."

I swallowed.

"Yeah, I know I was," I said quietly. "It was a mistake, obviously."

"A mistake because of what you tried to do," he asked, "or because it didn't work?"

I took in a long, slow breath. There was definitely a right answer to his question and a wrong one, but the words he wanted to hear weren't readily apparent.

Clearly, I cannot choose the glass in front of you…

I went for honest.

"It didn't work," I said.

He laughed, clasped his hand on my back, and turned to one of the goons next to him.

"You hear that, Nathaniel?" he said. "Here's a man who will let you know right where you stand."

"Yes, sir!"

"Don't you *yes, sir* me, you little shit," he yelled so loudly and without warning that I had to take a step back. "You can't give me a load of pleasantries when you're skimming my profits!"

A moment later, a shot rang out, and Nathaniel lay on the floor near Landon's feet. While my ears rang, Franks placed his gun back in its holster at his side and turned back to me.

"He tried to fuck me over last year," Franks said with a shrug. "He had his one chance, but he tried to pull that shit again. You understand what I'm saying here, Stark?"

I looked into his steely eyes and nodded.

"Yeah, I get it," I said. "I'm not a problem for you."

"Good!" he said, all smiles again. "Now let me get this party started."

Slightly shaken, but unwilling to show it, I moved off a little and watched as the body was hauled out of the back door of the barn. Landon looked over at me, and for a moment, I thought I saw relief in his eyes, but it was probably just the long halogen lights, hanging bare from the ceiling, playing tricks on my perception.

As I stood off to the side of Franks' group, I checked out the final set of Chicago-based mafia cohorts—Rinaldo Moretti and his crew. There were several of them, including three bodyguards and a woman who must have been his daughter, Luisa. The guy with Rinaldo Moretti was an interesting one. Slim, wiry, and tall, he looked more like a schoolteacher than someone mixed up with organized crime. I was too far away to hear what they were talking about, but whatever it was, Moretti kept glaring at him. I didn't pay much attention, though—my focus was on the other person standing with him.

Evan Arden.

I knew him both from the picture and from our brief encounter at the beach. He stood near Moretti at attention with his hands clasped behind his back. There was a shoulder holster over his arm, but it was empty. From the look of him, I was pretty sure he wouldn't need a weapon if push came to shove. He wasn't anywhere near my size, but he was a well-built guy—lean and muscular. I had the feeling that wherever he'd been hiding out, he'd kept up on his training.

Unlike I had.

I remembered Landon's instructions about doing what I could to mess with Arden's head. I thought about how he had looked on his knees with his hands bound behind his back as the guy next to him was shot in the head. He'd been a POW, and I wondered if bringing up the video might throw him off or if that was something he'd heard often enough already. I thought about what else I could say to him.

Not a fucking tongue-twister, that was for sure.

Franks called out to the room, and all six families gathered around the large table in the center of the barn. The three Chicago-based families, the reason we were all here, sat as far away from each other as possible. Gavino Greco and Rinaldo Moretti I knew from a multitude of tournaments, but the two Russian guys weren't people I had seen before today. Igor Severinov and the other, Sergi Dytalov, had taken over when the Russian mob's predecessors had retaliated against a stolen shipment of caviar by invading Moretti's home. When the invasion turned into a bloodbath, people on all three sides had been killed, and the tension in the city had escalated to war.

I could feel the hatred between them anytime one of them made eye contact with another.

The six contestants, myself included, sat next to their bosses. I was between Franks and Landon. John Paul stood off to the side, watching intently, as Franks got the meeting started.

"This is going to be a little different, boys," Franks said.

Maria Hill, the leader of the LA outfit, sat on the far side of the table and raised an eyebrow at him.

"And ladies," he said with a smile.

"Oh, no," she said sarcastically, "I'll just sit over here and look pretty for you, how's that? No, not too likely, huh?"

Franks ignored her and her tone.

"You'll each be dropped with weapons in hand," he said, "weapons chosen by your bosses and ones you've proven to be most effective when using."

It was unusual to start a tournament armed, but not unheard of. There were many times when there were weapons to be found around the tournament grounds, but being dropped with them wasn't usually part of the plan.

"Arden will have the firearms of his choosing," Franks said as he looked over a list in front of him. "Dytalov, three Kunai throwing knives and a Busse Combat Team Gemini."

He stopped and looked up at the dark-haired man near the Russian group.

"Whatever the fuck that is," he added.

"You want me to go get it and show you?" Erik Dytalov volunteered.

"Shut your mouth," Severinov said, "or I shut it for you."

"Mister Hunter will be armed with a compound bow in addition to a handgun," Franks said, "and Reaper will have her brass knuckles."

He looked over to the woman sitting next to Chambers.

"Is that all?"

"I don't need anything else," she responded.

Hunter laughed.

"I got somethin' else you need."

"Bring it over here," she challenged with a flash of her dark eyes, "I'll show you just what I can do with it."

"Enough," Chambers said quietly. The guy was always as cool as a cucumber, even in the past when I'd just walked out of a game with his guy's blood all over me. He'd hand over his cash with a slight smile and not another word.

"Tyrone Chimes will have a variety of blunt objects, and Mister Sebastian Stark…"

He looked over to me and smiled.

"Mister Stark will maintain a single weapon—the garrote."

No guns, no knives, nothing but a fucking piece of piano wire.

Maybe he does want me to lose.

There were a few murmurs from the group before Franks continued.

"Your location," Franks said, "is Buckingham Island in the Canadian territory of Nunavut. It's about as unfriendly a place as you can imagine, but we don't have to worry about you running into any tourists. It's about six miles across in the center, and you'll be dropped around the floes near the southern tip."

"This will have to be a fast one," Greco commented. "Everyone will freeze to death if it takes too long."

"True," Franks said. "Consider it added incentive to stop warring with your neighbors."

Greco glared but didn't comment further.

"Some weapons don't function well in the cold," Evan Arden remarked.

I watched him closely. There was no concern in his eyes; he was just stating a fact.

"Then you better have a backup plan, Mister Arden."

I couldn't see any reaction in the eyes of Moretti's hit man. He was completely calm and expressionless. Both Hunter and Reaper smiled nasty little smiles in his direction, but Arden didn't seem affected by that either.

Fuck me. He wasn't going to be easy.

I considered the location of the fight and understood the choice of weapons for me. For one, I had been damn effective strangling people in past games. Moreover, it wouldn't require any additional or complex equipment—nothing to misfire, no bolts to lose, and no possibility of it getting jammed in the cold. In fact, it was nearly the perfect weapon under such extreme conditions. I could use it without the loss of dexterity the others would experience through gloves and heavy clothing.

Maybe Franks wanted me to win after all.

I looked around the table to see the reaction from the others to the location. The Russians seemed pleased, Moretti and Greco annoyed, Chambers unaffected, and Hill downright pissed.

"The Arctic Circle?" she inquired. "Really? This is your best idea for the games? I mean, it's not like the closed circuit is going to work too far a distance, so we'll all be freezing our asses off. Oh, and let's not forget surfer boy, here."

She indicated Tyrone.

"He'll lose his tan during the trip."

A few snickers rang out as the dark-skinned man looked over at his boss and raised an eyebrow.

"She has a point about the closed circuit," Moretti pointed out. "As Mister Arden said, equipment has a tendency to malfunction in extreme conditions."

"All taken into consideration," Franks said dismissively. "You'll find our accommodations most pleasant as long as you stay indoors, and you can rest easy about the mechanical concerns—we're bringing in only the best. It's designed to handle the environment."

There were a few more grumbles from the bosses, but Franks answered all of their concerns quickly and efficiently. I could hear Landon in his words and figured they had rehearsed all of this. Landon was a planner, and he wouldn't let any matter get lost in the details.

The meeting came to a close as each of the bosses was handed an encrypted thumb-drive with all the pertinent information on it. Franks and Landon moved off to the far side of the barn to discuss something. Hunter watched with narrowed eyes as John Paul moved quietly up behind Reaper and leaned close to her to speak. I couldn't hear their words, though, and didn't really care.

My thoughts were on my main opponent.

Following Landon's instructions, I ignored the other fighters and made my way over to Arden. He was near Rinaldo Moretti, looking at the man intently and nodding his head every so often. I stood a little way away from them as they finished their conversation but was just close enough to hear the tail end of it.

"…will have an effect on the weapons. Mountainous terrain increases the possibility of an avalanche when I fire, too."

"I can ask," Moretti said, "but I think everything is set now."

"He's done this intentionally to give himself better odds," Arden replied.

"Possibly," Moretti agreed, "but there isn't anything to be done about it now. It has to be this way, son."

I took note of how Moretti addressed Arden and looked at both of them a little more closely. Moretti was short and stocky, whereas Arden was tall and sculpted with lean muscle. His eyes were blue, Moretti's brown. Arden had light brown hair, cut short against the sides of his head in proper military fashion, and a slight, scruffy beard, but Moretti didn't have enough hair to determine what color it might have been in his youth. I couldn't see any resemblance, but that didn't always matter.

"I understand, sir," Arden replied.

Moretti stood and headed over to the group that included Franks and Landon, and I took the opportunity to talk to Arden. He looked up as I approached, his face as passive as it had been during the meeting.

"Mister Stark," he replied politely. He stood and reached out to shake my hand then sat back down at the table.

"I don't really see Moretti as a bird-man," I said as I sat down across from him.

Arden looked at me, and I saw him stifle a slight smirk.

"Rinaldo's more than he appears," he said. "Like many people in this room, underestimating him is usually a mistake."

"You aren't really his kid, are you?" I asked.

"Not by blood," Arden said simply. "Not that it matters."

I nodded slowly. His loyalties were set, no doubt about that. He clearly wasn't someone who was going to turn on his boss. He wasn't in this because of blood or for the money but a deeper sense of commitment and allegiance.

"You still think I'm a pheasant for plucking?"

Arden stared at me, his face blank. I saw his chest rise and fall slowly, as if he were centering himself.

"I think at the end of this, it's going to come down to you and me," he said. "After that, it's no more than a matter of will."

He looked me over briefly.

"And aim," he added.

"You think that will be enough for you?" I asked.

"More than," he replied. There wasn't any bravado in the

statement; he simply thought it a matter of fact. He had no doubt in his abilities, and I needed to throw him off his game.

"It didn't keep you out of enemy hands in the past," I said with a shrug. "It sounds to me as if you have a habit of letting people get the jump on you."

His eyes tightened but only slightly and briefly. I was hoping for a stronger reaction, but frankly, I wasn't accustomed to playing mind games. Any reaction at all out of this guy seemed to be a win.

Arden stood, took two steps to get around the table, and leaned over slightly to look me in the face.

"I hear you're fighting for a kid," he said softly. "Maybe when I'm done with you, I'll put a bullet in his skull, just like his mother's."

Instantly, my hands were balled into fists. Once that happened, there was no more control left in me. I swung at him, made contact with his jaw, and sent him flying backward. I was on my feet and going for him a second later, but that was all it took for two of Moretti's goons to grab my arms to try to hold me back.

It didn't work.

I wrenched one arm out of the grasp of the guy on my right and used it to pop the one on the left hard enough to make him let go. I started to head back to Arden, who was on the floor and rubbing his chin but starting to stand back up again. Another hand grabbed my arm, but I couldn't shake it off.

"Stop." Landon's voice rang clear in my head even before I realized he was the one holding me back. John Paul was on the other side, telling me to take it easy, that there would be a time and place for this, but not here, not now.

"Motherfucker," I growled. I shook them both off of me though John Paul kept his hand on my shoulder as I stomped toward the door of the barn. I didn't get far. A moment later, Landon was standing in front of me, blocking my passage.

"Just let me get the fuck out of here!" I snarled.

Landon glared, and I felt someone else walk up beside me. I turned quickly, and found myself looking at a very irate Joseph Franks.

Fuck.

"You press too far," Franks growled in my ear. "I might need you for now, but don't you pull something like that again, or I'll blow your brains out and find myself another fighter."

I wasn't sure if the threat was serious or not, and I wasn't going to take the chance that he was bluffing. Anything I said could be used against me, Raine, and my son at any time. Deciding to go for contrite, I glanced at the ground, then back up to him.

"I know," I said, "I got it. Don't you worry about a fucking thing—I'm taking all these motherfuckers out."

"That's more like it," he said with a smile. It didn't touch his eyes, but it was an effort, at least.

Deciding it was best to get out as soon as possible, John Paul escorted me out the door and back to his car.

"You are out of your fucking mind," he said as he started the engine and began to back around the other vehicles. "That was seriously stupid."

"Fuck you," I muttered. I knew he was right, but I wasn't about to admit it. I just wanted to get home to Raine. I leaned back in the seat, closed my eyes, and pretended to sleep the rest of the way back to Miami.

There was no question about it—Evan Arden was my primary concern. The others were going to fall quickly and easily, either to me or to Arden. A couple of them would probably take each other out, which was just fine by me. I wasn't counting frags here; only winning mattered.

Last man standing.

As he had said, it would come down to the two of us. When that happened, it was going to be a matter of who found who first—a matter of my hands or his scope.

Unfortunately, he'd already gotten the drop on me once down at the beach. I couldn't let that happen again. It wouldn't have happened if I had been on alert. I wasn't going to fail in that respect when it came to the tournament. There was far too much on the line.

If he was serious about going after Alex…

I wondered if he had something to lose as well though, or rather, someone. Somehow, I doubted it. He didn't seem the relationship type, and I couldn't imagine any chick falling for a guy who was so cold, so blank. Yeah, I'd killed more than a few people in the past during tournaments, and I was going to do it again with good reason, but he'd killed a lot more people in service to Moretti and his family. What kind of girl would put up with that?

Well, Raine put up with my ass, so maybe it was possible.

Ultimately, it didn't matter. Even if he did have someone he cared about out there, it wasn't as if I could use that to my advantage —not now. The games were set, the territory chosen, and all there would be now was preparation for the fight. Once it was announced, no one was allowed to screw with the odds of which player would win.

My direction was clear. At least for now, Evan Arden wasn't my concern.

Chapter Nine

Ice and snow surround me. I'm climbing the sheer face of a rocky cliff as the wind tries to blow me from the edge. I reach up and find purchase on the rocks above. As I pull myself up, I hear a shot ring out.

Across the plateau, I see a body. I rush to it, but I know it's too late.

"Raine!"

What is she doing here? She shouldn't be anywhere near the fighting...

I kneel down and reach for her cold hand. She doesn't move. The sound of snow crunching underfoot catches my attention, and I look up to see the barrel of a rifle pointed in my face...

I woke in a cold sweat with a constricted chest. I had rolled away from Raine and all the way to the other side of the bed at some point during the night. I quickly fixed that by curling up against her side and pulling her fast against my chest. I threw my leg over the top of hers and just held on. For a few minutes, I panted and told myself over and over again that she was safe and warm.

A dream; not real.

It had felt real. Really fucking real. I had to fight against my body's desire to shake uncontrollably as I calmed myself down and looked Raine over to make sure she was fine.

She was, of course. It was all in my fucked up head. When I had relaxed enough to allow myself to release her, I went out to the balcony for a cigarette. The smoke filled my lungs, and the nicotine relaxed my mind. The alcoholic inside of me tried to tell me to take a little drink to calm myself some more, but I told him to fuck off.

After watching her eyes when she'd found me drunk, there was no way I was ever going to put myself in the position to cause that particular look on Raine's face again.

I smoked a cigarette and a half before I went back inside. I took a quick shower to wash myself of the nightmare and the stench of smoke before I crawled back into bed. I didn't think I'd be falling back asleep anytime soon, but I was content to just hold Raine and tell myself that she was fine.

I'm going to make sure she stays that way.

When morning came, I didn't say anything to her about my nightmare. She probably knew anyway because I looked like shit whenever I had been up most of the night. She also made an extra-large pot of coffee when she went into the kitchen, but she didn't ask why I hadn't slept. She knew I'd tell her when I was ready.

I didn't think I would ever be ready to think about that one again, though.

I finished breakfast and placed the dishes in the sink to soak a bit. Raine came up behind me and circled my waist as I stood at the sink, and I turned around to face her.

She reached up and ran her fingers through my mussed up hair.

"You okay?" she asked.

"Sure," I said. I didn't think she was buying it, but I was going to try to keep myself together. I still needed to get to the beach this morning, and it was getting late. Even if I were inclined to talk, it would just mean delaying my morning run.

"Take a nap if you want," Raine suggested.

"With you hanging all over me?" I replied with a smile. "Not a chance."

She wrapped her arms around my neck as I leaned down to kiss her. Kissing led to fondling, and before long, we were headed back to the bedroom with our clothing strewn across the floor.

I backed up against the bed, and Raine pushed against my shoulders until I was on my back. She climbed over me and leaned across my chest to press her lips against mine. I ran my hands over her bare ass and pulled down to press her core against my rigid cock.

Raine rocked her hips against me, and I arched my back to increase the friction. We kept kissing deeply as we moved together, and Raine's hands were gliding over my chest and abs, sending tingles through my skin. When she raised herself up a bit and broke the kiss, she was breathing hard, and I couldn't wait any longer.

With Raine straddling me, I grabbed a hold of my cock and guided it inside of her. She let out a sharp breath as her body encompassed me, and for a long moment, she just kept herself there, balancing with her hands on my chest.

I leaned back and let her have control. She moved slowly over the top of me, and I was glad of it.

I sat up and took her hips in my hands, raising and lowering her over me. With this angle, we could look right into each other's eyes, and I could feel her inside of me as much as I could feel myself inside of her.

Our mouths meshed, and our tongues slid over each other's as we moved together. Raine held on to my shoulders tightly as she pressed her lips to mine and moaned quietly in time to our rhythm. I reached up and enveloped one of her breasts in my hand, lifting it slightly as I rubbed the nipple with my thumb.

She moaned louder, and I wrapped my arm around her waist, twisted us both, and landed on top of her. Raine gasped as I entered her again, swiftly and deeply. I held myself inside of her, reveling in the sensation as she reached up to grip my back. I nipped the skin of her neck with my lips as I started to move again.

For a while, I could pretend there was nothing outside of the bed, nothing that was threatening to harm either one of us. If I closed my eyes and listened to the sound of the surf coming through the window, I could pretend we were on our isolated island, far away from everything else.

I moved inside of her slowly, wanting the feeling to last. I listened to Raine's short breaths and felt the beating of her heart under my hand. I cupped her breast in my hand, sucked at the nipple, and then switched to the other one. Raine grasped the back of my head and arched her back to meet my thrusts time and time again.

It was heaven.

Knowing her body so intimately, I was well aware when she couldn't last much longer. As her face turned pink with desire, I ran the backs of my fingers down her side, reached between us, and stroked her until she was panting and twisting below me. With my fingers pressed against her clit, Raine rocked, moaned, and called out as she came apart around me. I glided my hand up her side and to her shoulder, braced myself against her, and thrust forward quickly. She cried out again, and I repeated the motion over and over again until my head was spinning with the sensations inside of me.

My legs began to quiver, and my arms began to shake with the strain of holding myself up. As I struggled to keep myself from falling, I quickened the pace. My body quaked, and I groaned as I filled her deeply and collapsed on top of her. I panted against her shoulder for a minute as I collected myself and then rolled to the side so I wasn't crushing her. I wrapped her in my arms and pulled her close to me.

"You're fucking phenomenal," I informed her.

Raine giggled.

"You're not so bad yourself," she said, "except for the whole smooshing me afterward thing."

"You love that, too," I said. "You know you'd miss it if I didn't do it."

"Probably," she admitted as she tucked her head against my shoulder.

Warm and calm in her presence, I stroked her back for a couple of minutes. When we were like this, everything was right inside the charred world of my head.

Raine turned her face to look at me.

"I'm scared," Raine whispered.

"Don't be," I said. I tightened my grip around her. "I've got you."

"I'm more scared for you than for me," she admitted. "You might get hurt, or...or..."

"Shh, baby." I pulled her against me. Seeing her so upset tore at me inside, making me wish I hadn't told her anything at all. If I hadn't gotten myself drunk, maybe I could have avoided putting her through this.

I'm such an asshole.

"I'm going to be fine," I told her. I tilted her head so she was looking at me. "I always win."

"You haven't played in years," she reminded me. "You have been exhausted after working out with John Paul. What if you can't…"

Her voice trailed off, and tears started to form in her eyes.

"Nothing is going to happen to me," I told her as I stared intently into her eyes. "I'm going to be just fine. I'm going to win this tournament, and then we're going to take Alex as far away as we can. Landon said this was it—they'd never ask anything else of me. Soon, it will all be over."

I could still see doubt in her eyes, but she sniffed and nodded her head. Though I didn't want to remind her of her attackers on the island, it occurred to me it might be a good idea.

"Remember the guys on the beach?" I asked. "The ones who went after you?"

It was kind of a stupid question. It wasn't like she was going to forget being attacked.

"Yes."

"You remember what I did to them?"

She shuddered a little. I could see in her eyes that she was remembering the whole thing—how they'd come up to her on the beach, and she had mistakenly thought they were a rescue party. They'd grabbed her, and when I got to them on the beach, I'd beaten every one of them to death with my hands. She'd been terrified, and I hated making her recall the memory, but I needed her to remember what I was capable of doing.

"I didn't even have a weapon then," I reminded her. "I hadn't played in the games for years then, either. I'm in much better shape now than I was on the island, and this time I'll be armed."

"With what?" she asked. "Will you have a…a gun?"

I shook my head.

"Don't need one," I responded. "I like the silent weapons. Guns just tell everyone where you are."

Raine considered this information for a moment with narrowed eyes and creased forehead. She didn't ask for more details, and I was glad for that. Instead, she ran her fingers up my arm, squeezing a little at my bicep. I flexed, giving her a little smile in the process.

Yeah, baby—I'm that good.

I wiggled my eyebrows at her, which made her smile and shake her head. She didn't let go of my arm, and her smile faded quickly. She didn't want to think about some of the things I had done in the past, but it seemed more important for her to know I would be all right than to think I was going to get myself killed.

Hurt was a whole other thing. I'd get hurt, no doubt about it. It would be a rare thing to escape a tournament without some kind of injury—a broken bone, a nasty cut, or even worse. That didn't matter though. Staying alive was the only thing that counted.

Raine was apparently thinking the same thing.

"You could still get hurt," she said. "You could get cut again."

She ran her hand up my side, tracing some of the many scars on my body. Some were from knives, some from fists, and others from bullets. I'd had my skin torn open so many times there was no point in trying to count the scars.

"I'll be careful," I told her. "There are only five others, and I've got a lot more experience than any of them. Some of them have never even competed before. No one is going to touch me."

She didn't seem convinced, so I sat up and reached for her wrists. I pulled her up into my lap and grasped her face with both hands.

"I have you at stake," I told her. "You and my kid. There is nothing out there that can stop me from doing what I need to do. You understand me? Nothing."

Raine's eyes widened a little as she looked at me and considered my words. For once, I must have said something right, because she ran her hands up my arms until she was gripping both biceps.

"I believe you," she said.

Appeased by my words, Raine placed her head on my shoulder and squeezed my arms again. She still didn't like it, but I couldn't blame her for that.

"I hate this," she said quietly against my skin.

"I know." I held her closer. "Just focus on Alex. If you can deal with me, you'll be able to deal with a kid. I'm practically a child myself."

I finally got a genuine smile out of her with that one. She relaxed against me, and I kissed the top of her head. She turned to meet my mouth, and we kissed gently as I cupped her face with my hand.

"I love you," I whispered as I stroked her cheek. "You're my life. I won't let anything happen to us. I swear."

She accepted my words this time even if she didn't like how her safety would be secured. We lay back down with her head on my chest. I leaned against the pillow and closed my eyes for a while longer. I was tempted to doze off again, but the sun coming through the blinds made it impossible. I couldn't sleep during the day even if I hadn't slept at all the night before. It didn't matter, though—I still felt at peace with her in my arms, and that was rest enough.

As much as we both might have preferred to stay in bed, we eventually got ourselves up. Raine headed to the kitchen while I pulled on my jogging shorts and a T-shirt. I laced up my shoes, took a piss, and then went out into the main room.

Though it was Saturday and Raine usually took the day off from homework, she had her school stuff spread out in neat piles on the couch and coffee table. I had to hand it to her. In spite of her apprehension, she kept her priorities straight. She had set a goal and was sticking to it. So had I.

She looked up as I came in the room.

"Running?"

"Yeah," I said. "I need to keep building up my endurance."

She cringed a little.

Fuck me. I'd just given her another reminder of what I was going to do, which wasn't my intent. I didn't know how I was supposed to avoid it outside of lying to her about what I was doing, and she would see through that immediately.

Huffing a little breath through my nose, I went over to her and crouched down. I touched her face with my hand and looked closely at her for a moment. The need to reassure her kept my focus where it should be—right inside of her heart. If I could keep that in my head at all times, I'd be able to do this.

"Love you," I said as I brushed my lips against hers. "Everything is going to be fine."

She nodded, resigned to accept my words even if she didn't completely believe them.

"Love you, too," she said.

The power of her mental strength impressed me, as it always did. Tiny thing that she was physically, when it came to dealing with shit way out of her control, she was a beast. She took everything in stride, even when she hated every moment of it.

I was reminded of how she cared for me on the raft when I went through alcohol withdrawal. I'd been in such bad shape, she didn't know if I was going to make it. If I had died, she would have been left alone on that raft and probably would have perished shortly afterward. She'd suffered starvation and dehydration, not to mention putting up with my obnoxious tendencies, but she'd dealt with everything that came at her. She'd persevered through it all, and usually with a smile on her face and some kind word about how I was better than I thought.

In my own fucked up way, this was how I would thank her for everything she'd done and everything she meant to me. I'd get us through this the only way I knew how—with brute force and violence. It wouldn't be pretty, but it was a task I was uniquely qualified to do.

I gave her a brief hug and a kiss on the temple before I headed off.

If I had known then, I would have held her longer.

No, if I had known, I never would have let go.

But ignorance is bliss, so I tromped down the stairs in my running shoes and headed off to the beach even though it was late in the morning and the whole place was already filled with people. Even so, I ditched my shoes in the sand and ran barefoot.

Two little red-headed girls in pink bikinis bounced up and down in the waves, screeching like seagulls every time a whitecap splashed over them. Sunbathers worked on their already ridiculously dark tans, and numerous tourists splashed in the morning surf.

I felt odd the entire time I ran through the sand, but I couldn't put my finger on why, just that I felt strange. I tried to shake it off as nothing, but something in the back of my head kept telling me I was being watched. I needed to keep my head focused on training and the upcoming tournament, but something kept nagging at me.

Maybe my paranoia was going to drive me right into the loony bin before I ever had a chance to fight. Then again, maybe Evan Arden was up on a rooftop somewhere with a sniper rifle aimed at my skull, deciding that he didn't need to play by the rules after all.

His threat against Alex was still echoing through my head. I'd gone up to him with the intention of mind-fucking him, and he'd turned it around on me faster than I could process. It pissed me off, and I wasn't sure if I was mad at him for doing it, myself for letting it happen, or Landon for making the damn suggestion I try to screw with Arden in the first place.

If he had me this much on edge before the tournament actually began, what was the fight itself going to be like?

One thing at a time.

Tomorrow we'd be leaving for whatever area Landon had picked out for training. He wouldn't tell me where it was, only that I needed to dress for the weather. I didn't even own any clothes suited for temperatures less than sixty degrees, so I didn't know what the fuck he expected me to pack. It wasn't like there was a great shop on the beach to buy a winter coat.

I finished my run with the paranoid feeling still in the back of my mind. I glanced around at the rooftops near the beach, but those buildings high enough to obscure someone on top of them were plentiful. If Arden was up there somewhere, I'd never see him.

Shaking my head at myself, I collected my shoes and walked back down the street to the condo building. I glanced at Bar Crudo, which wasn't open so early in the day, but the lines of bottles behind the counter were still visible through the window. Every time I looked at them, my stomach lurched as I pictured Raine's expression when she walked in on me, drunk off my ass.

I had no desire to ever go into that place again.

My confidence that I was going to beat the whole alcoholic thing made me feel a little lighter, and the nagging feeling in the back of my head disappeared as I took the steps two at a time to reach our condo. I was even whistling as I unlocked the door, stepped inside, and dropped my shoes on the nearby mat.

It was quiet inside.

The television wasn't on. There was no sound of water running from the bathroom and no sound of Raine collecting laundry in the bedroom.

"Raine?"

I was answered by complete silence.

The cold, debilitating fear that crept over me was like nothing I had ever experienced before. All the blood in my body felt as if it had dropped to my feet, and I couldn't move. I couldn't take a step forward or backward, and I couldn't utter a sound as my eyes took in my surroundings.

Raine's textbook on Everglades conservation was on the floor, face down, with its pages creased against the carpet. There was a highlighter on the couch, cap off, and pressed against the back cushion as if it had rolled there. There was a paper beside it with a faint yellow streak across the margin.

They weren't exactly signs of a struggle, but they were enough. It was plenty of evidence to leave me no doubt. She had been studying on the couch. No one had buzzed the condo or knocked on the door. If they had, she would have at least set her book down right-side up, not dropped it on the floor, and she would have capped the highlighter.

Someone had surprised her. She'd dropped everything she was holding. Now she was gone. She had been taken.

Arden.

Oh fuck, fuck, fuck! Is she dead? Did he fucking kill her?

"RAINE!" I screamed her name as I found the ability to move again. I knew she was gone, but I couldn't stop myself from checking every little place in the condo, even the closets. Every time I put my hand on a door, I was sure I'd find her curled up in a ball with a bullet in her head.

I wasn't here... I wasn't here for her... When she fucking needed me, I wasn't here...

I had promised to keep her safe. "I've got you," I had told her. Now someone else had her, and I didn't know if she was dead or alive. The possible scene unfolded in my head as I came back to the living room and looked at her scattered items, and my gut summersaulted. She had to have been so fucking scared, and I wasn't here for her.

I'd failed her.

I didn't even put my shoes on as I ran at full speed down the stairs to the parking garage. I jumped on the bike and topped one-twenty on the short trek to Landon's hotel. Not giving a shit what happened to it, I dropped the bike on its side, keys still in the ignition, and ran inside to pound on the elevator button until it arrived.

The button to the fourteenth floor glowed passively at me as I mentally noted Landon was really only thirteen stories up. I rocked back and forth on my feet as adrenaline pumped through me, and as soon as the doors opened, I was running down the hall to his room.

The door was propped open by a little metal bar attached to the frame, and I didn't think about what it might mean as I burst into the room where Landon sat at the round table just inside, sipping from a glass.

"They fucking took Raine!"

Landon just stared at me, his eyes filled with disappointment. I was expecting a bigger reaction out of him, considering fucking around like this was definitely something that could affect the outcome of the games.

Then I realized why he wasn't surprised.

I also saw the gun in his hand.

It wasn't pointed at me, but he was gripping it lightly in his right hand as he sipped from his glass with his left. He was so calm; my words had not surprised him in the least.

If Evan Arden or anyone in any of the organizations had taken Raine, he would have been pissed off. It fucked with the odds of the game when tournament players screwed with each other prior to the match, which influenced the odds of which player would win. It was the death match equivalent to counting cards and simply not tolerated. If Landon knew and wasn't upset about it, then he also knew she wasn't abducted by one of the other families.

There was only one other answer.

"You have her," I said quietly.

He nodded, and I felt a trickle of cold sweat run down the back of my neck. I glanced toward the closed door to the bedroom of the suite.

"Is she here?"

"No."

I looked back to him. His finger still rested on the trigger of the Glock in his hand, but he didn't raise it. It was nothing more than an insurance policy in case I decided to be unreasonable.

"Why?" I asked.

"You pissed him off," Landon said with a shrug. "You embarrassed him by not being able to control yourself in an official meeting."

He leaned forward and pointed one of his fingers at me.

"Do you know how much he wanted you dead?" Landon asked.

"The other day or from the beginning?"

"Not in the beginning," Landon said as he shook his head. "He loved you back then. You made him a shitload of money and never got yourself into too much trouble outside the tournaments. That bullshit with Jillian was the start, and then you turned on him in the worst possible way. Now he's decided to give you another chance, and you fuck it up."

Franks has Raine.

It occurred to me that in his hands, she might actually be worse off than in Arden's.

Holy shit.

"I'll apologize," I said, barely able to form words in my tightened throat.

"I don't think he's interested in your apologies," Landon said simply. "He wants your mind on the game. He wants to make sure you're going to win and not let other shit get in your way.

"She's not in the way."

"She's not now." He continued to stare at me. It was a challenge and a warning. He wasn't going to hesitate to shoot me if he needed to, but he also knew at this point that I wouldn't make a move on him. Not when I didn't even know where she was.

"I want to see her." My words came out with a low growl.

"No." Landon sat back in his chair and waited.

This was it. This was the impasse I couldn't overcome. I could feel my heart pumping in my chest, and the start of the anger and fear inside of me threatened to block all my sensibilities. I took a step forward as I curled my hands into fists.

"If you touch me, you know what will happen."

To emphasize his point, he laid the gun on the table and picked up his drink with his right hand. That action alone was enough for me to realize how fucking helpless I was when it came to him, Franks, and their conniving.

I'll have to kill them both but not now.

"She's alive?" I asked. I knew she was; I just needed to hear him say it.

"Very much so," Landon said with a nod. "Sit down a minute, and let me tell you how things have changed."

In the interest of keeping my head free of holes, I dropped my ass to the plush chair several feet away in the room. I lowered my head to my hands and attempted to breathe normally.

"Trying to keep tabs on her is a distraction," he said. "I can't let you have any distractions, so I removed that one from the equation. Franks' ordering it just made it happen a little sooner than I had planned. Regardless, she's perfectly safe—safer than she would be under your care—and actually providing a bit of a service to Franks himself."

Service?

All the worst possibilities threatened to send me into a blinding rage.

"He…he'd better not…"

"No, no," Landon said quickly as he realized how I had taken his words, "nothing like that. She's doing a little babysitting, actually."

Babysitting?

"Alex?"

"Naturally." Landon polished off his drink and dropped the glass to the table. "She appears to be getting along with your son quite well, actually. She's an interesting woman—very calm in a crisis. I can see why you are so attracted to her."

The image of Raine and a child—my child—emerged in my head and calmed me. They had a reason to keep her safe for now, not just because I'd fucking quit on them if they hurt her, but also because Franks didn't want to have to deal with a kid while he ran his games. His selfishness would be her salvation.

Holding them both captive was also another reason I had to win.

Strangely enough, I started to see Landon's point. With Raine secured somewhere away from the tournament, I wouldn't have to worry about her safety until after the fighting was over. I wouldn't have to think about Arden going after her. I wouldn't have to wonder what was happening to my kid because I knew she would take care of him just as if he were her own.

"I want to see her," I said again. "I want to see both of them."

"Eventually," Landon said. "Right now, we're going to head to the airport."

He stood up, crossed the room, and reached into the briefcase sitting on the desk. He walked over to the chair and handed me a boarding pass.

"Where are we going?" I asked as I looked it over. The boarding pass clearly stated the flight was headed for New York, but I doubted that was our final destination. Traveling with Landon always involved connecting flights to make it harder to track his movements.

"Connecting flight to Thompson, a city in Manitoba," Landon said. "We can get you properly attired there."

He looked down at my bare feet.

"I suppose we need to at least acquire you some shoes before we leave."

I glanced down at myself. Lack of footwear aside, I was dressed in a pair of shorts and a T-shirt. I certainly wasn't prepared for cold weather, and there weren't any parka shops anywhere around Miami. Landon didn't want to waste any more time but allowed me to pick up my bike. There was a big scratch on the body where I had dropped it, but at least it hadn't been stolen or towed.

I took the motorcycle back to the condo and then went inside to grab my shoes. I tried not to think about Landon coming in here unannounced and dragging Raine off, because if I thought about it too much, I was going to go back down there and kill him in the parking lot. I doubted he'd given her any time to pack anything, so I tossed a few essential items for both of us in a small carry-on bag and dragged it out with me.

Landon was waiting for me at the back entrance, and without a word, we headed to the airport in Ft Lauderdale. I followed blindly as Landon led the way through security. I was a little stunned at how quickly everything was happening and was having trouble just keeping my thoughts from going too crazy. Before I knew it, we were sitting in our first class seats on the plane, and one of the flight attendants was offering me a drink.

Yes, I want a fucking drink. Several, in fact.

"No, thanks," I said quietly as I shook my head.

Landon ordered one, the bastard. I could see in his eyes he was doing it just to fuck with me. He probably thought it was good for me to have to exercise self-control when I was around the stuff. As soon as the flight attendant moved away, he started giving me more information about where we were headed.

"We'll be training near Thompson for the next three weeks so you can get acclimated to fighting in the colder climate. After training, we'll take several small planes to reach Resolute, way up in the northern territories. It's near the island where the games will be played."

"Where's Franks?" I asked.

"He'll join us in Thompson," Landon said.

"And Raine?" I'd been pressing him for more information since we'd left the hotel earlier that day, but he hadn't given me much.

"She'll be there eventually," he said.

"You have to let me see her," I said, trying to urge him to comply, "or just talk to her. I need to know she's okay."

More than anything, I wanted to hear her voice. I wanted to tell her everything was going to be all right and that she didn't have to be scared. I'd promised to protect her, and I was already failing in that respect.

"Eventually," he said for the millionth time.

"Landon…" I growled in warning.

He just chuckled under his breath.

"You were always so impatient," he said quietly. "You still need to get some control over that. She's safe; I told you that much. It's enough for now."

It wasn't. It wasn't anywhere near enough. I needed to be able to tell her myself that she would be all right because she wasn't going to believe anyone else.

She might not believe you either, asshole.

"Just give me two minutes on the phone with her," I said.

Landon tossed into my lap the in-flight magazine full of great shopping deals I could get without having to pay duty. I scowled at him.

"Get your mind on something else," he instructed. "Don't dwell on the things you can't control."

"Asshole," I muttered. He obviously wasn't going to budge at this point. I opened the magazine and stared at some strange contraption that was guaranteed to teach cats to shit in the toilet.

The plane began to taxi. At least for now, I would take Landon's advice.

Chapter Ten

"When are you going to let me talk to her?" I asked.

It was freaking freezing, and we'd been hard at training for three days straight outside a tiny, nearly deserted old mining town called Leaf Rapids. Landon had said it was near Thompson, but that was a load of shit. It had taken us more than three hours to get here. It was just about as uninhabitable a place I had ever seen, and the location of the tournament was supposed to be far more remote.

Landon let out a sigh. I grabbed a canteen of nearly frozen water and tried to recover from my latest jaunt across the icy land. I dropped my ass down on a tree stump near the lake and pulled a cigarette out of my pocket. It was slightly crushed, but serviceable. I had to take my hand out of my glove to light it, though.

I'd asked the same question at least a dozen times since we began training. I'd been met with silence or some comment about patience being a fucking virtue.

Landon looked up at me, glared at the cigarette, and then looked toward the setting sun.

"You make that your last cigarette today," he said, "and you can call her tonight."

I felt like a kid at fucking Christmas time. A kid with a real family and real parents who gave a shit and made sure there were presents wrapped up in red and green paper and a plate of cookies and milk for the elf dude. It was the kind of thing I'd never experienced, but I wanted to make sure I knew what it was supposed to be like so I could give all that to Alex.

I wanted to give him everything.

Knowing Raine was with him, even if it was against her will, made me feel like there was some actual hope for the future. It made me believe when this was all over, we could make it work.

That night, as I shoveled logs into a wood burning stove, Landon came up behind me and handed me his cell phone.

"Five minutes," he said.

I took the phone from his hand and placed it up to my ear.

"Raine?"

"Bastian? Oh my God, Bastian!"

"It's me, baby," I said. I could hear her crying. "Are you all right?"

"I'm okay," she sniffed.

"Where are you?" I asked.

"Somewhere in Canada."

"Thompson?"

"That might be it."

I looked to Landon, and he nodded once.

"I'm just a few hours away from there," I told her. "Everything is okay, baby."

"That man," Raine said with a shushed voice, "that Landon man —he came to the condo. He grabbed me and…and…"

"I know, Raine," I said as I glared up at him. "I know what he did. I didn't know he was going to do it, but he did it to protect you."

"Protect me?" Raine practically yelled. "He hauled me out of the building with a gun in my back!"

I placed my hand over the mouthpiece of the phone.

"You took her at gunpoint?" I hissed.

"I couldn't haul her out kicking and screaming, could I?" Landon said with a shrug.

I growled and went back to Raine.

"I'm sorry," I said, though I didn't know what the fuck made me apologize for him. "He never should have done that. Maybe if he had just *talked to me*"—I raised my voice and looked over at him pointedly—"we could have worked it out a little better."

Landon rolled his eyes. I knew he hated it when I used logic against him.

"You're safe now," I told Raine. "No one there is going to hurt you, I promise. They're just making sure you're not in the line of fire or anything like that."

"Like you are," she said quietly.

"I'm fine," I reassured her. "I'm just freezing my ass off while training. I'm going to make sure Landon takes me to see you soon."

"You're with him?"

"Yeah, I am."

"Well, tell him I said he was a fucking bastard."

If I had been drinking, I would have spewed whatever it was all over myself.

"I'll relay the message," I replied through my grin.

"You do that!" she spat back.

Landon made a little motion across his neck to let me know my time was up.

"I have to go," I told her. "I just wanted you to know it was all okay. Alex is with you, right?"

"He is," Raine said, "but it's not all okay, Bastian."

"It will be, baby," I said. "I promise."

As Landon reclaimed the phone, I wondered if my promises still meant anything to her.

⚬⚬⚬●◗◆◖●⚬⚬⚬

Snow, ice, and training; trying to scale rocks with my fingers so cold, they could barely move, let alone grip a thin ledge through the gloves; running mile upon mile with the frozen air coating my lungs and my legs so tired I couldn't even feel them anymore. This was apparently Landon's idea of fun.

"You should have been with me when I was training in the Navy," he said. "We'd go from areas like this to the Caribbean in the same week. I thought I was going to die from the change in temperature."

He laughed.

"I'm pretty sure you aren't right in the head," I mumbled.

"That's why I like you," he responded. "We're the same. Let's go over it again, shall we?"

I took in a breath of frigid air and nodded. I followed Landon down the gravel road away from the trees and lake to where his Jeep was parked. There were a couple of downed tree trunks off the side of the road where he had parked, and we sat on one of them.

"Buckingham Island is far above the tree line," Landon said, "so don't plan on finding any trees for cover. There isn't much in the way of vegetation or animal life at all, just a few lichens and mosses, but don't eat the lichens—they won't do you any good."

"I figured," I said with a nod. "This is going to have to be fast. I should be able to carry everything with me."

"You'll have to," Landon agreed. "You're also going to have to stop and eat frequently. In twenty-four hours, you'll burn seven or eight thousand calories easily just trying to stay warm."

That would explain why I had been so ravenously hungry every day we had been here.

"Temperature this time of year is right about negative five," Landon continued. He pulled a roughly drawn map from his pocket and laid it out on the gravel in front of us. "It could get as low as negative ten to fifteen with wind-chill. The only landform is Mount Windsor, which is pretty much the entire island. It's a volcanic formation with deep vertical ridges going from the top down to the ice floes. Those are going to be your best friends when it comes to securing yourself from the sniper."

I looked over the terrain on the map. It was pretty fucking boring—nothing but rock and ice. I could see the ridges Landon spoke about, running up and down the sides of the mountain.

"They'll offer some protection," I agreed, "but also the possibility of getting myself trapped. If someone's above me, they'll have a definite advantage."

"Maybe," Landon said. "When it comes to pure strength—either that in your hands or the strength of exceptional firepower—taking the high ground will give you the advantage. When it comes to strategy, that's what everyone is going to assume."

I sat back a bit and looked at him, realizing almost immediately what he meant. We'd had this conversation many times over the years I had trained with him.

"I should do the opposite."

"It will be the unexpected," Landon said with a nod. "You can pull that off where others can't. Remaining hidden is what will bring you victory."

"I got ya."

"I've got one other thing to help you out."

Landon stood and headed over to his Jeep. He opened up the back and pulled out a large duffel bag, which he dropped at my feet before leaning over to open it.

"Kevlar," he stated simply.

I looked over the rough-feeling black vest.

"Arden is definitely a one-shot-one-kill man," Landon said, "but this could still help you out."

"He goes for the head shot every time. He doesn't miss often."

"If he does, this could save you."

"It'll work against Dytalov's knives, too," I noted.

"It will," Landon agreed. "It will also give you a little extra warmth in the torso, which you're going to need."

I slipped off my parka and put the vest on underneath it. It was a little snug, but I could move well enough. If it managed to keep me from getting cut or shot, it would definitely be worth it.

"Let's call it a day," Landon said as I slipped the vest back off. He packed it in the duffel and handed the bag over to me.

I looked up at the sun, which didn't seem to make any perceivable difference in the temperature. It was still high in the sky.

"Kinda early, isn't it?" I wasn't going to argue with him or anything. I was already gathering up my stuff to make sure he didn't change his mind. We'd been hard at it for days upon days, and my head was overloaded. I wasn't even sure what the date was anymore.

"Well, it's a long trip into town."

"We're going into Leaf Rapids?"

"No," Landon said, "Thompson. Franks wants to chat, and I thought you deserved a little reward for your efforts."

Twenty minutes later, we were in Landon's Range Rover and heading down the snowy back roads to highway 391. The trek to Thompson was long and uneventful, which made it seem even longer. Knowing Raine was going to be on the other side of the journey didn't help with the perceived passage of time at all.

I'm going to see her—really see her, talk to her, touch her.

We hadn't spent more than a few hours apart since the night I pulled her onto the raft and away from my sinking ship. Being without her was physically painful.

We drove past the airport, into the city from the north side, and then headed south all the way through town. Landon maneuvered the vehicle off the main road and headed towards a cluster of buildings near a quarry.

I rubbed my hands on my pants nervously. I wasn't sure why I was feeling so jittery except out of a desire to see Raine. Maybe it was because I'd only spoken to her once since Landon had hauled her out of our condo. I didn't really know how I was going to be received or what she had been through since I last saw her.

My skin prickled at the thought. If there was a scratch on her, someone would end up paying for it in blood.

Landon drove around the main building and parked in the back near a cluster of smaller sheds. I jumped out of the car and followed him across the gravel to one of the doors. It appeared unguarded, but when I looked around, I could see several people around the area with weapons. They were watching us as we approached the door.

Landon knocked, and I shuffled the gravel around with the toe of my boot until someone opened the door and let us in.

"Mister Stark," the man behind the door said.

I looked up but realized he was talking to Landon.

"Hello, Roger," Landon said politely. "Where's Franks?"

"In the back," the man indicated with a pointed thumb over his shoulder. "He's expecting you."

"Do me a favor," Landon said, "and take Sebastian here over to the other building. He's going to visit with Miss Gayle."

"Sure thing." Roger held out his hand, shook mine, and then took me over to the slightly smaller building behind the one Landon had entered. My heart started beating faster as we approached.

She's in there.

Despite the cold, my palms were beginning to sweat. I watched as Roger took out a key and unlocked the padlock on the outside of the door. I wondered if the lock was more to keep her in or others out.

He opened the door.

The inside of the building was set up like a small apartment. There was a couch, loveseat, coffee table, and television on one side and an eat-in kitchen off to the left. A short hallway led directly away from the door, and I could see four openings into other rooms, presumably bedrooms and a bathroom.

Raine was sitting on the couch, dressed in jeans and wrapped up in a long, blue sweater. She looked up as the door opened, and her eyes went wide.

"Bastian!"

"I'll leave you to it," Roger said quietly as he took a backwards step to remove himself from the shed and shut the door behind me.

Raine nearly tackled me as she wrapped her arms underneath mine and grabbed me in a death-grip. I tightened my arms around her and tucked my face into her hair. I'd almost forgotten what she smelled like, and the scent of her hair and skin was overpowering. I squeezed my eyes shut and held her to my chest as her arms came up around my shoulders, anchoring me to her.

"I'm here, baby," I told her. "I've got you."

Just the words coming out of my mouth drove red-hot anger through my body. My teeth clenched as my hands gripped her back. Like the sacred promise I had vowed to her in the life raft when there was no fucking hope for survival, I'd held her to me and said, "I've got you." But I hadn't been there for her. When she really needed me, I wasn't there.

"I'm so fucking sorry for all of this," I said.

She shook her head against my chest.

"Not your fault," she claimed.

"I'm hardly blameless," I countered. "I never should have told you anything about my life. If I hadn't, maybe they would have left you alone."

"You don't know that," she said. "They very well could have come after me anyway. You know they could have."

She was right. Even if she knew nothing about my connections to organized crime or the death-match tournaments I'd completed to entertain the far-too-rich-for-their-own-good sycophants of the underworld, Franks and his group still could have decided it was best to get her out of the way.

"I missed you so much," Raine said quietly.

"I missed you, too."

"We've never been apart before," Raine said. "I don't like it."

"I know. I hate it."

I breathed in her scent again, trying to force the memory to lodge in my brain somewhere so I could keep it with me. I felt both better and worse being in her presence—better because I could touch her and be with her, but worse because she was being held prisoner in a fucking shed in the middle of Nowhere, Manitoba.

I pulled back a little and looked her over.

"Are you okay?" I asked. My chest tightened as I waited for her answer.

"Yes," she said. "A little annoyed by all of this, but I'm all right."

"No one hurt you?" I braced myself for her answer. If anyone had laid a hand on her, I'd be ripping out throats before the tournament began.

"No," she said. "Scared me a bit, but no one hurt me."

I breathed a sigh of relief and held her closer.

"Do you have everything you need? Are they getting you plenty of food and whatever else you want?"

"Mostly." Raine scowled.

"What is it?" I demanded. If Franks' cohorts were holding back something she needed, they were going to have to answer to me.

"They won't let me have internet access," she said with a sigh. "I didn't have my phone on me when Landon showed up at the condo, so I can't call anyone. I can't reach my professors, and exams are next week. I'm going to fail the whole semester."

Raine's schooling had been the farthest thing from my mind. If I was totally honest, I couldn't have cared less about it. She could fucking drop out, and it wouldn't make any difference to me. There was nothing in the foreseeable future that was going to require her to have a degree in ecology.

It was important to her though, and it was obviously stressing her out. She'd worked hard and nearly had straight A's in her classes. Though I didn't ultimately care, I could understand why she wouldn't want all that work to be wasted.

Kind of like building a kick-ass shelter out of nothing and then having a helicopter haul you away from it all.

"I'll see what I can do," I said.

"If I could just get a hold of them and tell them I was… *indisposed*, maybe they would let me make up the work in the summer or something."

There was no way in hell Landon was going to let her talk to anyone, but I didn't want to bring that up just yet. I had a couple of ideas I thought might work.

"I'll take care of it," I told her. "I don't know exactly how just yet, but I'll figure something out."

She nodded, and I was glad she took me at my word. Considering what I had gotten her into, she had every right not to believe a fucking thing that came out of my mouth. I wouldn't have blamed her. Even if she had come to understand that all of this was for her own protection, it was still a shitty way to live, even temporarily.

Raine reached up and ran her fingers over my jaw.

"How about you?" she asked. "How have you been sleeping?"

I shrugged one shoulder.

"I've been so exhausted," I told her, "I've pretty much dropped off as soon as training was done for the day."

It wasn't completely true, but I didn't want her thinking I wasn't sleeping at all. The last thing she needed was to worry about me. It didn't work, though, and as Raine eyed me, it became clear that she wasn't buying it.

"I wake up cold at night," I admitted. "I reach out for you, but you're not there. I usually can't get to sleep again after that. I guess the plus side is there isn't enough time for nightmares."

I gave her a half smile, hoping she'd see the joke in it, but she didn't return the gesture.

"I can't sleep, either," Raine said with a nod. "I keep thinking of all the times I woke up with you practically on top of me, and how annoyed I would get because you were sweaty. Now I wouldn't mind that at all."

"I like making you sweaty," I said with a raised eyebrow.

Raine leaned her body against mine and wrapped her arms around my neck. I held her around the waist as she placed her cheek on my chest and just stood there for a minute.

I looked over her head and around the room. It wasn't too bad, really. It was spacious enough, but I had to wonder if the television actually got any reception out here in the middle of nowhere. I couldn't imagine anyone had gone through the trouble of connecting cable for her.

Next to the couch, there was a small pile of Legos.

"Bastian," Raine said softly as she looked up at my face, "there's someone you need to meet."

"Alex?" I swallowed hard as I kept looking at the plastic bricks.

"He's in the other room," she said, indicating one of the doors down the hallway.

I nodded and relaxed my grip on her. I took a deep breath and started to step away, but Raine grasped my arm.

"Bastian?"

"Yeah?"

"He's *amazing*." The way her eyes lit up told me everything. She loved him already, and loved him deeply.

I didn't ask for any more information but took a few steps to the bedroom door. Inside were a twin-sized bed and a small dresser in dark wood. There was a mismatched nightstand with a small light in the shape of a turtle. A bookshelf lined with Doctor Seuss and *Captain Underpants* books stood in the corner near the closet. There were a dozen or so books on the floor in front of the bookshelf with a few Star Wars action figures poised on top of them.

In the center of the chaotic room, a tow-headed boy sat at a small plastic table. The table was cluttered with crayons, markers, and colored pencils, and the boy was bent over a piece of paper scribbling madly. He didn't look up. He was completely focused on his task.

For a few minutes, I just watched him as he worked, observing everything I could about him. He was right handed, and even with the way he was bent over, I could tell that his eyes matched mine exactly. There was something about how he leaned into his work and the intense expression on his face that was also very familiar.

I didn't have any pictures of myself from when I was a child. Apparently none of my foster parents ever took any, or if they did, they didn't give them to me. I never really considered what I had looked like back then, but now I knew. I could see myself as a six-year-old, sitting there at that table in a room just like this one.

I couldn't quite see the drawing Alex was making, and when I took a little step forward to get a better angle, he looked up at me. For a moment, we stared at each other without speaking. He tilted his head to one side to study me, and I realized I was making the same motion as I watched him. He dropped his gaze down to my feet and then raised it back up to my face.

"You're tall," he said.

I grinned. I started to open my mouth, but I realized the sentence that had formed in my head included an F-bomb, which probably wouldn't be a good idea. I quickly thought of something else.

"Maybe you're short," I suggested.

Alex looked up at me and let out a long, exaggerated sigh as he tossed his hands in the air.

"I'm only six," he replied. "Someday I'll be bigger."

"I bet you'll be as big as me when you're older."

He tilted his head to one side and looked at me intently.

"Maybe," he said. He turned back to his drawing.

"What are you making?" I asked as I took a second step into the room.

"A picture."

"Of what?"

"You."

My heart skipped and my diaphragm constricted. For a moment, I couldn't breathe.

"Me?" I finally choked out.

He nodded and went back to coloring.

I stepped the rest of the way into the room to get a better look. The drawing was definitely of a person, but I wasn't too sure anyone would think it was me. The figure's head was just as big as his body, and Alex had colored in red shorts over stick legs. The arms were large balloon shapes, and the hands were little round balls with five tiny sticks coming out of them.

I couldn't help but smile.

"How do you know it's me?" I asked.

"Right here," Alex said as he pointed to the blue dots on the oversized head. "Your eyes are the same color as mine. Raine said so."

"She did, huh?"

"Uh huh."

I wondered what else she had told him.

I pulled out the extra chair from the other side of the table and dragged it around to sit next to Alex. My ass barely fit in the seat, and I was a little worried it was going to break under my weight. I shifted a little, deciding the chair would at least hold me for a while, and looked down at the simple piece of printer paper covered in crayon marks.

"What are these?" I asked, pointing to a couple of objects near the feet of the figure.

"Dumbbells," he said. He looked up, and his eyes traveled over my arms. "You work out a lot. That's why your muscles are so big."

He pointed at the balloon arms.

"Well, that makes sense," I said.

We sat in silence as Alex continued to draw. I knew I ought to say something else, but I didn't know what it should be. I hadn't spent any time around kids since I was one myself, and I had no idea how to interact with them. He obviously knew something about me, but how far that knowledge reached was a mystery. Did he only know about me through Raine, or had Jillian divulged information as well? If she had, what would she have said?

I was totally lost, so I decided sticking to something simple would be best.

"It's a good drawing," I finally said.

He stopped drawing and looked at me with a creased forehead and slightly narrowed eyes.

"Are you going to be my dad now?" he asked bluntly.

Whatever he had been told, it was enough for him to understand some of what was happening. I wanted to ask him what he knew about me and the death of his mother, but I couldn't bring myself to change the tone of the setting quite so much. It was the first time we had ever laid eyes on each other, and I wasn't going to fuck it up.

"I'd like to be," I said.

"Okay." He turned back to the drawing and started to make a second figure in the picture. This person was smaller than the image of me, with no balloon arms but the same blue dots for eyes.

"Who's that?" I asked.

"Me," Alex said as he shrugged his shoulder. "If you're going to be my dad, I have to be in the picture, too."

Apparently, that was all there was to it.

"I guess that makes sense," I replied with a nod. "Will anyone else be in the picture?"

He placed the end of the crayon up against his lip, creating a little depression there. He stared down at the picture in contemplation.

"I think maybe Raine, too," he said. "She's not my mom, though. She's your mom."

"Raine's my *mom*?" I had to laugh at the idea.

"She's not?" His brow furrowed.

"She's my girlfriend," I corrected.

"Oh."

The news didn't seem to faze him at all. He studied the picture for a moment before switching to a purple crayon and adding a shirt to the picture of himself. He made his pants yellow and his shoes blue.

I couldn't help it—there were some things I just had to know.

"How do you know I'm your dad?" I asked. "We haven't met before."

"Raine told me what you looked like."

It wasn't exactly what I was going for, but this was all new territory for me. I was having a hard enough time keeping my language clean. I knew what I couldn't say, just not what I *should* say.

"I meant, how did you know…or did you know…"

I bit my tongue to stop the natural curse that formed there. It hadn't been very long since Jillian had been killed, and the last thing I wanted to do was upset the kid at our first meeting. Still, I needed some answers.

"Did you know that your mom's…your mom's husband…did you know he wasn't your dad?"

"Yeah," Alex said without looking up.

"How did you know that?"

"Mom and Ian yelled at each other a lot," Alex explained. "When she was mad at him, she'd say he wasn't my real dad. I didn't know who my real dad was until Raine told me about you."

The idea that Jillian had picked fights with her husband didn't surprise me in the least—that woman could be a hellcat. I was a little pissed she had obviously fought in front of Alex but not necessarily shocked by it.

"What did Raine tell you?" I asked.

"She said you were strong," Alex said. "She said you had big muscles to always keep us safe. She said even though you weren't here yet, that's what you were doing. That's why we had to stay here, so you could make us safe again."

I looked Alex over carefully, trying to determine any signs of distress, but I couldn't see any. His words were matter-of-fact, like he'd practiced saying them or at least had been thinking about them frequently. I couldn't figure out if he was scared or not, and that bothered me. I wanted him to know that he would be okay.

"That's exactly what I'm going to do," I said definitively. "Just like Raine said—I'm going to make sure both of you are safe, and then maybe we'll find a house we can all live in together. What do you think of that?"

"That would be okay," Alex said. "Raine said we were going to find a house on the internet, but there isn't a computer here."

"Well, when we find a house for all of us," I said, "I'll make sure you have the best computer out there. You can play games and do your homework on it."

"Ugh!" Alex cried out, startling me. He arched his back halfway over the chair and splayed out his arms. A couple crayons fell to the floor. "I hate homework!"

I grinned as I looked around the room at the books, action figures, and stuffed animals all over the floor.

"I bet you don't like cleaning up your toys either, do you?"

He rolled his head to the side, keeping himself bent backwards over the chair.

"Of course not!"

I laughed at his display.

"I bet Raine makes you clean them up though, doesn't she?"

He took in a big breath and let it out in a huff.

"Yeah."

I grinned.

"I'll tell you a secret," I said as I leaned closer to him.

"What?" he asked, his interest piqued.

"She makes me clean up my stuff, too."

I was rewarded with a smile.

"I'm going to go talk to Raine," I said to Alex. "Will you show me the picture when it's done?"

"Sure." Alex righted himself in the chair and went back to his work.

When I came back into the main living area, Raine was in the kitchen with bread and peanut butter on the counter in front of her. She stopped and looked at me as I came out.

"You were right," I said. I couldn't stop the smile on my face. "He's awesome."

"He really is." Raine's expression mirrored my own. "I see more and more of you in him every day."

"What does he know?" I asked. "I mean, he said a little, and you must have told him I was his father…"

"I didn't tell him; Landon did," Raine informed me. "When he brought me here, and Alex came out of his room, Landon told him I was going to take care of him until his dad got here."

"Fuck," I muttered. "How did he react?"

"I think he already knew Jillian's husband wasn't his father," Raine said. "He didn't seem surprised, just took it all in stride. I tried to talk to him about his mother a little, but he doesn't say much. He knows they're both dead, but I can't get much of a reaction out of him. I kind of think he's in shock about it all."

"Why don't you know who your parents are?"

"I don't remember them."

"How can you not remember your own parents?"

"I just don't, okay?"

"Everyone remembers their parents. Are yours dead?"

"I don't know."

"How can you not know that?"

"Just shut the fuck up!"

I tried to shake the memory from my head, but it lingered a while. If anything, it solidified my resolve to win this tournament and give Raine and Alex some kind of normal life—the kind of life I never had. There was no way I'd let Alex be bombarded with the kinds of questions I always had to deal with as a child.

No fucking way was that going to happen to my kid.

"Bastian? You okay?"

"Yeah," I said. "Just thinking. I don't want him to grow up like I did."

Raine lowered the knife full of peanut butter and walked over to me. She coiled her arms around my back and held me against her. I brought my arms up and returned the embrace.

"He's so smart," Raine said quietly. "You won't believe how smart he is. I think as long as he knows we're going to take care of him, he'll be just fine."

I wasn't sure if it was going to be that simple or not, but I was willing to believe it. I wanted to believe it. I wanted to know he was going to be all right when all this was over.

Assuming any of us were all right.

I heard the sound of the lock at the door and turned to find Landon motioning me outside. I told Raine I'd be right back and went out into the bitter wind to speak with him.

"It's set," Landon said. "The tournament will begin the day after tomorrow."

"What's the plan?"

"Stay here tonight," he said. "In the morning, we'll get on the plane and head up there. The usual pre-tournament party for the elite is tomorrow night, and then it's on."

I nodded.

"I'm staying with her."

"I figured as much," Landon responded. "Don't let it distract you."

I ignored his tone.

"Give me your phone," I said to Landon.

"Why?" he asked with narrowed eyes.

"This little party has fucked up Raine's semester at school," I said simply, "and I'm going to fix it."

He debated only a few seconds before handing me the phone.

"I don't have to tell you to use caution, do I?"

"Nope," I responded.

I browsed the university website on the tiny screen until I figured out how to reach the first of Raine's professors.

"Doctor Michaels?"

"Speaking."

"This is Detective Masterson from Miami Dade," I said smoothly. "I'm calling regarding one of your students, Miss Raine Gayle."

"Yes, sir," he replied. I could hear from his voice that he was already intrigued. "Is she in some kind of trouble?"

"I'm afraid I can't discuss the details with you at this time," I replied. "I just need your understanding and cooperation. Miss Gayle will be in protective custody for the next few weeks pending an important trial out of state. Needless to say, she won't be finishing her semester, but she's concerned about the hard work she's already done in your class specifically."

"Of course!" Michaels said. "Anything I can do to help. Miss Gayle is an excellent student. I've been wondering what happened to her."

"She's perfectly fine," I said. "We just need to do what we can for her right now. Would you be willing to collect all her remaining schoolwork for the class and forward it on?"

He agreed completely, as I figured he would. Her remaining professors did the same, and Landon helped me arrange to have her work picked up at the university student center by a courier under Franks' control. She'd have it all within a few days and had until the first of May to complete and return it. That gave her plenty of time.

It also gave her something else to think about besides what I had to do.

Tomorrow's activities were set. At least for now, I'd spend my time with my family.

Chapter Eleven

Back in the apartment Franks had set up for Raine and Alex, I sat awkwardly at the table in the kitchen while they ate sandwiches. Raine offered me one, but that was junk food in my book, so I declined.

"Can't you give him something healthier?" I mumbled.

"He's just a kid, Bastian. It's peanut butter and jelly, not candy bars."

I looked over the sugar content on the label of the jelly jar and cringed. The bread Raine had used for the sandwiches was that squishy white stuff, too.

"Jesus, Raine," I said, "this is pure shit!"

"Watch your mouth!" she said with a hiss.

I rolled my eyes, but I knew she was right. I looked over at Alex, but he was face-deep in peanut butter and not paying any attention.

"He didn't hear me," I said.

"Maybe not *this* time," she countered.

"It's still crap food."

"Well," Raine continued, "this is what they give me. It's not like I'm doing the shopping myself. You know I don't usually buy this kind of stuff because you always throw a fit."

All right, I couldn't argue with that. I could tell the assholes in Franks' employ to get her some better quality food though. Of course, I had no idea what kids liked to eat—weren't they supposed to be picky eaters or something? Was I going to have to spout a plethora of arguments about why vegetables had to be eaten?

I'm so unprepared for fatherhood, it's not even funny.

As I sat there and thought about it, I realized just how correct that statement was. I didn't know what I was doing. Raine seemed so natural with Alex, and I didn't even know what he'd want to eat for dinner. I'd spent years of effort pushing the memory of his existence as far into the back of my mind as possible; I never even considered needing any information about children. I couldn't exactly use my own past as a delinquent skipping from one foster home to another as a model.

I had no clue what a six-year-old was like. I didn't even know where to start.

"Fuck," I muttered under my breath.

"Bastian!" Raine snarled. "Stop it!"

I was about to take myself out of the room to let out a good string of cuss words when Alex spoke up.

"You aren't supposed to say bad words, Dad."

That single word melted me. It flowed over my flesh like warm bath water and sunk into me so deeply, I could feel it in my core. My throat felt like it was closing up on me, and there was burning pressure building up behind my eyes. I felt Raine's fingers brush over my thigh, and I forced myself to swallow.

"You're right, Alex," I finally said. "I shouldn't."

Alex and Raine finished their sandwiches, and we spent the rest of the day sitting on the living room floor with Alex, placing little plastic bricks together in such a way that they ended up looking like little spaceships. There were astronaut figures to add to the cockpits, and Alex flew them around the room, sparking memories from my own fucked-up past.

With a plastic airplane in my hand, I make buzzing sounds as I hold it high above my head and run in circles around the room. It's the very best plane from the box. All the others are scratched up or rusty.

Jared, the new kid in the foster home, finishes the wooden puzzle he's been working on and looks over to me.

"It's my turn to play with the plane!"

"No, it isn't," I say. My skin quivers through my body as I hold the toy close to my chest. He'd played with it all day yesterday. I've only had it for a few minutes, and I'm not about to give it up now.

It is a something. It is a something important, and if I give it to him, I have nothing.

"It's my turn!" Jared insists. He looks over to Miss Janet and yells to her. "Sebastian's not sharing!"

"Share the toys," Miss Janet says without looking up from the crossword in the newspaper. She scribbles in a word then purses her lips and erases it again.

"She said you have to share," Jared says with a sneer.

My hands shake as I hold the plane tightly in my fingers. I won't give it to him. I won't.

Jared reaches out and tries to grab it from me, but I push him away. He lands on the carpet and cries out.

"He pushed me!"

Miss Janet tells me to stop in the same, tired voice.

Jared stands and comes at me, and I shove him again—harder this time. The plastic wing of the plane is cutting into my fingers a little as I hold it tightly. I take a step forward and kick him in the side.

"It's mine!" I shout. "You can't play with it!"

"Sebastian!" Miss Janet yells as she looks over at me. "Give Jared the plane!"

The shaking in my hands travels through the rest of my body. It's all I have. Jared has everything, even parents who are just waiting for the court system to say their house is in good enough shape for him to come home. He has them, he has a home, he has his own toys, and I have nothing.

Screaming at the top of my voice, I throw the plane against the wall. The shaking turns to pressure in my head and chest as I watch it fall in little pieces to the floor.

"You see what you did!" I scream at Jared as I launch myself at him.

Shaking the memory away, I swore to myself again that Alex was not going to have the same kind of life that was forced upon me as a child. I wasn't going to let that happen to him.

Promptly at eight o'clock, Raine coerced Alex into taking a bath. I watched as he floated little boats around in the water and Raine washed his hair. Seeing her with him made me feel proud of her but also extremely inadequate. How did she know how to do these things? I was at a total loss.

"Can you grab some pajamas for him?" Raine asked.

"Where are they?"

"Second drawer."

I went into his bedroom and dug around through the dresser until I came up with a faded pair of PJs with Spiderman all over the fabric in various heroic poses. Alex held onto my shoulder as he stepped into them, and Raine dried off his hair and handed him a toothbrush.

"Can Dad pick out a story to read?" Alex asked.

I looked to Raine, nearly panicked. I'd never read a story to a kid in my life.

"Of course he can," Raine said. She grinned at me and leaned close. "He likes the one called *The Hungry Thing*."

After a little digging, I found the book on the floor beneath Alex's dirty clothes. I tossed the clothes in the hamper near the door and pulled one of the plastic chairs to the edge of the bed. Alex settled in, and Raine pulled the blanket up to his chin.

I held the book in my lap and chewed on the edge of my thumb, unsure of how to begin. Raine raised her eyebrows at me and nodded her head toward the book. I took in a deep breath, opened the cover, and began to read in a shaky voice.

It was a weird story about a creature coming into a town and demanding various things to eat, but it never said the words right. Only one kid in town was able to understand what it wanted. Alex laughed every time the creature demanded a new dish.

When I arrived at the end of the story, Raine kissed Alex on the forehead and told him goodnight before she walked out of the room. I stood there for a minute, not sure if I should do the same or not.

Apparently tired of my hesitation, Alex looked at me and held out his arms. Glad for the invitation, I reached down and gave him a hug.

"'Night, Dad."

"Goodnight…son." I choked.

Raine was standing in the hall with a grin on her face.

"That was pretty good," she said.

"I've never done that before," I admitted.

She placed a brief kiss on my cheek.

"You're a natural."

I wanted to deny it. I wanted to tell her I had no fucking clue what I was doing, and watching how good she was with Alex was a little intimidating. That little, abused kid inside of me wanted to remind her that she'd be better off finding some dude with a regular job who could drink an occasional glass of wine without losing control of himself.

I didn't.

Her hand brushed over my cheek, and I didn't want to say those things. I didn't want her to find someone else.

I wanted to be that man.

Well, probably sans glass of wine with dinner, but everything else.

Could I do that? Was there any chance I would be able to give her everything she deserved to have in life without my past always getting in the way? I'd dwelled on it for so long, allowed it to make me into someone who couldn't handle a fucking dinner party with his girl's friends, that I wasn't sure I could ever be any other way.

Fuck that.

She deserved more, and I wasn't going to deny her. I could never let her go, but I could change myself. I could be what she needed most. I could be a father to Alex, one worthy of the title, and in the process, I would make myself into a man she would be proud to call hers.

I would do it, but first, more than anything, I wanted to show her something else I was a natural at doing.

"Get in that bedroom," I said. "Now."

Raine's eyes darkened as she swept her tongue across her lips. She turned quickly to comply. I followed, closing the door behind us.

I grabbed her waist before she could even reach the bed, turned her around and covered her mouth with mine. I was hungry for her, the weeks of not having her body pressed to mine overwhelming me with sudden intensity. I needed her more than I ever had before.

Raine broke away, trying to catch her breath as I moved my lips down her neck. I grabbed at the bottom of her shirt and yanked it up over her head and down her arms. Reaching for her lace-covered breasts, I found her shoulder with my mouth and sucked at the skin there as she wrapped her arms around my head.

"I missed you so much," she said.

"I'm going to make up for that right now," I promised. I tore off my shirt and released my cock from my pants. Raine pushed them down my legs, and I kicked both the pants and my boxers out of the way.

Grabbing the waist of Raine's jeans, I pulled them off and tossed them on the bed. Her panties and bra followed quickly, and I pulled her against me again, my cock pressing hard against her bare stomach.

Lifting her in my arms, I pressed her up against the wall. She circled my waist with her legs, gasping as I slammed into her with a grunt. I looked into her eyes as I pulled back and thrust forward again.

"You feel so fucking good," I said. "You ready to take this?"

"Yes!" Raine cried out and then lowered her voice as she glanced toward the door. "Please, Bastian!"

"Beg me," I whispered against her ear. I sucked the lobe into my mouth. "I wanna hear you beg for my cock."

I pulled out nearly all the way, just leaving the tip inside of her. I moved back and forth with shallow thrusts from my hips, teasing her.

"Ugh, Bastian! Please…please…more. I need more!"

I pulled back again, then slowly buried myself inside of her, pinning her body to the wall with my own.

"You want me to move?"

"Yes!"

"You want it fast and hard?"

"Please!"

I wrapped one arm around her ass as I placed the other against the wall. I didn't bother building up, just pulled back and slammed inside of her again as she tried to keep her cries low. I tightened the muscles in my arm with every movement, bringing her ass up to meet my blows. I could feel every tendon flex in time with the pounding of my cock.

Our lips meshed together, and our tongues found each other inside her mouth. I scraped her lips with my teeth, growling and pressing my hips hard against her body as she held on to me as tightly as she could. She flexed her legs with each thrust, bringing me deeper into her.

"So fucking good," I groaned. "Jesus, Raine…so good…"

"More, Bastian…please…"

I could have sworn my dick hardened more at her words.

Stepping back from the wall, my cock slipped out of her as I turned us around and threw her face down on the bed. Raine scrambled to her hands and knees as I crawled in behind her, tapped her legs apart with my knees, and drove into her again.

Pulling back, I grasped her hips in my hands and shoved into her as hard as I could, making her jump and cry out. She pressed her forehead against the mattress and tried to stifle herself as I moved in and out, twisting and shifting my hips to change the angle and pressure. I wanted her to be sore in the morning. I wanted her to remember every fucking second of my cock being inside of her.

For all I knew, this would be our last time together.

I flipped her over on her back and entered her again. Reaching for her wrists, I held them both in one hand over her head as the other hand caressed the skin up and down her side. I gripped one breast, then the other, never stopping the strokes inside her body as she lay below me, gazing up with hooded eyes.

As we moved, I could see in her eyes everything she had been through since we were last together: her kidnapping and imprisonment in this little shed of an apartment; her forced motherhood; the willpower she maintained to embrace it all for my sake. Everything she had, she offered to me with her eyes.

As her strength flowed into me, she made me feel more powerful than I ever had before.

Through her, I could endure anything thrown at me. I'd do it for her gladly because she was counting on me to do so. She needed me now more than ever.

I intended to deliver. I would never leave her side again once this was through. I'd be there for her forever and always. She'd get a real house and a degree in whatever field she wanted. I'd stop being such a moody asshole and be the kind of man she deserved to have at her side. I'd fucking ask her to marry me if that's what she wanted.

When all this was over, I was going to give her the fucking world.

Raine arched her back and bit into her lower lip. She moaned in her throat as she tried to keep herself from crying out. I felt her body shudder under me and picked up the pace. Squeezing my eyes shut, I leaned into her and pounded furiously until the buildup was too much to hold back, and I exploded inside of her.

Raine's legs fell from my hips, and I slowed and finally stopped, exhaustion coming over me. I dropped my head to Raine's shoulder for a moment before pulling out and rolling to my back beside her, panting. She rolled with me and raised herself up on her arm before she leaned over and placed her lips to mine.

Closing my eyes, I relaxed against the pillow and let her kiss me softly and gently, over and over again. I ran my hand up and down her back, soothing both of us.

"Dad? Raine?" The door to the bedroom opened slightly, and Alex's tousled head peered in.

Raine moved faster than I think I had ever seen as she rolled off of me and grabbed for the sheet. She pulled it up to her chin, glanced at me with widened eyes, and then back at Alex in the doorway.

"What is it?" she asked him.

"I can't sleep," Alex said. "I heard a funny sound."

I had to bite my cheek to keep from laughing out loud.

"I'm sure it's nothing," Raine said. "You know the wind outside can make things sound funny."

"Nothing, was it?" I snickered under my breath.

Raine elbowed me in the ribs.

"I don't think it was the wind," Alex said. "Can I sleep in here? I'm scared."

Raine looked to me again, and I shrugged. Whatever the protocol was for having a kid catch you in bed was beyond me. I grinned at Raine as she bit down on her lip, trying to think of something. Finally, she did.

"Alex," Raine said as she peered out from under the sheet, "did you remember to floss your teeth before you went to bed?"

"Um…no."

"You go do that, and then you can come in here."

"Awww!" Alex stomped off down the hall toward the bathroom.

"Get your shorts on!" Raine said quickly as she started scrambling around the floor, trying to find her clothes.

I tried to hold in a laugh as I retrieved my boxers and pulled them up my legs. Raine barely managed to get her clothes back on before we could hear small footsteps coming back down the hallway.

Alex crawled into the bed next to Raine but wasn't content to stay on that side. Instead, he clambered over her and wedged himself between us before pulling the blankets up to his chin. He looked up at me and grinned before shifting his shoulders back and forth to make more room for himself, shoving me a little farther toward the edge of the bed.

He rolled to one side, facing me, and closed his eyes. He was sound asleep a moment later.

I tentatively reached over his body and placed my hand on Raine's hip. I couldn't bind her to myself like I usually did at night with Alex between us, but the sense of contentment I felt inside of myself told me it didn't matter. I had both of them with me, secure and protected.

Raine reached over and placed her hand on top of my forearm, right above where Alex slept.

"You okay?" she asked quietly.

I looked from her to Alex and back to her again. Blinking a few times, that warm feeling came over me again.

"Yeah," I said. "Better than okay, actually."

Raine smiled, settled herself, and soon joined Alex in slumber.

I watched them both for a few minutes as I tried to work out what was going on in my head. I didn't have any words for it, so I gave up, closed my eyes, and had the best night's sleep of my life.

<hr />

I rose early the next day and went over the travel plans Landon had left with me. In a couple of hours, we'd head to the Thompson Airport. A plane would take us over to a small airport on the edge of Hudson Bay. From there, we would head up to a remote airfield located somewhere in the Northwestern Passage. It was an area so inhospitable that it didn't allow for any road traffic, only aircraft. The last leg of the trip would carry us to Resolute Bay by prop plane. The tournament would take place just south of the airfield there.

I was more concerned with spending as much time as possible with Raine and Alex before I left for the games than with our travel plans. However, they both seemed content to sleep in, and I couldn't bring myself to wake them.

I drank black coffee as I sat at the small kitchen table and realized I didn't even want a cigarette. That made me smile. I sipped up the last of the coffee, started another pot brewing, and began to make breakfast.

The smell woke Raine, and she shuffled down the hall, rubbing her eyes and yawning. Her hair was bunched up all over the place, and she tried to tame it with her fingers, but it wasn't working well.

"Morning," she mumbled.

"Morning," I replied with a smile. "You're beautiful."

"Ha," she said.

"You are."

"If you say so."

"I do."

She poured herself some coffee and sat at the table to watch me flip omelets.

"Find some acceptable food?" she asked.

"Reasonably," I said. "There isn't much to put in the omelets except for these orange squares claiming to be cheese, but it shouldn't be too bad. I used more whites than yolks."

"How did you sleep?" Raine asked.

"Pretty good," I said. I looked back over my shoulder at her. "Really good, actually."

Raine returned the smile over the rim of her coffee mug.

A blurry-eyed Alex wandered into the kitchen and plopped down on one of the chairs. At first, he seemed a little startled at my presence but smiled a bit when I put a plate full of bacon and a cheese omelet in front of him.

"Can I have toast?" he asked.

I rolled my eyes at the only bread in the kitchen but toasted it for him anyway. He proceeded to use it to make a giant sandwich out of the eggs and bacon.

"He likes sandwiches," Raine said with a shrug.

"Apparently."

Raine took her plate and sat down next to him, and I sat on the opposite side. My food went a little cold as I watched him eat, seeing small traits within myself with nearly every movement he made.

It was surreal.

When he completed his breakfast and headed to the carpeted area of the living room to play with his Legos, I continued to observe him, both stunned and pleased to recognize myself in his mannerisms. I could have watched him all day, but before Raine was even done clearing away the dishes from breakfast, we were interrupted.

There was a short knock at the door, and it opened a moment later. Raine looked up, and her face darkened. I didn't have to check —I knew it was Landon, and Raine and I both knew what that meant.

It was time for me to go.

"Hey, buddy," I called over to Alex. "Come here a sec."

He sighed, put down his Legos, and thumped over in his stocking feet. When he got close enough, I put my hands on his shoulders and peered into his eyes.

"I need you to do something for me, kid," I said seriously.

"What?" he asked.

"I have to leave for a while. That means I need you to help take care of Raine while I'm gone."

"Take care of her?" Alex asked through narrowed eyes. "I'm six!"

"Yeah, you've still got a bit of growing to do," I replied with a half-smile, "but you're the man of the house around here while I'm gone. You take care of Raine by doing what she tells you to do. You also need to watch her really closely."

"Why?"

"Because sometimes she needs a hug, and I won't be here to give her one. I need you to do it for me."

Alex pondered a moment.

"Do I have to kiss her?"

I snickered and rubbed the top of his head with my hand.

"No, no kissing required."

"Good, 'cause kissing is gross."

"Yeah, we'll see how you feel about that when you're older."

"Gross," he repeated.

I laughed. Alex's eyes suddenly lit up, and he ran to his room. When he came back, he held out the drawing he'd been working on the day before.

"This is for you."

I took the paper in my hand. He had added Raine to the picture, her figure to the side of mine. Her hair was drawn all the way to her waist, and the brown dots for her eyes stared out at me.

"You should take it with you," Alex said. "That way, you'll remember what we look like until you come back."

I had to swallow pretty hard to find my voice.

"Thanks," I said. "Yeah, it'll be nice to have with me."

I folded the paper carefully and tucked it into the pocket of my jacket before I reached over and gave Alex a quick hug. He squirmed a little, and then he ran back to his toys. Raine had stood off to the side, watching our exchange with a bemused look, but now that Alex was occupied again, her expression changed.

"You're going now?" She already knew the answer to her question, but I nodded anyway.

"I'll be back before you know it."

She nodded as she brought her hands up around herself and held onto her arms. She looked over to Alex and sniffed.

Glancing at Landon, I saw him tap his watch twice as he turned and exited through the open door, giving us a moment of privacy. I stood and crossed the kitchen and took Raine's face in my hands. Bending down, I placed my lips against hers, kissing her slowly. When we parted, I could see the beginning of tears rimming her eyelids.

"Before you know it," I whispered as I stared into her eyes.

"Please be careful," she said.

"Always," I said. "I'll be fine."

She nodded her head and gave me another squeeze. I kissed the top of her head, then took her chin in my hand and placed another firm kiss on her lips.

"I love you," I told her.

"Love you, too." Raine's eyes moistened as she looked up at me, bit down on her lip, and ran her hands down my arms. She grasped my fingers with hers for a moment before stepping back.

I took a long breath, committed her face to memory, and turned to go out the door. Landon was waiting outside for me along with Roger, Franks, and two of his bodyguards.

"Let's go," I said, and Landon tilted his head in acknowledgement as Roger pulled the key to the padlock out of his pocket to lock my family securely inside until all of this was over.

Before the door managed to close, Raine shoved her way past Roger and grabbed my arm. She pulled me to her and wrapped both arms around my neck. Her grip on me tightened so much, my air supply was limited.

"Don't go," she said, her voice breaking. "Don't do it, Bastian—please. Just don't…don't…"

"Oh, baby." I held her shoulders. "I have to. You know I have to."

"No, you don't!" she said, her voice rising. "You don't have to do this! Stay here! Please!"

"Fuck, Raine…" I could feel her tears against my skin as she begged and sobbed. It couldn't have hurt any more than if she shoved her fist through my ribcage and ripped my heart straight out of my body.

"You might die," she cried. "Oh God, Bastian, please, please just stay here!"

I held her as tightly as I could and tried to come up with anything to say to calm her, but nothing was working.

"Sebastian," Landon said from behind me. His hand tapped my upper arm as he spoke my name.

"I know," I said. I shrugged his hand off of me and grabbed Raine's shoulders, holding her back a bit so I could look into her face. I brushed tears from her cheek and touched my forehead to hers. "I have to go."

"No," Raine said, shaking her head rapidly. "We can just leave… go far away…please!"

"You know I can't do that, baby. You just have to hold on a little longer. This will all be over soon, and then we'll go. We'll find the perfect place for all of us to live together, and everything will be normal again. I promise, Raine. Everything is going to work out."

"You don't know that." Fresh tears spilled down her face as her head shook slowly back and forth. "You might get hurt; you might… you might…"

"Shh…" I brought her against my chest once more, which was probably a mistake. She'd latched onto me so tightly I wasn't sure how I was going to get her back inside so I could leave. Talking sense into her wasn't working. "You have to let go, baby. I have to leave."

"No!" She wouldn't let go, and though it nearly killed me, I pushed her arms away from mine as Roger grabbed onto her and kept her from grabbing me again. I stared into his eyes for a second, silently warning him to be gentle with her. I could tell by his expression that he understood my meaning—he'd pay for a single bruise.

I looked back at Raine. I knew she was trying to get herself together, but it just wasn't working.

"I love you, babe," I told her. "I'm going to be back soon."

"No! No, Bastian!"

I closed my eyes as I turned around and followed Landon. Raine's cries tore into me with every step.

I could still hear her as we drove away from the quarry and through town. I could hear her pleas echoing in my head as I boarded the first plane and buckled myself in. In my mind, I could see Roger holding her back as the plane took off into the early morning sky. Her tears continued to burn my skin through the entire journey north.

Landon glanced over at me from time to time, but he said nothing.

My mind was in a daze the entire trip. Even as Landon went over strategy and technique for the hundredth time, I was barely responding to him. I already knew it all, anyway. It was as committed to my soul as it was to my brain.

Despite Raine's fears and the imminent danger, as we switched planes near the frozen northwest side of the Hudson Bay, I began to tingle with excitement. My muscles flexed and released as I thought of past tournaments, blood, and victory.

I wanted to fight. At least for now, I desired blood.

Chapter Twelve

I carefully descended the stairs out of the plane and looked around at our final destination. Other small prop planes were unloading passengers, and I could see a bunch of people bundled in fur-lined parkas heading over to a large, obviously recently constructed building with smoke coming out of several chimneys.

Franks and his bodyguards headed for the building, and Landon motioned for me to follow the group. As we approached, I began to recognize all the people who had been present at the initial meeting. Each family was represented, but also along with them were many others.

Investors.

These were the people who tossed in all the cash to make the tournament happen, bet on individual players, and ultimately reaped the rewards through our bloodshed. Each of us would be fitted with a camera, and the gamblers would watch on closed-circuit television as we slaughtered each other for their amusement.

In the past, I hadn't thought about them much, but now I did. What kind of people considered this entertainment? What sort of society spent all their illegally earned cash to watch us fight to the death so they could feel power through our bloodied hands?

Sick fuckers, that's who.

We walked through the wide doors and into the building. Inside was ridiculously luxurious, especially considering the location. There were fireplaces along every wall to warm everyone with ambiance. Crystal chandeliers hung from the ceiling, and every table was decked out with fancy linen and centerpieces filled with flowers and colorful LED lights. There were several open bars set up around the edge of the room, and it even had a dance floor with a DJ in the back. People milled around in suits and cocktail dresses like they were at a ball following a Hollywood red carpet event.

Except it wasn't a movie—*we* were the event. I was equally disgusted and electrified by it all.

It was still early evening, and most of the groups were divided by their loyalties to a particular family. Landon and I milled around with Franks' people near one of the bars, and I got myself a glass of water when Landon ordered a scotch. I scanned the room to locate the other tournament players. They were easy to spot because they stood out in the center of every group.

Though it wasn't my style, tournament players usually dressed for their parts. Erik Dytalov and Reaper looked like they came out of *Blade Runner* or some violent computer game. Both were dressed in black, and she had eye makeup painted over her lids in bright colors and studded jewelry around her wrists and neck. It made sense, in a way. We were essentially a live video game to the people around us. Dressing for the role came naturally to a lot of players. Erik displayed his knife skills to anyone willing to watch, and Reaper posed for pictures with some of the men in suits.

The displays were ridiculous as far as I was concerned, but the investors obviously liked it. There were three women currently hanging off Hunter, who stood taller than anyone else around him. He wasn't dressed elaborately like some of the others. In fact, he was shirtless, and I wondered if he was planning on freezing to death before the game started. The women milled around him, running their hands over his chest and asking for explanations of his many tattoos. There wasn't any blank area on his whole upper body, and I wasn't sure how he could even keep them straight.

Glancing away from Hunter and his group, I found Tyrone Chimes. He was near a buffet table lined with hors d'oeuvres, standing with a woman in a bright red dress. He was in a cut-off T-shirt and ripped up jeans. All he needed was a little zombie makeup, and he could have been an extra in *The Walking Dead*.

I didn't see Evan Arden at first because unlike the other players, he wasn't decked out in ridiculous attire. When I spotted him, he was wearing a high-quality, tailored suit and standing near Rinaldo Moretti. In his hand was one of those electronic cigarettes, and he looked the part of crime lord rather than contestant. As I watched, he smiled and clinked glasses with Moretti.

I reminded myself that this wasn't his thing—he wasn't a tournament player. This would be his first. It would also be his last.

As far as I was concerned, all of them were here for their last party.

I couldn't feel any pity for them or any regret for what I planned to do. Not only were they here by choice but they also knew the risks and the potential outcome. It was kill or be killed, and I had more reason to win this game than any tournaments in the past.

"Any concerns?" Landon asked as he took a step closer to me.

"None," I said.

"What about Arden?"

"You were right from the beginning," I said. "He's more dangerous than the rest, even if this isn't his thing. As long as I can keep to cover, he shouldn't be able to get a lock on me."

"Not going to be easy," Landon replied. "There won't be a lot of cover in that landscape."

"The ridges on the mountainside should work. I just have to keep moving. I'll have to do that for the warmth anyway."

"Water is your biggest concern," Landon said.

"Isn't it always?" I mused. Flashes of my time spent bobbing around the middle of the Caribbean Sea with Raine on a life raft swirled around in my brain. "I don't think I'll run out of water. This whole thing is going to go down fast. It has to before the cold takes us all out."

"With the exception of Reaper, you will have the advantage when it comes to weapons. The others will have problems using them effectively and keeping their hands warm at the same time."

I kept my eyes on the other players throughout the evening. Even when a multitude of women came up to ask me questions about prior tournaments and offer me their beds to stay warm for the night, I barely made any conversation past what had to be said. I answered their questions, politely turned down their offers, and steered the conversation toward the food.

The food was actually really good. Death row inmates couldn't have demanded better. It reminded me to give Franks shit for the food in Raine and Alex's kitchen. He laughed but told me he'd do something about it.

"It's good to have you back, Sebastian," he said. "In many ways, I've missed you."

There was way too much potential for double meanings in that statement to give me any feeling of comfort. I wondered how long he'd looked for me after the trial and what made him eventually give up. I considered asking him but figured it was in my best interest to let all of that go for now. I knew in my heart that he would never truly forgive me for trying to bust him, and I knew in my mind that the only way I could ever get out from under him was to end his life.

Get through the tournament first.

Franks moved off to chat with some of the other bosses. I sat back at one of the tables, tipped a couple of oysters down my throat, and watched the people around me. Some came up to talk to me, and I was as polite as I could manage. Eventually, they moved on to harass one of the other players. Hunter and Reaper had moved closer to one another, and though I couldn't hear their words, their sexual chemistry was evident as they eyed each other. It was obvious they would spend the night together.

Stupid.

Then again, it would be their last opportunity for a tryst. It made me think of last night and Raine's body underneath mine, and I closed my eyes for a moment. The memory of her scent and the feel of her skin in my hands warmed me.

I would be with her again. I had to be. I wouldn't let her down ever again.

I opened my eyes and continued to watch the crowd. After a while, Landon returned from wherever he had been.

"Heard something interesting," he said as he sat beside me. He waved one of the servers over to our table and ordered another scotch.

"What's that?" I asked.

"Moretti and Arden talking," Landon said. "Arden actually sounds a little concerned."

"Huh," I responded. "Even punching him in the face didn't get a rise out of him."

"Well, apparently the arctic mitts and gloves *do* get a rise out of him."

"What do you mean?"

"They're fucking with his aim," Landon said. "He was primarily concerned about equipment malfunction in the beginning. It's possible for the primer in the rounds to have problems firing under extreme cold. What he hadn't considered was how many layers you have to wear up here just to keep from getting instant frostbite. The thicker clothing is interfering with mounting his rifle to his shoulder. He has to keep adjusting his rifle to hit his target. His gloves or parka shift a little, and his aim is off again. If I had to guess, I'd say he's a little pissed off about it."

"You said that could happen." I remembered his words during training when we had been going over all the supplies I would need.

"I did," he said with a nod. "Arden didn't think of it before they arrived up here yesterday. He must be living somewhere far north from the way he was talking, but not this far north."

"No one lives up here."

"Exactly," Landon agreed. "He didn't consider how much it might impact his accuracy."

"That's a point in my favor."

"A big point."

"Did you catch anything from any of the other players?"

"Dytalov is nervous," Landon said. "He hasn't done this for a while, and I can see how uneasy he is. Tyrone as well, though I think that's because this is only his fourth tournament and all the others have been held indoors. He's definitely uncomfortable in the cold."

"I'm not worried about either of them," I said dismissively. "I'm pretty sure I could kill them in my sleep."

Landon agreed with a nod.

"I'm pretty sure Hunter and Reaper have been fucking each other," he said. "That should provide some entertainment during the games."

"Yeah, that's inadvisable," I said with a snort.

"You should know."

"It never affected me."

"It came close." Landon leaned back in his chair and took a sip of his drink.

"You always said 'close only counts in horseshoes and hand

grenades,'" I reminded him.

"And you said you'd never let another girl get close to you," Landon retorted.

"Raine's different." I turned a little away from him, wanting to shut the conversation down, but Landon wasn't having any of that.

"You're different around her," he said. "Not like you were with Jillian. I've never seen you quite like this."

I looked back at his face.

"Is that a good thing?"

"Not sure yet," Landon replied. "Are you going to let it interfere with your focus?"

"She is my focus."

"Then that could be a problem."

"No," I said, "it won't. In fact, it's the reason I'm going to win."

Six in the morning.

I'd been up and dressed in my gear for an hour, trying to keep myself close enough to the door not to overheat and start sweating. The only thing worse than the cold in this environment was being wet; the combination was deadly. I had four layers of warmth on my body, including the Kevlar vest and a double layer of gloves and mittens for my hands. A canteen of water was looped to my side. The many pockets in my parka held everything I needed—macadamia nuts, pats of butter, tubes of food that could be easily ripped oven without removing my hand coverings, and three long pieces of piano wire—my only weapons.

Inside my left breast pocket was the picture Alex drew of the three of us.

The other contestants milled around in the same area, eyeing each other. Erik Dytalov and Tyrone Chimes looked nervously at me as they met my stare. Hunter and Reaper stood at opposite ends of the doorway, glaring at one another.

Arden stood quietly and stoically with his eyes focused on the airfield. The long sniper rifle responsible for his infamy was strapped across his back, and a shorter assault rifle rested between his arm and body. He was the epitome of calm.

Outside, six helicopters rested on the runway near the planes. Landon was talking to the pilot who would take me from Resolute to Buckingham Island, but the wind was too loud for me to overhear anything he was saying. After a few minutes, he waved me over, and I joined him next to the aircraft.

"You set?" he asked.

"Ready," I said. "Anything change since last night?"

"No—all's clear."

"Good."

The helicopter's engines roared, and the blades began to spin. Landon adjusted the camera attached to the goggles across my eyes and made sure it was transmitting properly. Once he was satisfied with it, he shook my hand as he leaned close to me.

"This is it," he said. "Now you go fuck those guys up."

I nodded and turned away without another word. The wind was burning my cheeks, and I pulled the loose-fitting mask around my face as I climbed aboard the helicopter.

We rose into the air and above the ice floes.

The scene would probably have been considered beautiful under other circumstances. Even though it was insanely cold, the sky was clear and the sun was peering out over the horizon. Everything below us was white, grey, and a thousand shades of blue.

The helicopter veered to one side and began to descend close to the ice floes near the bottom of the mountain. Chunks of ice floated in the open water near the island's edge, and the wind blew snow into the air all around us as we neared the surface.

"Ready?" the pilot called out over the noise. "I can't actually set down here, so you're going to have to jump!"

"Got it!" I called back.

The helicopter descended, and I held onto the bar near the open door. As the pilot maneuvered the aircraft close to the ground and hovered, he gave me a thumbs up sign, and I jumped to the white surface below.

It was only about six feet to the ground, and I tucked and rolled easily against the icy surface. It was somewhat jarring, but I at least managed to get back on my feet without injuring myself. I checked my compass, looked out over the rocky ground leading up to Mount Windsor, the only real landmark on the island, and took off at a quick pace.

Game on.

Looking up into the sky, I saw the other five helicopters rise into the air and head back north to the airfield. I mentally marked the positions beneath them as they departed, noted the closest one to my location, and headed that way.

I didn't know which helicopter held which fighter, but it didn't matter much to me. Everyone would be heading to the peak of the mountain—the place with the highest and most desirable vantage point. I intended to come up from behind.

Let's do this.

My body and mind were ready. At least for now, I knew exactly what I was doing.

Chapter thirteen

Gauging the area between the closest helicopter drop-off and the most logical way up the mountain from that point, I made a beeline directly across the lower face of Mount Windsor until I found what I was looking for—slight depressions in the snow. Even with the wind quickly covering the impressions, I could see the outline of footprints. They were smaller than mine, and I guessed they belonged to either Erik or Reaper. I gazed up the mountainside, but I couldn't see anyone.

Looping one of the pieces of piano wire around my gloved and mittened fingers, I adjusted my goggles and followed the tracks silently as the frozen wind whipped around my face, keeping close to the tall ridge on my left. It didn't take long to catch up to the owner of the footprints, and even less effort to actually locate her. Reaper wasn't exactly stealthy about her battles.

I could hear loud scuffling and grunting as I approached. Staying crouched, I maneuvered myself off to the side to get a good view of what was going on without being seen. As I got close enough to see through my goggles, I witnessed Tyrone swinging in a wide arc with a crowbar at Reaper. He towered over her form, but she ducked away from his swing and rolled to the side.

She was quick and agile, moving around him in fast steps as he tried to make contact with her. Tyrone moved from left to right as he swung the crowbar at her, but he missed every time. Reaper danced away, laughing as he missed again.

"You suck!" she called out though Tyrone refused to acknowledge her verbal taunts. He only glared and took a stance in front of her. "You think you're fighting with your boyfriend? I bet my dick's bigger than yours!"

I checked behind me and then up higher. I couldn't see any forms or movement, and I was fairly sure Arden wouldn't have had enough time to reach the mountain peak to fire down on me just yet. I figured I was still a good two and a half miles from the top, and even with his fancy sniper rifle, I'd still be out of range.

Unless he went for another tactic.

I heard a loud grunt and looked back to see Tyrone take a hit from Reaper's brass knuckles as she yelled out in glee. Blood spewed over the ice from the bottom of Tyrone's facemask. A moment later, Reaper was on top of him, pounding her fist into his face. He brought his hands up to her arms, trying to hold her off, but the chick was a lot stronger than she looked. He managed to pull them both into a roll, but she still came out on top.

Her fist slammed into his trachea, and he sat part way up with a jolt. He dropped his hands from her arms and clawed at his collapsed windpipe. Reaper jumped off of him and stood her ground, fists up and ready. Tyrone clutched at his throat, rolled to his hands and knees, and started crawling away from her.

Bad move.

Reaper was on his back in a second, slamming her metal knuckles into the back of his head over and over again until he collapsed with his arms splayed out on the cold ground. She didn't stop but kept pounding his skull.

"Yeah! Take that, bitch!" Reaper cried out.

Her victory was short-lived.

With all the noise she was making, anyone on the island could have heard her. By now, she'd led everyone to her position. From way off to her right—the farthest point from me—a crossbow bolt flew through the air and slammed into her shoulder.

Enraged, Reaper turned toward the direction of the bolt and ran several feet. She didn't even bother to try to remove the bolt as she dropped to the ground and rolled. Another bolt whizzed over her head and slammed into the ice a few feet away from me.

Never one to turn down an extra weapon, I grabbed the bolt out of the ice and headed up the ridge to get a better view of the fight. It took a few minutes to reach a place I could scale over—the mountain cliff was sheerer at this location—and I had to be careful about my steps to keep from falling down the outside of the ledge. I wouldn't fall very far, but the landing would be a rough one. The sounds of the fight were louder here and coming from slightly below me. Harsh voices and the sound of scuffling brought me to the very edge where I looked down and saw Hunter and Reaper hard at it.

I settled back a bit, lodging myself partially between two rocks for protection from above and from the sides. If Hunter or Reaper looked up, they would have been able to spot me, but they were far too intent on killing each other. My vantage point allowed me to look directly down at the battle. As soon as one of them killed the other, I could jump in and finish it before the winner had a chance to recover.

"Why don't you just put that down and let me give ya a little of what you got last night?" Reaper danced around, her eyes wide open and wild.

"I figure once you're a piece of meat in the fucking dirt," Hunter snapped back, "I can fuck you in whatever hole still works!"

I could see the handgun shoved into a holster at his side, but he never went for it. As I looked closer, I realized why.

His right hand was completely exposed. I could see his crossbow lying a few feet away, broken in several pieces with the bolts scattered across the ground, and a lone glove lying near it. Without something covering his skin, the metal on the gun would instantly freeze to his hand if he touched it. Even if he won this battle, his fingers would be frostbitten before he could retrieve the glove. He must have removed his gloves to improve his aim with the crossbow.

Reaper continued to taunt him, and he just smiled and gave it right back to her. I wasn't sure if he was oblivious to the danger of exposed skin or just too high on the fight to give a shit. Hunter definitely seemed overconfident in his own combat abilities, which was fucking stupid. Even from where I was, I could tell Reaper was faster and deadlier than he, even if he had a good foot and a half on her in height.

Never fuck someone you plan to kill.

Reaper had the advantage of agility. She connected several blows to Hunter's head as she advanced on him. Each time he tried to hit her back, she ducked out of his way and hit him in the kidney.

He was losing, but he still didn't go for the gun. I probably would have, skin be damned, but he either didn't realize she had him, or he had just discounted the weapon altogether.

Reaper landed a fantastic blow to Hunter's face, and he stumbled backward, fell on his ass, and started to roll down the incline to the ledge below. He reached out with his bare fingers and grabbed at the edge of the rock, finally stopping his descent just as he was about to go over. He hung somewhat precariously, grasping at the rock and kicking with his feet to get a better grip. Reaper poised herself just above him, taunting the giant of a man.

"Is that all you got?" she sneered. "I thought a man like you was going to give me some kind of challenge! You couldn't even give me a fucking orgasm!"

"Bitch!" Hunter growled as his hand began to slip. "I'll give your ass a good pounding!"

She slammed her metal knuckles into his fingers. He lost his grip and started sliding down the rock again, barely keeping his balance on the lower ledge. He crouched and allowed himself to drop, managing to fall only a few feet before he found a place for his boots on the ledge below. Scuttling off to the side, he hoisted himself up a few yards away from Reaper and began to run up the side of the ridge, passing the area where I was hidden.

I got up on the balls of my feet, my heart beating in anticipation.

"I thought you wanted to play, asshole!" Reaper yelled as Hunter disappeared into the rocky landscape behind me. She started to head after him, but as she got a little closer to me, I decided now was as good a time as any to take her out.

I jumped from the top of the rock and landed on her back, sending us both to the ground. As we began to roll down the side of the mountain, I flipped the piano wire over her head and around her shoulders. With a quick jerk, the wire lodged under her chin.

I wasn't quite cutting off her airway, and Reaper leaned against me, struggling to get her head out from around the wire. Though I couldn't seem to get it positioned right to strangle her, she couldn't get it off either, so she began to punch upward toward my face, hitting the side of my head. My ear rang with the blow, but my grip didn't falter.

That's when she went for the oldest trick in the book.

Oldest because of how effective it was.

She dropped one shoulder, brought her arm up, and slammed her elbow into my balls.

Not even Kevlar can stop that shit.

"Motherfucker!" I cried out as I tried to keep myself from doubling over.

Even through the thick clothing covering my body, the impact of her elbow in my crotch was enough to make my stomach clench and for a wave of nausea to wash over me. It was also enough to make me lose my grip on the wire completely. Reaper ducked out of it, turned partway to the side, and clipped me in the jaw with those fucking brass knuckles.

I stumbled backward but managed to grab her arm and take her with me. We tripped a couple of times before both of us fell to our knees, fighting for control over each other's blows. I grabbed at the crossbow bolt still in her shoulder and twisted it, causing her to scream in pain. Apparently, that just pissed her off because she managed another hard hit to my shoulder.

Damn, that woman could throw a punch!

Forgoing the wire altogether, I let it drop to the ground as I went at her again, grasping the bolt in her shoulder as I wrapped my arm around her throat. She bucked against me, and my hand lost its grip from the bolt's shaft, but the other arm stayed in place. I tightened my grip around her neck as I coiled my other arm around her head. My position was perfect, and all I had to do was twist to break her neck, but I didn't get the chance.

I heard the shot ring out, and had no doubt from whose gun it originated. I braced myself for the impact of the bullet, and when the impact came, I was momentarily stunned. The pain wasn't that of a bullet wound though, rather that of simple blunt force. Instead of feeling an exit wound in my own back, Reaper went limp in my arms.

Thank Landon for Kevlar.

I dropped to the ground and rolled, bringing her on top of me just as another shot rang out, making her torso jump in my grasp. Glancing down her form, I saw a pair of bullet holes in her body— one in the center of her chest, the other slightly below. Beyond her feet, I could see a rocky cliff jutting out from the mountainside just a couple hundred yards away. Right at the edge was Arden, tossing his sniper rifle to the ground as he reached up over his shoulder and brought the assault rifle around and pointed it in my direction.

"Fuck!"

Blasts ricocheted off the ground around my feet and up the side of Reaper's body as I ducked my head beneath her shoulder. A line of bullet holes ripped their way through the thick layer of clothing up Reaper's leg, and I felt a searing pain in my thigh.

Cursing, I rolled again, hauling her body along with me for cover, until I could get myself upright and back behind the rocks. Out of Arden's line of sight, I quickly evaluated my leg and determined it had only been grazed. I paused and remained as silent as possible as the echoing blasts of gunfire faded around the cliffs.

Listening closely, I tried to make out any sound of footsteps coming closer to me. I heard nothing, so I dropped Reaper's body, knelt down to remove a set of brass knuckles from her cold fingers, and slipped them into one of the many pockets in my coat. I didn't intend to use them, but I didn't want anyone else to have the opportunity to use them against me.

I need to get the fuck out of here.

Since Arden already knew my location, my best chance was heading up, taking away his high-ground advantage, so that's what I did. Carefully making my way around the rock cliff, I stayed low and went as quickly as I could up the mountainside. As soon as I was a little way up, I ran to my right and jumped over the next ridge, then began to slide down. It wasn't steep at this point, but my leg was throbbing a bit from the exertion, the slight wound making the journey more difficult. It wasn't bad, just annoying enough to make me want to slow down.

Another shot rang out, but there was no pain and no blast in the ground near me. Either Arden was just trying to freak me out, or he was aiming at someone else. I didn't figure him for mind games, and I wondered if he'd found another target. That seemed more likely, but I couldn't be sure of it.

I was tempted to stop my stealthy trek and check out my wounded leg.

I didn't.

I couldn't.

Aside from Arden, there were still two others out there with bloodshed on their minds—Erik Dytalov and Hunter. If I paused long enough to attend to the bullet scrape, I might as well strangle myself and get it over with because the chances of one of them finding me when I was vulnerable were too great right now. I'd just have to ignore the ache.

Pain is weakness leaving the body.

Push on. Always push on, no matter what you feel.

Get your fucking ass up and move!

Fuck it all. I couldn't stop because I had to get back to Raine.

⊶•••◗◍◖•••⊷

A mile or so up Mount Windsor, I finally found a place secure enough to briefly peel back the leggings around my right thigh and take a look at my leg. It wasn't bad—just a scrape, as I had figured. I cleaned it up a little and got the bleeding to stop before covering myself back up again. The possibility of frostbite was more dangerous at this point than a scratch.

I was covered with Reaper's blood, and the stench burned my nose as I peeled back the facemask to get myself some water and nutrition. There was only silence around me. From where I was perched in the center of a grouping of rocks, I could see all the way to the ice floes below. Somewhere nearby, there were still three other people out to kill me, but for now, it was quiet. I took the time to center myself, remember my objectives, and concentrate on what I had to do next.

Far below me, a pod of whales surfaced, blew streams of water out their blowholes, and disappeared below the ice again. The giant marine mammals were the only signs of life to be seen in the harsh environment, save a few crusty lichens on the north side of the stones. There weren't even any trees anywhere on the island.

Franks couldn't have found a less hospitable place in the world.

It was probably a fitting place for such activity, though. I couldn't begrudge him that. There was no habitation on the island. There were no settlements of people and very little vegetation to attract any animals. Only those creatures that actually adapted to live in the Arctic Ocean could be found here.

Knowing there were no living creatures around except for the people trying to kill me did nothing for my peace of mind, of course.

Every time I heard a rock tumble across the ground, I had to assume one of my opponents was nearby.

I drank from my canteen of frigid water and then pulled a tube of gel packed with vitamins, protein, and carbohydrates out of my pocket. It was supposed to taste like chocolate and peanut butter, but it didn't. It just tasted nasty, but I downed it anyway along with a handful of high-fat nuts. I hadn't seen anyone for an hour and was grateful for the break though I still remained on alert. I had heard one additional shot ring out from high up the mountain, but that was twenty minutes ago. There had been nothing else to see or hear since then.

Lack of knowledge was my biggest enemy. I had to locate the other three players before they found me. Their best chance was to catch me off guard, and I couldn't let that happen. I had to keep moving.

The sun was high in the sky but did nothing to warm me as I hauled myself out of the rock cluster and started up the ridge again. I kept low to the ground, watching everywhere around me—especially farther up—for any kind of movement. I walked several hundred yards without seeing anything and then found myself at the bottom of a short cliff. The high ridges on either side of me would have been as difficult to scale as the rocks in front of me, so I decided to climb up to the top.

Climbing was difficult with the mittens over my gloves, but it was a move I'd practiced with Landon a thousand times over the past few weeks. As I hauled myself to the edge of the small plateau and looked all around, my skin tingled. I couldn't see anyone, but every instinct inside of me told me someone was there. I examined the area, trying to identify the places large enough to hide a person. There were two groups of rocks on the left, a depression in the ground to the right, and another ledge up above.

I considered the options.

If I was in Arden's sights, he could take me out at any time. That went for most anywhere I could go. Without cover from above, he could take a shot anytime he found me in his crosshairs. To climb farther up the mountainside, I either had to get across the plateau or drop back down to find another way up. I'd waste time and energy— energy I couldn't spare—if I headed back down again. If one of the others was up here, and I was pretty sure someone was, they were going to try to jump me as I crossed the open area. It would be either Hunter or Erik.

I was fairly certain Hunter wasn't much on stealth—he relied on his brute strength, which usually worked in a tournament setting. Here, it was wise to be cautious as well as silent. If Hunter was close by, I would have heard him already. That left Erik and his knives, some of which could be thrown. This would be a perfect place for him to plan an ambush. A throwing knife could definitely be deadly at a distance but not when you're covered in Kevlar.

Knowledge is power, so says Schoolhouse Rock.

I decided to chance it.

My instincts were rarely wrong.

I was halfway across the plateau when the knife lodged in the center of my chest, right up against the Kevlar vest. I glanced at the blade, grabbed the hilt in my hand, and looked up in the direction it pointed as I pulled it out with a smile.

Erik didn't duck behind the rock fast enough for me not to see him. Wasting no time, I raced in his direction. He must have heard me coming because he stepped out from behind his shelter to throw another knife. Before he even released it from his hand, I could see the panic in his eyes. I was too close, and he knew he'd lost his advantage. The knife that flew from his hand went wide and disappeared over the cliff.

With a grin on my face, I tossed his throwing knife back toward him. I watched him clench his fingers and crouch down to retrieve the blade, looking up at me with incredulity. As he hesitated, I charged.

There was no taunting or banter as Erik and I moved around each other in a circle on top of the plateau. He held the Busse in his left hand and the throwing knife in his right. I didn't know what was going through his head, but his eyes remained wide and his steps unsteady. For an experienced tournament fighter, he was acting like a newbie. Something had changed since his last fight. He didn't have the confidence I was expecting.

Good.

When it came to those who were unsure of themselves, the waiting game always worked to my advantage. He tossed the last knife at me, but we were too close for a projectile weapon like that to be effective. Losing it only gave me an additional advantage. He was sloppy and afraid, which made me calmer and surer of myself. He was hoping for me to make a move, but I won on patience. Eventually, he took a step closer to me, jabbing with the Busse.

He was quick but not quick enough.

Stepping to the side, I gripped my fingers around his wrist and stopped the forward motion of the weapon. With a quick spin, I twisted his arm around and brought it to his side, shoving the blade through his parka and inner clothing and into his gut just below his ribcage. As I felt his hand go slack, I pushed the blade sideways, cutting through his abdominal muscles as he screamed in pain.

I let go of the handle and quickly wrapped the piano wire around his neck. Erik moved fast, grasping the wire with his thinly gloved fingers before I could tighten it completely. I slammed my knee into his back near his kidney, and he gasped at the blow. If he hadn't been suspended from the wire around his neck, he would have fallen to his knees.

With a quick movement, he slammed the back of his head into my face, and we both went down as pain ripped through my jaw. He fell on top of me, but I didn't let my grip falter. The muscles in my arms strained as he fought against me. His hand was lodged between the wire and his neck, so I couldn't get the proper grip to strangle him. I could see the wire was cutting him on one side as I pulled harder and harder, but his strength remained enough to try to talk.

"Motherfucker!" He twisted and turned, but I kept my grip on the wire around his neck. Blood oozed from the space between his fingers as the wire cut into his flesh beneath the gloves.

"Give it up," I said quietly. "It's over. You're done."

He screamed and lurched to dislodge me, but he didn't have the strength as his blood poured from his side onto the ground. I tightened my grip, further cutting his skin even though I couldn't quite find purchase against his trachea. As his struggles weakened, so did his voice.

"I have a kid…" he groaned between panting breaths. "A girl… she has…no one…fuck, no…"

I released my grip on the piano wire with my left hand and shoved myself backward with my feet, letting his head drop to the snow as the wire slipped from around his hand and neck. Blood seeped from the area where the wire had entered his skin near his jugular but not in a grand enough stream to make me think I'd severed it. It didn't matter. The skin exposure from the cut through his clothing and the blood pouring from his stomach were more than enough to kill him.

His words felt like a stab to my own gut.

Erik tried to roll to the side, but he couldn't manage it. He struggled to pull the knife from his body as I stood a few feet away, watching him bleed to death. I should have stepped in and ended him faster, but I couldn't quite bring myself to do it. The wounds he had suffered were the end of him. It wasn't as if there were any emergency medical personnel coming.

He turned his glazed eyes to look up at me, and his mouth opened to form additional words, but nothing intelligible came out. I crouched to keep low to the ground and caught my breath as his blood puddled below him. He choked out a couple more breaths before lying still.

Where's his daughter?

The thought rumbled through my brain, but I had no way of knowing. I could only hope she was with someone who would care for her because her father wasn't coming home. It was the price he paid for being a part of this. It was the price any of us could pay.

Not me.

I looked into the dim red light at the top of Dytalov's goggles, knowing there was a room filled with people watching me right now. They could see my face through his camera and his through mine. If I could have seen them, I would have witnessed the passing of large bundles of cash back and forth as losers forked over their money to the gloating winners.

I glared at the light, wanting to give them all the finger, but I couldn't do that without removing the mittens. I had to be content with a look. It was only three hours into the game, and half of the players were gone. If I kept up the pace, I could be sleeping with Raine again tonight.

A tiny voice inside of me—one that sounded like Raine—told me I should regret what I had just done. The same voice tried to tell me what I was doing was wrong. I had no argument against it, but I couldn't bring myself to feel any remorse either.

My resolve was set. At least for now, the blood on my hands was of no consequence.

Chapter Fourteen

It had been an hour since I had killed Erik Dytalov, and I hadn't seen either Arden or Hunter. A few minutes ago, there had been two more gunshots coming from the west. I was no gun expert, but I was fairly certain the shots had been from handguns, not Arden's sniper rifle or AR. I'd pinpointed the direction from where the sounds had originated, and I was heading that way.

Reaching up with both hands, I pulled myself to the top of a ridge and looked over cautiously. A dark shape below lay on the ground, face down. From the size of him, I knew it was Hunter. He looked dead, but I wasn't taking any chances. I approached slowly with the piano wire wrapped around my covered fists. As far as I could see, the huge lump of a body wasn't moving at all, but possum tactics were common in tournaments, and I wasn't stupid enough to make any assumptions.

I looped the wire in one hand, the circle large enough to slip over Hunter's head, if necessary. In the other hand, I gripped Reaper's bloody brass knuckles. Slowly and quietly, I approached the mound lying on its face on top of the ice-covered rock. When I got close enough, I could see a neat bullet hole in the back of Hunter's head. His face was nothing more than a mess in the snow.

In his bare hand, he held his gun. Kneeling, I reached for it, but his skin was practically grafted to the handle. I could have pulled it away from him, ripping skin from his dead flesh in the process, but I didn't. I dropped his hand and the weapon back to the snow.

I was better off with what I had.

I looked up, wondering where that bastard of a sniper was and if he was still looking down on this spot. The only way I would have found out was if I heard the shot before I died. I paused just a little longer than I should have, testing him or myself; I wasn't sure. In the end, it didn't matter. No shot rang out.

"Just you and me, Arden," I whispered into the icy wind.

<hr>

Exhaustion was setting in. As much as I wanted to push on, I was too fucking cold.

This should have been over by now.

I had no idea where Arden was, and I could only hope he didn't know where I was either, or rather, that he didn't figure it out before I found him. Every time I stepped out from the cover of a ridge, I tensed and waited for a shot to ring out.

Maybe he's dead already.

It was an errant thought, and one I discounted immediately. If he was dead, they'd know from his camera and would send the helicopter for me. Since I didn't hear any helicopter, he was definitely still alive. I'd just have to keep looking.

Time was running out.

Most of the day had passed, and the sun was low on the horizon. The only saving grace was the time of year—there would be no sunset or darkness in this part of the world. That wouldn't stop the already icy temperature from dropping significantly. I wasn't sure how much longer I'd be able to fight in the cold as the wind picked up and my rations depleted. Unlike other terrains, there was no vegetation or animals to eat. Maybe I could have traveled all the way to the bottom of the mountain and tried my luck at fishing, but the amount of energy I would spend in the process wouldn't make it worth the effort.

There was also no real place to make a shelter on the rock and ice ridges of Mount Windsor, which meant I had to keep moving. The only thing that kept me from panicking was the knowledge that Arden would be in the same predicament. Unlike me, he hadn't played in the games before and wouldn't be as adept at adapting to the environment. My chances of surviving in the open were better than his.

Don't underestimate anyone.

If the dude could handle being tied up in the desert as a POW, maybe he'd be just fine out here in the cold. I certainly couldn't count on him freezing to death. If he did, I'd still be stuck here until morning. The helicopter wouldn't come looking for me with winds this strong.

Gotta find him.

I hauled myself over another ridge and stood on top of it. It was a stupid place to be, but it gave me a much better vantage point. If Arden was anywhere near me, I might be able to locate him before he got a shot off.

Nothing.

I crouched and placed my hand on the top of the ridge, gauging the distance to the flat ground below. I inhaled and then jumped…

…just as the shot rang out.

Startled, I landed awkwardly on my shoulder but still managed to roll effectively and get myself on my feet. Without thought, I ran to the far ridge for cover as another shot pierced the ground near my feet, throwing shards of ice into the air and back toward the ridge from where I had just jumped.

He's in front of me.

I ducked, trying to keep my head low and in front of my chest, and zigzagged to impede Arden's aim. I heard another shot but didn't see where it hit. I only knew it hadn't hit me. Leaping my final stride, I slammed into the side of the ridge and dropped low.

Glancing up the side of the rock, I couldn't see any dark shape that would indicate Arden's location. This was good because it meant he probably couldn't see me either. However, it also meant I still didn't know exactly where he was.

No time to waste.

I headed up the mountain, and my boots crunched in the icy layer on top of the snow. It was steeper and more difficult to make progress as the terrain turned from ice, dirt, and rock to ice, rock, and snow. I trudged on as quickly as I could, always looking up and over my shoulder for any sign of my opponent.

The higher I went, the deeper the snow became. I had on proper boots to keep myself from sinking too much, but it made the trek much more difficult. I was panting and starting to sweat, which was a bad combination. I had to slow down to keep from overexerting myself.

I reached the top of the high ridge and clambered over another outcropping of rocks and snow. My foot slipped a little. The snow here wasn't as packed as the ice farther down. It was grainy powder, and there were dark patches of rock jutting out all around me. I took another tentative step, and the powdery snow gave way and rolled down the ridge, taking a few rocks with it. As I watched, chunks of snow rolled out of sight around the rocks before I could pull my foot back and find another place to stand.

Fuck.

I reclaimed my footing and held on with both hands as I steadied myself. A few more ice-covered rocks rolled down the mountainside below me as I took a deep breath and pulled. My muscles strained to lift my weight up and over the ledge.

Keeping low, I scuttled over the small, flat shelf and up against the ridge. There was another ledge above me, offering cover from the higher points of the mountain. I didn't think Arden was much higher than I was and began to look all around.

Still nothing but precarious rocks and frozen terrain.

I shivered, grabbed a handful of macadamia nuts from my pockets, and started up and over the next ledge. The snowpack was even more unstable as I went higher, and I kept close to the top of the ridge, hanging onto the established rock as I crawled up the mountainside.

I reached the top of the southern edge of Mount Windsor. Looking north, there was a deep gorge of smooth snow separating the south and north sides of the island. The cliffs heading down were extremely steep, and there was no way to safely head down from where I was.

I could see the entire island around me, all the way down to the Arctic Ocean. White snow, grey ice, and brilliant turquoise water looked so peaceful from my vantage point, I could almost forget the bloodshed that had already occurred in this remote, serene location. I couldn't spend any time enjoying the scenery though—I had to keep moving.

I walked slowly on top of the precarious edge of the ridge, looking all around me as I did. My feet slipped a couple of times, and I watched the loosened snow form small mounds and roll down the mountain face. Up ahead of me was a large standing of rocks, and I headed toward it.

Crouching in a crevice, I paused to catch my breath. I was taking too many breaks, wasting time, but the wind was starting to penetrate the layers of clothing covering me and was even beginning to sneak into the gap at the bottom of my face mask.

I tucked the mask's edges a little deeper into the neckline of my parka, making sure there was still plenty of room for my moist breath between my mouth and the fabric, taking care to avoid getting any part of my clothing wet.

My fingers were sore from the intense climb. I spent a couple minutes flexing them and making sure I hadn't hurt myself. I wasn't sure if I would even be able to tell; the frigid temperatures often masked injuries. I could barely feel the place on my leg where Arden's bullet had grazed it earlier in the day.

Out of the corner of my eye, a dark shape caught my attention.

I had no doubt who it was, and my heart rate increased as I watched Arden make his way over the top of the ridge two hundred yards from where I remained hidden between the rocks. The assault rifle was slung over his shoulder and held in one hand as he used the other to steady his passage across the unstable rocks. He looked back and forth down the side of the cliff as if he was searching for a way down.

It was the best chance I'd had all day.

I backed through the rock formation, keeping my eye on him the whole time. I couldn't risk losing sight of him. Slipping to just over the edge of the ridge, I held on with my hands as I moved from right to left across the narrow ledge, counting the hand-over-hand motions until I reached two hundred. Flexing, I brought myself high enough to peer over the ledge but had to quickly drop down again, careful not to make a sound as I did.

He was right in front of me.

I closed my eyes and counted to five, breathing deeply to center myself. Bending my knee, I found a stable rock ready to take my weight, and then launched myself to the top of the ridge.

Arden turned toward the sound, but I was already jumping down on top of him. He tried to swing the AR in front of him as we collided, but the shot he fired went far off to my right. We landed in the snow with him on his back and me straddling him.

My first punch went straight into his chest, the second into the side of his head. I could have gone for the piano wire at my waist, or even the Busse I'd taken from Dytalov's body, but I didn't. I wanted to hit him. In that instant, I blamed him for everything that had occurred over the last month.

Arden was as slippery as the ice near the shoreline. Every punch I threw at him made contact but not in a vital place. He had one hand on my chest, grasping at the front of my parka. The AR was still gripped in his other hand, but he couldn't maneuver it into position to fire.

He could, however, hit me with it, which is exactly what he did.

In the back of my head, I registered how good a hit it was. It takes a lot of strength to hit someone from a supine position, and he managed a sharp blow into my hip with the barrel of the weapon. It jarred me, and I started to fall to the side. Grabbing for his face, I tore off the mask protecting him from the wind as he shoved upward with both hands on my chest, and we rolled right into the base of the ridge.

We were both on our sides, each of us fighting to get on top of the other. I was bigger than he and more muscled, but he still managed to keep me at bay. He jammed the AR up against my side, and I barely managed to shove it away before he fired.

The blast went into the rock, showering us both with debris. The noise made my ears ring, and my body reacted by sending blood pounding through my head. My vision blurred, and I could feel my grip on him beginning to slip. As I ran out of options, I slammed my forehead into his.

It wasn't as sharp a blow with all the cold-weather padding we each wore, but it was enough to send him to his back. The rifle fired off into the rock again, and the whole mountain rumbled in protest.

Arden pulled his legs up and jabbed at my abdomen with both feet. The blow wasn't enough to knock the wind out of me, but his momentum was enough to send him rolling out of my reach. He was on his feet before I could do the same. By the time I had taken two steps closer to him, he was over the edge of the cliff.

I looked over the ledge and watched him slide down the steep incline through the snow. He was only barely in control of his descent and nearly hit an outcrop of rocks, but he had achieved his objective—to get the fuck away from me. Distance was his only advantage.

"Pussy," I mumbled down the slope. "You think that's going to save you?"

Speaking the words just made the answer obvious to me—yeah, that could save him. I had very few options in front of me: head down the mountain after him; look for a better way down; let him get away and start all over again.

"Fuck it," I grumbled. I knelt near the ledge and launched myself over. I had to catch up to him before he found a stable place to regroup and properly aim.

Rocks and snow cascaded down the cliff along with me. I ran parallel to the snow as it broke away, keeping myself to the edge of the small snowslide. Arden was far below me, trying to slow his descent and get his footing. As the sliding snow stopped, I turned and began to gain on him quickly, pulling the garrote from the loop at my belt as I descended upon him.

Arden stopped, placed his foot against a rock jutting out from the snow, and wheeled about. The AR came up to his shoulder, and I could see directly down the barrel.

I leapt into the air, heard the shot, and felt the impact against my side. The Kevlar stopped it from entering my body, but the blow put me off balance. I careened into Arden's side, grabbed hold of his arm, and we both began to roll down the mountain as snow slid around us.

With a grunt, my body stopped abruptly as I hit a patch of rocks. Arden's fist was in my face a second later, and as I lay stunned, he brought the rifle up to my face. We were too close for him to use such a long weapon effectively. I punched his arm as he tried to get the rifle in position and pulled up my knee to slam into his side at the same time. The blast rang through my ears as the bullet hit the rock next to me.

We struggled to make contact with each other and with the rifle itself, but neither of us was able to get the advantage. I took a couple blows from the barrel of the weapon and also landed a few into

Arden's side and face. He took every hit with barely a grunt.

Desperate to gain advantage, I let go of the rifle and grabbed hold of the piano wire with both hands. I looped it over his head and pulled his face to my chest with the garrote. I couldn't get it around the front of his neck, but he was at least unable to move enough to bring the rifle into position.

Growling, Arden swung the AR around and fired three shots in quick succession into the rock right below my face. He couldn't have actually been trying to hit me, but I knew immediately what he was trying to accomplish.

It worked, too.

My head throbbed as the blast so close to my ear left me deaf. I couldn't hear anything, but I could feel the ground beneath me as it rumbled.

A dozen things seemed to happen at once.

Flashes from Arden's weapon were followed by a shower of snow and rock right above my head. I blinked, but all I could see was Arden's body as a wall of snow slammed into his back and sent him flying over the top of me along with a wave of snow. My body twisted, and my legs were shoved up into my chest. I rolled backward and grabbed hold of the rock before I went over the edge.

There was nothing to see but white. It spun around and covered me as snow invaded my mask and filled my mouth. I felt the pressure against my body, my arms feeling like they were about to rip from their sockets. If I let go, I was going to be buried in the avalanche, just like Arden already was.

"*I love your strength.*"

Raine's voice whispered in my head, tightening my resolve as I held on. Bits of rock slammed into me as snow covered me, and the pressure increased again. There was nothing I could do. I couldn't breathe. There was no way to hold on. I wasn't strong enough.

I lost my grip. As least for now, I was heading down the mountain the hard way.

Chapter Fifteen

I rolled completely out of control. All I could manage to do was to tuck my head down and wrap my arms around myself to keep from slamming into the rocks with a vital part of my body. My vision was obscured by the snow, and the only perceivable change was seeing everything go from all white, to slightly blue, to white again, and then to black.

I kept falling. The back of my head hit something hard, and white flashes invaded my eyes, joining the darkened snow as my goggles first filled with snow and then flew off. I tumbled, tried to turn and straighten myself as the powdered snow deepened, and again I couldn't breathe. Remembering everything Landon had ever told me about avalanches, I started moving my arms and legs as much as I could in a classic Australian crawl stroke—trying to swim up and out of the snow before I lost all my breath.

The movement worked, and grey snow turned back to white. For a moment, my head was out from under the snow, and I could take a deep breath. It didn't last long, and I was buried again quickly. I kept swimming down the slope, gasping for air every chance I got.

The rumbling and shaking finally slowed and then ended completely as I came to a sudden stop when my lower body hit something hard. I couldn't see a damn thing, and I realized I was totally buried in the snow. My head pounded, and I wasn't even sure which way was up.

I couldn't feel my legs at all.

First things first. I need to breathe.

I moved my head from side to side and then forward, making a small pocket of air around my face. It wouldn't last long, though—maybe a minute or two—so I needed to get unburied as quickly as possible. To do that, I needed to know which way to dig. With my head still dizzy from the tumble, I had no idea.

Gathering saliva in my mouth, I looked down into my ripped up mask and let the spit escape from my lips. Following gravity, it dribbled straight down my chin, which meant my body was angled vertically. A damn good sign if I ever saw one.

I wriggled my arm up my body until my hand reached my face. I made a bigger air pocket before I continued to use my fingers to dig upward. The ice and snow weren't too packed, and it only took a minute before my hand popped through the surface. I was under about a foot and a half of snow, but at least I could see out and, more importantly, breathe.

I took a deep breath of chilled, fresh air. I still couldn't feel my legs, but at least I had oxygen. Step one accomplished.

I closed my eyes for a minute and tried to recall anything and everything I knew about avalanches. Everything I recalled just told me I was fucked. Normally in this kind of situation—not that being caught in an avalanche was normal—someone would be nearby, looking to help. In my case, I already knew there was only one person still out there looking for me, and I hoped to God Evan Arden was under ten tons of snow and ice right now. It wasn't the way I wanted to kill him, but it would still do the trick.

Arden's being dead didn't help me get myself out of where I was though, and I couldn't win if I couldn't escape. The loss of my goggles in the avalanche also meant the loss of the camera and GPS locator attached to them. None of the investors back at Franks' camp would be able to see what I could see. If Arden was completely buried, they wouldn't have any way of finding him either.

With images of Raine and Alex in my head, I started fighting through the snow.

Moving my arms around in the hole I had made near my head, I widened the pocket around me as well as the hole a few inches above my head. Part of the snowpack around me fell, dusting me with powder but also clearing the space in front of me. The hole let in more fresh air and gave me the ability to observe a little around me. There wasn't much more than sky to see, but it was a hell of a lot better than snow. What worried me the most was the view in front of me.

I was on my back at about a fifteen-degree angle with snow and ice all around me, but as the snow in front of my face fell away, I found myself looking out over a ravine. I was perched about a third of the way up the side of the mountain. Right below me was a wide rock ledge jutting out from the nearest mountain ridge. If I did manage to dig my way out, I was going to have to scale all the way down the cliff in front of me.

Thinking about scaling the cliffs also made me think about my legs. I was starting to be able to feel them again, and what I felt wasn't good at all. The left one was starting to throb like a bitch, and I was pretty sure it was either broken or at least badly cut from striking a rock. I wouldn't know for sure until I dug myself out, so I started scooping out the snow around my chest and stomach. It was slow going, and I couldn't turn my head to look around or anything, so I just focused on the ice and snow in front of me.

It felt like I was at it for hours though it couldn't have been more than a few minutes. The chill in my body had seeped into my core, and I was shivering, making it difficult to push the snow out of the way. There was a decent opening in front of me now, and I could see out a lot better. I shoved more of the snow behind me and away from my face, ending up with an icy pillow at the back of my head and added maneuverability for my neck.

Just as I thought I might get my shoulders free, I saw the slightest movement out of the corner of my eye. Near my right ear, I felt cold pressure pressed against my temple, followed by an audible click.

No.

Oh fuck no.

I couldn't move enough to turn around and even see him, let alone try to fight him off. I could at least hope that the sound of the firing gun would be enough to trigger another avalanche and end his sorry ass as I died in the snow, but there was nothing I could do to stop him.

Evan Arden had a gun at my head, and I couldn't do anything about it. My already cold body turned even colder.

Raine.

Fucking failed her.

Again.

Tensing my body in preparation for what was to come, I closed my eyes and tried to keep her face in my mind, but the business end of Arden's Beretta was too much to ignore.

Fucker.

"Aren't you supposed to give me some kind of 'ha-ha-I-knew-I-was-going-to-win-the-whole-time' kind of speech first?" I asked with a snarl.

I heard him snort a little laugh behind me.

"Not really my style," he said.

The barrel of the Beretta pressed a little harder against my skull, and without another word, Evan Arden pulled back on the trigger.

There was a click—louder than the one from the hammer—but that was it.

No gunshot. No continued avalanche. No bullet in my brain.

"Fuck," Arden muttered.

I relaxed my muscles.

"Run out of ammo?" I asked. I chuckled softly because the fucking irony was perfect and because I figured it would piss him off.

"No," he said in a deadpan voice. "Jammed. Probably from the ice or a rock or something."

I felt my insides churn. Arden was way too good to be stopped by a jammed gun. He would have it working again in a few seconds, which wasn't nearly enough time for me to get myself dug out enough to turn around, take the gun, and beat him to death with the blunt end. It was only a delay of the inevitable.

Raine.

I closed my eyes again and tried to be grateful that I had a little time to picture her face, think about the way she smelled, and remember how her skin felt in my hands. I hoped and prayed that Landon would just let her and Alex go, now that he had no use for them.

I took a long, shuddering breath and waited for the inevitable.

But it didn't come.

"Motherfucker," Arden mumbled, and I realized I'd been

thinking about Raine for quite some time now, and I still wasn't dead.

"Having a problem?" I hoped my smirk was evident in my voice.

"A bit," he said bluntly but didn't elaborate.

I had the feeling talking wasn't one of Evan Arden's strong points.

"Something I can help you with?"

Arden took a deep breath, and when he exhaled, the water vapor wafted over me. I heard and felt him shift in the snow, and I realized just how close to me he was. We had both been stopped by the rock ledge directly below us. If I could get myself turned around enough to reach back behind me, I might be able to snap his neck.

Why isn't he just beating me to death?

Before I could act on one thought or consider the other, he bashed me in the side of the head with the blunt end of his weapon.

"Ow! Motherfucker!"

The angle was bad, or he would have knocked me unconscious. He smacked me again, but I managed to move my head a bit to the side at the last moment. Gritting my teeth, I listened to the scraping sound as he moved his arm. Concentrating, I waited for the sound of the crunching snow to enter my ears, reached up behind my head, and grabbed for his wrist.

I ended up with two fingers and part of the gun, which I twisted backwards in an effort to break his fingers. My wrist scratched against a rock, but my thick clothing preventing it from scraping off my skin. He tightened up, prepared for the move, and I waited for him to grab me with his other hand, but he didn't. He tried to pull away, but I wasn't having any of that. As painful as it was, I held onto his fingers and slammed my hand at an awkward, backward angle against the rock behind my head.

Arden grunted, our hands parted, and the gun fell from his grip, cascading down the cliff and bouncing high in the air as it hit a rock. Spinning silently, it dropped out of sight, no longer a part of Arden's arsenal.

"Fuck," he muttered, completely monotone.

"Why didn't you just fucking shoot me?" I snapped.

"Still jammed," he replied.

"I thought you were a fucking gun expert," I challenged. "You telling me you can't unjam a gun?"

"Not with one hand," he replied in the same tone.

One hand…did he lose a fucking arm in the avalanche? It was possible, and I hoped it was true. In this cold, bleeding to death would take quite some time, but having him end that way sounded pretty good to me.

I shifted my shoulders against the snow behind me, trying to create a little wiggle room. I was only mildly successful, but it gave me just enough space to be able to turn and see him.

Evan Arden was lying on his side, facing me, with one arm not just below him but completely buried under rocks and snow. Unlike my icy tomb, Arden's was made of more rocks than ice, and he was definitely pinned down. He had one leg trapped as well.

I let out a short laugh.

"Well, you're fucked," I said simply. I went back to digging at the snow around my lower half. If I could get out, I could finish him off without a lot of resistance.

A half hour later, I was panting, sweating, freezing, and still completely unable to dig myself out. I dropped my head back into the snow behind me and watched my breath rise in puffs around my mask and over my head.

I turned my head to see Arden's stoic face as he laid his head against a rock and stared out over the cliff. There were a lot of marks in the snow where he had obviously tried to free his arm, but the rocks and ice were too thick there. He'd need a fucking bulldozer or at least some help, which I wasn't about to offer.

His gaze shifted to me.

"This is supposed to be my fucking retirement," Arden mumbled.

"Ha!" I snorted. "Mine, too."

"Oh yeah?" He shifted his head lower to rest it on the snow and sighed again. "What are you doing here, then?"

"Killing your ass is the plan," I answered simply.

"I've heard that before," he replied. "Everyone who ever said it is floating in the Chicago river."

"Everyone I've ever said it *to* is six feet under."

He moved his eyes to me and gave me a slight nod.

"So I've heard," he said, "but you've been out of the games for a long time."

I didn't comment. My leg was starting to throb, and I was

convinced it was broken. Conversation was distracting, pointless, and pissing me off. I needed to get myself out of this and kill the guy beside me. Even then, my chances of getting back down the mountainside with a busted up leg were growing slimmer by the minute.

I was cold. Really fucking cold.

I closed my eyes and tried to think of Raine, hoping thoughts of her waiting for me would give me a little more motivation and maybe even warm me a little. Thinking just made the back of my head throb, and I reached up to rub at it. There was a good knot back there, and touching it made me dizzy.

Fucking fabulous.

I set my head back against the snow bank to catch my breath. I needed energy, so I dug down a little by my side until I could reach the pocket with the tubes of nutritional goo. I sucked it down my throat and then ate a few nuts to get rid of the taste of the overly processed shit in a tube.

"Why did you agree to play?" Arden asked. "If you're supposed to be retired, why come back now? This is all about the Chicago war, not Seattle."

"It wasn't exactly by choice," I said with a sigh. I was too tired to yell at him, and wasting energy was a bad idea anyway. "Why are you here? You were never a tournament player before."

"Nope, never was," he confirmed.

"So, why?"

"Rinaldo asked me to do it," he said simply.

"You always do what he asks?"

"Pretty much," Arden confirmed.

"Why you?"

"I killed the guy who would have otherwise done it," Arden replied as he stared up into the sky.

"You killed one of your boss's men?"

He moved his eyes slowly to mine. He didn't need to respond verbally.

"You got balls," I muttered.

"He was an asshole," Arden said.

"There are plenty of those around. You can't kill them all."

"Maybe." He kept looking at me, and his cold eyes reminded me a bit of Landon's. They were the wrong color—much too dark. In fact, they were pretty close to the shade of blue in my eyes. "So why are you here?"

I ignored him. The last thing I wanted to do was have him thinking that I had someone out there to make me vulnerable. Not that it mattered at this point—only one of us was going to get out of this alive.

If even that.

Closing my eyes, I tried to find my focus again. Getting free was paramount, but my body was exhausted and half frozen. I licked my lips, and it felt like the cold was freezing the saliva to my mouth. I needed more focus to stop myself from giving in to the temptation to just give up and lie back in the snow.

Incentive.

Struggling a little due to my mitten-covered hands, I reached under my parka and into my breast pocket to pull out the drawing Alex had made. I unfolded it carefully and stared at the figures in the picture. I traced the bottom of the picture where Alex had drawn his feet in blue tennis shoes and long, crazy laces and then brushed the edge of Raine's face with my thumb.

When I glanced back over my shoulder, Arden was still looking at me. From his vantage point, he would have seen the picture clearly. For a moment, I felt a touch of panic because every one of the people watching over the closed circuit had just seen it, too.

But Arden's head was free of his goggles as well. We had both lost the cameras used to broadcast back to Resolute. There was no beacon being transmitted from our location at all. They didn't know where we were or what we were doing. Their last images would have been the avalanche taking us both down the side of the mountain.

We were fucked—completely and totally. It didn't matter what he knew now.

"They got my girl," I said quietly. As the words came out of my mouth, something inside me flipped. It was over. There was no way I was going to be able to get out of this without help, and as much as I didn't want to admit it, I was done. I couldn't move. My leg was broken. This was going to be an all losers tournament.

Arden didn't respond, and I looked over to him. He was staring blankly into the snow in front of his face with his jaw tight.

"You're never going to see her again," he said, "not the kid, either."

My muscles tightened at his words. As much as I wanted to deny it, I knew he was right. I'd come to the exact same conclusion. I wasn't about to admit it out loud, though.

"Fuck you," I growled. "I'm getting out of this, fucking you over, and going home to them."

"No, you aren't," Arden said. "You know it, too. You just figured it out."

"How do you know that?" I snapped back at him.

He shrugged with his one free arm.

"Your posture just changed," he said. "You slumped down, and your eyes dropped. There's no way to dig yourself out, and we aren't going to help each other, so there will be no winner for this tournament. You were looking at that crayon drawing when you realized you'd never see her or your kid again."

I couldn't hide the shock I felt.

"Wha…?"

He moved his shoulder up and down again.

"I'm pretty perceptive," he said numbly.

I mentally gathered myself together.

"Well, it's bullshit," I said, trying to convince myself of the words. "I'm just giving myself a little break before I haul my ass out of this snow bank, beat you to death, and head back home. All I have to do is make it down that mountainside, and then I'm done for good."

"You'll fight again," Arden said. "Well, you will if you ever get out of this, which you won't. If you did, this still wouldn't be your last tournament."

"Fuck you," I said with a snarl. "I don't quit in the middle of a fight. This *is* my last tournament, and it ends in victory just like my first fight and every one of them in between."

"It never ends," Arden said. "Franks won't let you go any more than Rinaldo will let me go. Once they got you, they got you. You never get away from them completely, even when they tell you that you can."

I might not have been as perceptive as he was, but I still knew he wasn't talking about me anymore. He was talking about himself.

"Landon isn't going to fuck me over," I said. Everything Arden was saying rang true, aligning with my own thoughts, but I refused to agree with him. "I know him. He told me this was it, and he wouldn't go back on his word. He's like my fucking father."

Arden chuckled.

"Yeah, I got one of those, too. He's the reason I'm here, retirement or not."

Arden pulled his arm across his chest and placed his hand under his head to get it off the snow. He looked into my eyes again. For a second, he didn't look quite as emotionless as he had before. His eyes tightened a bit, and his jaw flexed as he spoke.

"We're too good for them to just let us go," Arden continued. "Even if they really want to, they're always going to need us for something *one last time.*"

I stared at him as the words sank in, and I knew deep inside that he was right. If I did get out of this, Franks and Landon would let me off on my own for a while, but eventually there would be something else—just *one more thing* they needed for me to do. One more favor. One more fight.

"Fuck you," I grumbled through clenched teeth. "I've got bigger priorities now."

Arden nodded slightly, sniffed against the cold, and looked back to me.

"I got a girl, too," he finally said. "Lia. Never thought that would happen."

"Heh," I chuckled, "tell me about it."

The statement was rhetorical, but it seemed to put Arden in a more talkative mood.

"She doesn't know where I am," he said. "I sent her off to visit her mom for a couple of weeks. She's going to come home, and I won't be there."

My mind played through the scenario he described, only with Raine and myself as the subjects. I pictured her coming into the condo and finding it empty. I thought about what she would do when it stayed empty through the night. I wondered at what point she would start looking for me and what she would do when she couldn't find any trace of where I had gone.

She'd freak out. She wouldn't know what to do, and there wouldn't be anyone she could call to get any information. How long would it be before she gave up? Weeks? Months? Years?

"Lia came after me once before," Arden said. "I ditched her in Arizona, but she still managed to find me again. She's stubborn."

"That sounds familiar," I said. "I don't think I've ever known anyone as stubborn as Raine."

"Raine?"

I tapped the edge of the picture.

"That's her name."

Arden huffed a breath through his nose.

"At least she'll have her kid," Arden said. "Lia's stuck with the dog."

"He's not her son," I said quietly.

"Oh, right. Sorry."

I remembered his words from our first meeting with all the families when he'd threatened to come after Alex when this was over.

"You knew that," I said accusingly. "You knew his mother was dead."

"Yeah," Arden said. His eyes were blank again. "Forgot. My mind's a little preoccupied."

His eyes flashed over to the side, narrowed, and he shook his head slightly as if to clear it.

"Did you kill her?" I asked bluntly.

"No," he said. "Franks put the hit on her. Rinaldo told me about it."

I didn't see any trace of a lie on his face. I clenched my teeth a bit. I shouldn't have been surprised. Franks would choose profit over family, obviously.

"Fucker," I muttered.

"He won't be on his own," Arden said as he nodded toward the picture.

"Yeah." I shrugged though I wasn't sure he could see the movement from where he lay on the snow. I stared back at the drawing for a minute. "She treats him like he's hers."

"Well, you got that at least."

I didn't want to go into the detailed story about Jillian and all that shit. He didn't need to know any more than he already did, and I didn't want to spend my last few hours thinking about that woman. I wanted to keep the image of Raine in my head, so I kept talking about her.

"She's a fucking saint," I said. "I suck at being a boyfriend. I can't even get along with her friends."

Arden nodded his head, and his eyes darkened.

"Lia doesn't really have any friends," he said. "That's my fault. To keep her safe and away from all this shit, I had to isolate her. I did it to protect her, but…yeah, well, she doesn't have anyone but me. Once she figures out I'm not coming back, she'll probably move back to Arizona with her mom."

Raine would at least know what had happened to me. Landon would tell her I was dead, and she could move on with her life. Lindsay would be there for her, and she'd have a shoulder to cry on if nothing else. I couldn't even imagine how she would deal with it all if she didn't have Lindsay around, and I felt like a shit for being nasty to her and Nick all the time.

At least they could take care of her and help with Alex.

"I don't know if Lia is a saint or not," Arden said, "but she puts up with me. Even when I'm…well, when I'm not the friendliest person around, she still hangs in there. It doesn't seem to matter how fucked up I am in the head, she always stands by me."

"Raine's like that, too," I replied with a nod. "I can be a total asshole, and she still has my back."

"Lia knows just when to back off and when to be there," Arden said. "She knows I'm fucked up, but I guess she just…I dunno… ignores it? She doesn't like it, but she never gives up on me. She also thinks I don't do hits anymore, but I do."

"How do you do that without her knowing about it?"

"She's in school," Arden said. "It's mostly online, but sometimes she has to go to conferences or meet with her professors in person. I plan my hits around those."

"So you hide it from her?"

"Yeah."

"You're crazy."

Arden laughed.

"Yeah, I've got the diagnosis to prove it."

I stared at him a minute. It didn't seem like an off-hand remark; it seemed like he meant it. He looked back at me and nodded.

"PTSD," he said. "I'm a certified nut."

"From being in the Marines?"

"From being a POW, yeah." He was silent a moment. "Why are you such a dick to your girl?"

"I just…have a nasty temper. I used to drink to make up for it."

"Not anymore?"

"That's the one thing she'd leave me for," I admitted. "If I drink, she's gone."

"And that's enough to keep you off it?"

"Yeah," I said. "Well, mostly. I've fucked up but just once."

"She forgave you?"

"She did."

Arden pondered a minute.

"I don't think Lia would be so forgiving if she knew I was still in the business."

"If she's anything like Raine, she'd have your balls."

Arden laughed.

"Sounds like they are a lot alike," Arden mused.

I had the feeling we were both thinking it, but neither of us said anything about how that probably meant he and I were a lot alike as well. I thought about how he fought—as if none of the blows I'd made to his face mattered. Arden really believed that as long as he was alive, there was still a chance.

If we were so much alike, why wasn't I thinking the same thing? I wasn't dead yet, dammit. I was just in a totally fucking hopeless situation with no conceivable way out. I'd been in similar situations before.

"Fuck that," I muttered.

"What?"

I didn't answer him.

Reaching down with my hand, I dug at the space near my hip. It was nearly frozen solid, and I couldn't get much of the ice away from my body. I placed both hands against the frozen ground and tried to push myself out of the hole, but I couldn't get enough leverage, and my legs wouldn't budge.

Pain rippled through my left calf as I tried harder. As I attempted to move, it became clear that my leg was not only broken but also turned backward at a nasty angle, further securing itself inside the bank of ice and rock below.

Exhausted, I dropped my head back in the snow and tried to breathe through my nose. I could hear Arden behind me, shuffling against the ice, but he wasn't trying anymore either.

He kept thinking about giving up; I could see it in his eyes.

Normally, that would have been good news for me, but I didn't feel particularly happy about his predicament. Maybe I was just too tired to give a shit anymore, but the idea of beating his head in wasn't as attractive as it had been an hour ago.

"I want a fucking cigarette," Arden said suddenly.

I laughed. I paused for a moment and then dug through my pockets. I had three smokes wrapped up in a plastic baggie—my usual emergency supply—and I pulled two of them out. Moving my torn facemask to the side, I stuck both Marlboros in my mouth. I grabbed one of the matches from the bag and leaned down into the hole and away from the wind to strike it against the rock. I ran the flame across the ends of each cigarette until they blazed.

Reaching out over my shoulder, I handed one to Evan.

"Damn," he said, genuinely surprised. "Thanks."

I inhaled deeply and watched the smoke flow out around my face.

"If I get out of this, I'm going to end up running that whole organization when Rinaldo retires," Evan said. "I don't want it, but the war has made it clear that his daughter can't handle the pressure. Lia wants nothing to do with it. I'm going to lose her over the whole thing, and there's no other path before me. I think I'd rather die on the edge of a mountain than lose her over that. I'd rather she just wonder why I never came home."

"That's fucked up," I replied. "Raine would go bat-shit if I just didn't come home one night. She'd drive herself to an early grave wondering what happened to me. I may be a dick, but I wouldn't do that to her."

"I don't know what Lia will do," Evan said softly. "She'll be upset, but she'll get over it eventually, right?"

I looked over my shoulder at him and raised my eyebrows. I didn't know this chick, but she did sound a lot like Raine. Raine wouldn't just get over it. I knew that much. I figured Evan's girl wouldn't either.

"Fuck," Evan muttered. He took a long drag off the cigarette and stared out over the ledge. "I can't leave her like that."

"Well, why don't you help me get out, and then I'll make sure to let her know you're dead when I'm done with you."

"Thanks a lot," he said as he glared over the burning tip of the smoke. "I'm sure having the dude who killed me tell her all about it would be a great comfort to her."

"Just tryin' to help," I snickered.

"Yeah, I can do without that type of assistance."

"Wouldn't Moretti tell her what happened?" I asked.

"He doesn't know where she is."

"He knew how to find you, though," I said after a moment's consideration. "Are you saying he can't find her?"

"Rinaldo has people who could locate her," Evan said with a deep breath. "She'd be able to move on then, I guess."

He didn't seem convinced as I watched him drop his eyes to the ground. He blinked his frozen eyelashes a couple of times, and with a shiver, took another long drag off the smoke. I might not have been as perceptive as Evan was, but I could see it in his face—he didn't have any hope left. He was done. I wasn't even sure he wanted to survive.

The knowledge should have spurred me on. It should have encouraged me to listen to Landon's voice in my head and get my ass moving, but it didn't. For some reason, I didn't want Evan to give up though I wasn't sure at what point he became *Evan* in my head instead of just *Arden*.

"Landon's always told me that victory is in your head first," I said. "If you decide that's how it's going to be, then that's how it *will* be."

Evan took another hit on the smoke and tried to shift himself into a more comfortable position. He looked straight at me.

"Let' go over the possibilities, shall we?" he suggested.

"Okay."

"Most likely—we freeze to death right here," he said. "No winner. I don't know how this shit works when there's a tie, but it won't matter to us because we'll both be dead."

I didn't agree with him—what happened to Raine and Alex mattered a fucking hell of a lot regardless of how things turned out for me, but I didn't feel like arguing the point.

"Next option—one of us manages to get free, and the other one is still trapped," he continued. "Easy enough kill for either of us."

I had to concur with that one.

"They don't know where we are at this point," Evan said. "Neither of us has our cameras anymore, and they'd have to come looking for us. My guess is they've already decided to do that but are probably waiting until the wind dies down. I don't know what the protocol is. Rinaldo only filled me in on standard procedure, not exceptions."

"There aren't usually any exceptions," I said. "The tournament goes until there's only one player left. I've never been in the situation where the investors don't know what's happening, but I can guess. There was a tournament once—not one I was in—where the last two people were fighting with knives. They both cut each other fatally. The investors waited to see which one died first and declared the other guy the winner even though he died a few minutes later."

"What if they find us both dead at the same time," Evan asked, "or if they find us both alive?"

"As far as I know, that's never happened." I thought about it for a minute. "They might decide to start the whole thing over again."

My stomach churned a bit. The idea of having to do it all again actually sounded worse than losing. It would mean breaking one more promise to Raine. She'd never trust me again.

"How about we make a deal?" Evan said quietly.

I turned a little farther to get a better look at him. He was watching the cigarette burn as opposed to looking back at me, but his expression was quite serious.

"A deal?"

"Yeah," he said. "A deal where we both end up retired for real with the women we fight for."

"The only way that happens is when one of us dies," I reminded him. "There isn't a prize for second place."

"Yeah, I get that." Arden rolled his head to the side and stared into my eyes. "You can have the trophy—I don't give a shit about that. I just want to walk away with people thinking I'm dead."

I knew exactly what he was suggesting. Normally, it wouldn't be an option because the audience would be aware of any allegiances formed between tournament players and would put a stop to it. This time, they had no idea what we were doing. I still didn't see how it would work—they'd have to have a body to prove I'd won.

"Don't you think that kind of alliance has been tried before?" I asked. "They watch for that shit."

"Not if they think I'm buried on the side of the mountain. They'll only look for me for so long before they have to take your word for it"

"You're crazy."

"Already established."

"I mean *really* crazy," I countered. "You're living in some kind of fantasy world."

He glared at me a moment.

"Look over there," Evan said. He pointed with his finger out near the top of the ridge. "You see anyone?"

I glanced over for a second then looked back at him with narrowed eyes.

"There's no one for miles," I reminded him.

"Yeah, I know," he said softly, "but I still see him."

"Who?"

"A kid I killed in Iraq. He follows me everywhere. He'll go away for a while—sometimes for months—but he always comes back when shit gets real."

I stared at him for a moment until I realized my mouth was hanging open. I closed it quickly.

"Dude—there's no one there."

He shrugged.

"I know. I still see him. I have nightmares about killing him all the time. Not just him, but being in the desert, tied up in a hole for months. Sometimes I can't stop thinking about it, and when I do, I can't sleep at all—sometimes for days."

I could certainly relate to the nightmares. Before I had met Raine, I could only avoid them with alcohol. With her around, I slept better than I had since I was a kid. She drove the nightmares from my head.

The next phrase out of Evan's mouth would have knocked me to the ground had I been standing.

"When I'm with Lia, I sleep better."

I looked over to him quickly, trying to figure out if he had somehow used his skills of perception to know what I was thinking, but he seemed completely inside of his own head.

"Fuck," I muttered. "Seriously?"

"Yeah," he said. His eyes darkened as he looked at me.

"It's just…well, Raine helps with my nightmares, too."

Our gazes locked as we both considered this. I thought it was just me, and from the look on his face, Evan had thought the same thing about himself. Knowing we had such an odd similarity struck me right in the gut. I didn't know what to make of it.

"I couldn't deal with it if it wasn't for her," Evan said quietly.

"Me either," I said. "With Raine, I mean."

"All the more reason I should stay away from Lia," he said. "She deserves better, but I can't let her go. I also can't get out of my debt to Rinaldo. At some point, it will become either her or him, and I can't choose between them."

"You are fucked up." I took in a long breath and thought about it for a minute. Evan was fucked up because of a war and whatever happened to him over there. None of that shit was his fault. What was my excuse? Crappy childhood and a woman running out on me? It all sounded kind of lame to me now.

I was trying, though. I tried to keep myself off the booze even if I *had* failed. I wanted to be better for Raine, and I wanted to be a good father for Alex. I didn't have the slightest fucking idea what that entailed, but I fully intended to figure it out.

Evan was different.

He'd been cheating on his girl. All right, maybe not with another woman, but he was doing what she didn't want him to do with full knowledge that he was going against her wishes. I had the feeling that he would ultimately side with Moretti, if it ever came to that. It wasn't the same situation as mine. I'd had a momentary lapse of judgment under a stressful situation and taken a drink. He was actively planning his deceptions.

"That doesn't end my relationship with Franks," I pointed out. "Maybe that would secure your retirement, but I'd still be in the same situation."

"I'll kill Franks," he said simply.

I stared at him, unblinking, and considered what he was saying.

If I acted on my own, there was always the risk of being caught. If everyone thought Evan was dead, and Franks got knocked off a while later, it would never be traced back to me. As long as he was gone, Franks would lose his hold over me, and the organization would be in a total uproar as they tried to figure out who would be in charge. All my past transgressions would be forgotten.

"So, what do you think? Evan asked.

"Dude, I think you make me sound like a fucking angel," I said. "When this is over, I'm going to tell Raine how much worse it could be."

"You can't tell her that if you don't get out of this," he pointed out.

"True." My mind was spinning. What he was suggesting could actually work. It was fucked up and insane, but it could still work. It meant trusting him, which was probably a mistake, but I was out of options.

"So we should find a way to end it?" he pressed. "We both come out alive, but as far as anyone else is concerned, I'm dead."

I looked at him carefully. There was no deceit in his eyes. He was being perfectly straightforward with me. He wanted to figure out how to get both of us out of this mess and didn't give a shit about winning.

That's how we were different. I had to win.

There was no choice. At least for now, we were going to work together.

Chapter Sixteen

"So what's your plan?" I asked. My teeth were starting to chatter, which was a really bad sign. Whatever we were going to do, we were going to have to do it quickly. My head was throbbing as well, and I was pretty sure the dizziness and nausea I was feeling were indicative of a concussion.

"Neither of us can move without help," he said, stating the obvious. "I'm guessing you can't see what I see."

"A kid I've killed in the past?" I said. "No, I don't see that."

Evan shook his head.

"Not him," he said. "The position of the rock next to your leg."

I had to crane my neck and tilt my head over as far as I could, but I finally saw a glimpse of what Evan was talking about. To my right, below Evan, there was a channel of snow. The ditch would have been formed by the rocks lining one side of it—the same rocks that pinned my leg to the ground below me.

"I'm pretty sure I can move the rock up against your leg out of the way with my foot," Evan explained. "Once it's gone, you should be able to pull yourself out and keep your leg intact. Well, as intact as it is now. It's broken."

"Yeah, I can tell that."

He looked at me closely.

"That's gotta hurt like a bitch," he commented.

"It does."

The corner of his mouth turned up a little as he gave me an appreciative nod.

"It's gonna hurt worse when I move the rock," he said. "I don't have the best angle, and I'll probably end up crushing your leg more."

"Great."

"Beats staying where you are."

"I can't argue with that."

"You ready, then?" he asked.

We looked at each other for a moment before I nodded.

"Do it."

I held my breath, and Evan began to push down on the rock against my leg. I had to grit my teeth and squeeze my eyes shut as he did it to keep from screaming out loud. I felt it shift a little, and heard the bone crack.

"Fuck!"

"Almost got it," he said calmly.

"Fucking hurry."

"That'll hurt more."

"I don't give a shit!" I yelled. "Just fucking do it!"

I heard him take a deep breath and saw him pull his leg up close to his chest. As he thrust his leg forward, I couldn't hold it in—I screamed as I heard a rock tumble off the edge of the cliff. Reflexively, I yanked up my leg. For the first time, it actually moved.

My head swam and my vision went dark. I had to choke back the bile that rose in my throat as I felt the tendons in my knee tear. Forcing myself to keep my mouth closed, I squeezed my eyes shut again and just tried to keep my cursing to a minimum.

"I think that did it," Evan said.

"Fuck," I said with a rush of breath. "I should have asked for a bullet to bite on."

"I have a few," Evan said. "I should have offered."

"Bastard," I muttered.

Evan chuckled.

"Can you move it yet?"

"Gimme a sec." I focused on my breathing for a couple minutes, trying to force the pain into the back of my mind. I looked down at the top of my thigh, just barely visible, and tried to push more of the snow off of it. I twisted and turned my fingers right next to my body until I managed to make a large enough hole to grab my leg with my hands. "Here goes nothing."

I yanked, but nothing happened other than causing additional searing pain to run through my body. I told myself not to be such a fucking pansy and yanked harder. It moved a little more. With my arms straining against the pressure, I gritted my teeth and kept pulling. An inch. Another.

"Fuck!" I screamed as Evan kicked at another rock.

"You do like your F-bombs, don't you?" he mused. "There was one more in the way. Try again."

"Motherfucker!"

"Quit your bitching," he commanded. "Just do it."

I tried to remember what rank he had held in the Marines. He sounded a bit too much like Landon for my taste. The tactic worked though; I grabbed hold of my thigh and pulled as hard as I could, and my leg finally came loose.

Panting, I dropped my head back to the snow and tried to get myself together before I pulled out the other leg. With the extra space made from releasing my first leg, the second came out a lot easier. It also wasn't broken, though my thigh hurt like a bitch from the bullet wound there.

With my body free from the snow, I held myself up by my arms and pushed myself out of the hole, rolling off to the side and slamming into Evan in the process. He grunted a little but didn't say anything as I got up on my hands and knees.

I looked to him and observed his wary expression. This was it— the last real choice I had to make. Right now, I could easily kill him where he lay; there was no way he could stop me. I could break this allegiance and take him out, securing my victory.

But only temporarily.

If he lived up to his side of the bargain, Franks would be out of my way for good. It wasn't an opportunity I was going to pass up.

I let him wonder for a minute, though, because I'm an asshole.

"Shall we get you out?" I finally said with a grin.

His shoulders relaxed, and he closed his eyes as he nodded.

Using one of the loose rocks as a shovel, I dug around one side of Evan's trapped arm. It took a while to get through the ice and rock, but once his arm was free we both worked to release his leg, and he crawled out of the snow bank.

His shoulder was dislocated, but he stood still and silent as I shoved it back into place with a loud pop.

"You okay?" I asked.

"Yeah," he said, "I'm good. Your leg is a mess."

I looked down at it. It wasn't just fractured but cracked, and I thought the tibia was likely crushed. I couldn't even feel my foot, but that might be a good thing.

"How are you going to climb?" Evan asked.

"I'll manage," I replied. "How are you going to get out of here?"

"I'll manage," Evan said with a smile.

I laughed through my nose as I looked down the edge of the cliff. This was going to suck, no doubt about it, but at least I had the hope of someone finding me at the bottom. Evan was going to have to avoid that.

"Keep out of sight," I said.

"I'm pretty good at that." Evan looked me over. "You're going to tell them I'm dead, right?"

"That's the plan," I said. "I don't think they're going to spend much time looking for you."

"They won't," he said. "Rinaldo knows me too well."

I didn't know what he meant, but I was too cold and in too much pain to start asking a lot of questions now. Time was running out.

My leg hung loosely from the rest of my body. I couldn't put any pressure on it at all, and I couldn't see anything around to use as a splint. I thought about Hunter's crossbow, the body of which might have worked, but it was too far away. Then I remembered the bolt I had grabbed during his fight with Reaper.

I pulled it from my waist and held it up to my calf. It wasn't really long or thick enough, but it was better than nothing.

"I can do that," Evan said.

I looked up at him, and my paranoia set in. Would he try to betray me at this point?

I shook the thought from my head. If he wanted me dead, all he had to do was bash me with a rock or something. I wasn't in any shape to fight anymore.

"I do have some training as a medic," Evan said with a shrug.

It was my only option, so I let him splint my leg using the bolt and one of the pieces of piano wire I still had on me. He wrapped it securely but not tight enough to cut off any circulation.

"The thick clothing should provide a little extra support," he said. "Don't put any weight on it if you can help it. It won't hold you."

"Yeah, I can tell."

"It's going to have to be reset," Evan said. "A few more hours, and it'll have to be broken again to get it to heal right."

"Whatever," I said. "I'll deal with that when I get to the bottom of the mountain."

"Yeah, I was wondering how you were going to do that," Arden said. "I'm going up and over, away from where they might try to land a helicopter."

"You know there's no other way off this island," I said. "It's not like you can swim it."

"I have an idea," he said. "Don't worry about me."

"I'm not," I replied. "I don't give a shit about you, but I do have a vested interest in your survival now."

His mouth turned up in a half smile. The look was almost challenging, like he'd still be willing to fight it out, but I didn't acknowledge it. There wouldn't be any point.

I did give a shit, though, even if he wasn't going to take out Franks on my behalf. I wanted him to make it. He was in better shape than I was physically, but I didn't see any fucking way he could survive.

"I'm going now," Evan said.

"You're not going to make it," I said.

"Yeah, I will," he replied. He smiled as he looked at me. "You'll know it, too—as soon as you hear the news about Franks."

I nodded, still not completely sure I could trust him to go through with it, but I also knew it was a better option that what I had planned, which was nothing.

Evan reached out his hand, and I took it a little tentatively. We shook briefly, and he turned without another word to start up the slope. I watched him for a minute and then headed over the side of the cliff.

I probably could have brought myself down the side of the mountain with one leg and both arms on a good day, but it was rough going, considering the state I was in. I was still mostly frozen, and my body didn't want to do anything I told it to do. My arms and shoulders ached. My head was swimming and clouded, and there was a throbbing in the back of my skull that kept reminding me that I'd hit my head pretty hard.

Grasping the sharp rocks to scale my way down the cliff, my one good foot tried to find a decent place to rest as I caught my breath a little. The rock I stepped on held me, but it wasn't enough to let go with my hands. It only gave my shoulders a little relief as I leaned my forehead against the cliff and took some breaths.

Back to it.

I didn't know how long it took to get down. The sun never set; it only dipped low on the horizon before it started to rise again. By then, my body was done. Only my mind with images of Raine and Alex kept me from letting go in defeat.

Can't stop.

Hand over hand, balancing on one foot, and reliving my time on the island with Raine, I kept on going. I never looked down as I progressed and was surprised when the cliff flattened out somewhat and allowed me to let go of the rocks with my hands. As I did, I lost my balance and put weight on my left leg.

"Fuck," I groaned as my leg gave out from under me and I fell, rolling down the rest of the mountainside between two short ridges. I threw my arms out to slow my descent but continued to tumble anyway. I didn't have enough strength to stop and ended up just going where gravity took me. I managed to turn myself just enough to point my feet downward and try to dig in the heel of my good foot, but it wasn't enough. In the process, I slammed my temple into the ridge on my right, and my head jerked to the side. A moment later, I landed at the bottom, just short of where land gave way to the ice floes.

My lungs burned as I tried to get some oxygen into them. The pain in my head was excruciating, and I was sure I was going to throw up, but I couldn't even roll to my side. The exertion from the fall had been too much—I couldn't move anymore. As much as I tried, my body simply wouldn't listen.

I tried to get my bearings. I was at the bottom of the mountain and would be easily visible from the air. I was close to the water, and the ground was wetter here. I knew that was a death sentence, but I couldn't manage to do anything about it.

My body was done.

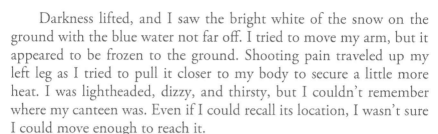

Darkness lifted, and I saw the bright white of the snow on the ground with the blue water not far off. I tried to move my arm, but it appeared to be frozen to the ground. Shooting pain traveled up my left leg as I tried to pull it closer to my body to secure a little more heat. I was lightheaded, dizzy, and thirsty, but I couldn't remember where my canteen was. Even if I could recall its location, I wasn't sure I could move enough to reach it.

I wasn't cold. That was bad.

After all this shit, I'm going to die waiting for them…

Curling into myself as much as I could, I closed my eyes and waited.

I never heard the helicopter; I just heard Landon.

"Give me a sign, buddy."

The word sounded strange to me. Landon wasn't one for terms of endearment. For a moment, I thought maybe I was hallucinating. Maybe if I opened my eyes, I'd see the imaginary kid Evan had gone on about. I wanted to find out for sure, so I forced my eyelids to open.

"There you are," Landon said quietly.

As I looked up into his face, I saw him smile. It looked strange on him. It wasn't sarcastic or snippy, but a real, genuine smile as if he were really, genuinely happy. I'd never seen him smile like that, and it made me think that I was hallucinating after all.

"Can you talk?" he asked.

I swallowed and opened my mouth, but nothing came out.

"Okay," he said, "don't try."

"Where's Arden?" another voice called out. "There's no sign of him."

I cleared my throat and licked my lips. Pulling air into my lungs, I managed to utter a single word.

"Dead."

"You sure?" Landon asked.

I nodded.

"Snow," I croaked. "Avalanche…"

"Yeah, I got that idea."

"Found his Barrett," another voice said. I couldn't tell who was speaking and couldn't move my head enough to figure it out. "The barrel's damaged, but I know he'd never leave this particular weapon behind, damaged or not."

"Are we calling this?" another voice asked.

"Not without a body."

"You want to dig through all of that?" a woman's voice snapped. "It's fucking freezing already, and the temperature is dropping."

"There has to be proof."

"If Moretti says Arden wouldn't leave without his rifle, that's good enough for me."

"Fine."

"Agreed. Get me off this fucking rock."

"Folks," I recognized Franks' voice as he spoke, "we have a winner."

There was a lot of motion around me, but I couldn't quite keep up with it. I heard myself scream as I was lifted and placed on a stretcher of some sort. The whirring blades of a helicopter filled my vision as I was maneuvered through the open door and onto the floor. Without the wind rushing over my body, I felt my muscles relax a little as the warm air inside the helicopter seeped into me.

Landon knelt beside me and began to release the fastenings on my parka. As he got it open, I warmed a little more. My stomach lurched as the craft took flight. Landon continued to remove my outer clothing.

"Shit, Sebastian," he muttered.

I felt his hand against my leg and then a sharp pain. I closed my eyes against the sensation and gritted my teeth as my head swam, and my vision went dark.

I didn't know how long I was out, just realized how sick I felt as I regained consciousness. I opened my eyes to look around, but everything was blurry. I knew I was inside a helicopter. From the motion, I could tell we were in the air, but I couldn't really identify anything I saw. There were human shapes moving around me, but I didn't know who they were.

"Can you focus on my finger?" Landon asked.

The voice came from a nondescript mass in front of me, so I assumed it was him. I tried to focus on his hand where he held it up, but there were at least three of them. I shook my head, but that was a big mistake.

The nausea that had been building inside of me took over, and Landon had to roll me to my side to let me puke all over the inside of the chopper. Once I was done, he rolled me to my back and straightened me out.

"Sebastian," Landon said, "I'm going to have to reset your leg. It's better for me to do it now; we won't have proper medical treatment for at least twelve hours."

I tried to nod, but wasn't sure if I managed it or not.

"You hear me?" Landon called out. I felt his hand on the top of my head. "Fucking answer me if you can."

"Yeah," I mumbled.

"I'm going to set your leg now. You want a fucking bullet to bite on?"

"No." I laughed, but it hurt like a motherfucker.

"Good."

Maybe I should have asked for one.

I heard the crack and then myself screaming. After that, everything went dark.

≫••••◗◯◖••••≪

Gunter Darke used to tell me what banging heroin felt like. He would describe it in great detail, everything from the needle prick in his arm to the pressure of the fluid filling his veins. Then he'd talk about the warm, sleepy feeling like it was the best fucking thing in the world, better than Christmas morning, better than rich desserts, better than orgasms.

I was sinking. I felt heavy everywhere though there wasn't any discernable pain. I was dizzy, and when I tried to understand why, I realized I didn't have any idea where I was or what had happened to me. My eyelids felt heavy as I pried them open.

I'd been in enough hospital rooms to recognize the setup. There were white walls, dimmed lights, and a lot of beeping machines. I was on my back with a sheet pulled up to my chest, but my arms were on top of the covers. One of them had an IV hooked up to it. My left leg was encased in a cast and elevated off the bed in traction.

"Bastian?" a feminine voice spoke.

I moved my eyes toward the sound, and a dark-haired, dark-eyed woman sat near me in an oversized chair. She was a tiny thing—petite in frame with long, straight hair flowing past her shoulders. She stood as I looked at her and moved close to the bed.

She was beautiful, but her eyes were sad.

I tried to place her, but nothing came to me other than pain and throbbing. My throat was dry, and I couldn't swallow properly. She reached over to touch my face with her hand. Her expression was so tender and familiar, but I couldn't remember who she was.

As I looked around again, I figured I must have recently finished a tournament though I couldn't remember the details. All the games kind of flowed together anyway. Obviously I'd won, or I wouldn't be here at all.

Where's Landon?

I couldn't speak to ask.

The woman's eyes filled with tears. Had I been sleeping with her before the tournament? She wasn't dressed like a nurse, but she seemed awfully concerned for someone who had just spent a single night with me. Maybe she was just like that. I wished I could remember her name.

"Can you hear me?" she asked.

I opened my mouth, but my lips were as dry and cracked as my throat felt. The woman reached over to the table beside the bed and held a glass of water with a straw up to my lips. I couldn't lift my head to drink, but she angled the straw for me to take a few sips.

"Are you in pain?" she asked.

I still couldn't place her. I thought about her question and did a mental evaluation of my body before I tried to speak.

"Leg hurts," I croaked.

"It's broken," the woman said.

I'd assumed so from the cast. I took a deep breath and focused on my other limbs. My right thigh felt a little strange, and I was achy almost everywhere. My head was pounding, making it hard to think.

"What else?" I asked.

She pulled a rolling chair close to the side of the bed and took my hand in hers.

"Your leg was basically crushed," she said quietly. "You've gone through two surgeries to fix it. The ligaments and tendons around your knee had to be repaired, too. You have a really bad concussion, and Landon said you…you…"

She choked up a little, took a breath, and went on.

"You were shot in the leg. He said it wasn't that bad, but it was infected by the time they found you. They had to give you a skin graft there."

I closed my eyes and focused on my right thigh for a moment. It was itchy, and I figured that was due to the graft; I'd had them before. I recalled a brief flash of the pain from the bullet, and I remembered the snow and ice surrounding me as I tried to clean it up. It had been too cold to leave my flesh exposed long enough to do it properly.

Cold. Ice. Snow.

"Avalanche."

"Right," the woman said with a nod. "You were caught in it."

A slight dizzying sensation overcame me as I remembered tumbling down the mountainside. The pain in my leg throbbed as I recalled the abrupt stop as I hit the rock ledge below. Visions of being trapped and unable to move traipsed along in my head together with images of a little piece of folded paper with a drawing on it.

It all came back to me like a bright and violent flash of lightning as it strikes a tree.

One final tournament in the frozen north. No one but me and a certified hit man left in the game. Certified and certifiable.

Evan Arden.

We had both been covered by the snow and had formed an unprecedented alliance to free ourselves. I had to survive. I didn't care about the money or a fucking trophy. I had to get back to her. To *them.*

"Raine," I whispered.

"I'm here," she said.

"Oh, fuck—Raine!"

Ignoring the tug of the IV needle in my hand, I reached out and brought her to me. I'd done it. I'd lived up to my promise to her. She was here with me, safe and protected again. Somehow, I had gotten out alive and back to the one woman who mattered in my world.

With the help of my key competition.

Did Evan make it? Did he get off that island alive? There was only one way I would ever know, and that was if and when I heard that Franks had been murdered. Assuming Evan made it, how long would he wait before taking action? Days? Weeks? Longer?

Would he even bother to fulfill his promise to me?

I only thought about it for a moment before deciding that yes, he would. Evan Arden was about as fucked up as they get, but I didn't think he was a liar. I also got the idea he was a guy of principle —he'd never back out of a hit. If he did survive, I had no doubt that he would get the job done. I'd just have to be patient.

Not my best attribute.

Raine was crying against my shoulder, and I placed my hand on the back of her head and pressed my lips to her temple.

"I'm all right, babe," I told her. "I got you."

"They said you might not make it," she cried against me. "They said even after the surgery, you might not wake up."

"I'm awake," I said. "I'm going to be fine, Raine. I'm going to be fine."

I had no idea if it was true or not, but I wasn't going to contradict myself. I made it down a fucking mountain with a crushed leg. There was no way I was going to die in a fucking hospital bed.

I held her as long as I could, but my head was aching, and I nearly passed out again. Raine summoned a nurse to tell her I was awake, and the woman checked my pulse, temperature, and the output of the various machines connected to me.

Raine stood to the side, wringing her hands and biting her lip.

"Where's Alex?" I asked.

"With John Paul," Raine replied. "They're in that building where we were staying."

"He's okay?"

"He's great," Raine said. "He and John Paul hit it off. I didn't realize that man was such a child at heart."

I smiled, but it hurt my head.

"Landon?" I asked.

Raine's face scrunched up at the mention of his name.

"He left a little while ago to get something to eat," she said. "He should be back in an hour."

A doctor showed up and checked me over in greater detail. She pulled back the dressing on my thigh, ordered the nurse to add something to my IV, and shined a flashlight in my eyes.

"How does your head feel?" she asked.

"Like shit," I replied.

"Bastian!" Raine snapped.

"Well, it fucking does," I muttered.

"Quite all right," the doctor said. "He's got a few reasons to curse. You might want to consider a safer hobby."

I wasn't sure what she thought my hobby was, but I figured it was best not to say anything else. Raine watched as the doctor finished up my examination and then left. The nurse came back with a bag of something to add to my IV drip, and Raine gave me a little more water.

"You okay?" I asked her.

"I'm fine," she said. "Just worried about you."

"No worries," I told her. "I always bounce back."

Landon appeared in the doorway just as the nurse was finishing up. He stood quietly near the entrance until she was done then asked Raine to give us a few minutes alone. She glared at him without responding but stood from her chair. She leaned over to kiss my forehead and run her hand through my hair.

"I'll be outside," she said sharply. "I'm going to let John Paul and Alex know you're awake."

"Thanks, babe."

Landon moved out of the way as Raine passed, a slight smile on his face. He watched her walk out before shutting the door and coming to sit by my side.

"You look a little better," he remarked. "There was a time I thought I'd have to convince them to give Raine your winnings posthumously."

"Thanks for your vote of confidence."

"You were in bad shape," he said. "You had hypothermia along with your injuries. Bad infection in your leg, too."

"So I hear."

"Prognosis is good, now that you're conscious. Your leg is going to need some physical therapy once it's mended enough, but you should be back to normal in a few months. You gained a few more scars."

"Just additions to the collection," I mused.

"If you are going for a record, I think you might have won."

I had to keep myself from laughing at his comment—moving hurt.

"Did you find Arden's body?" I asked.

Landon shook his head.

"No sign of him," he said. "Considering the depth of the snow, I doubt he'll be uncovered any time soon. We'll just have to wait until global warming takes its toll."

I gave him a half grin, but it hurt to do so.

"I saw him go down," I told him. "The only way I kept from being buried was from hitting a ledge part way down. That's what broke my leg, but it stopped me long enough for the rest of the avalanche to pass over me. He kept going to the bottom."

"Are you sure?"

"Positive." I hoped I sounded convincing.

"Any chance he could have survived?"

"Not as far as I could tell."

Landon took in a breath, filling his lungs deeply before he stood up.

"I'm heading back to Seattle," he announced. "John Paul is arranging for you to be moved to a hospital in Miami. It will take a day or two, but you can finish your recovery from there. You were in a skiing accident in case anyone asks."

"Good to know."

"I'll be in touch." He started for the door.

"Landon?"

He turned back to me.

"I'm done now," I said as I looked straight at him. "No more tournaments. No more favors. This was it."

Landon nodded but didn't look back at me. I had no doubt that he was simply agreeing because he knew it was what I wanted to hear. Evan had been right—there was no way out of this except to eliminate those who had leverage over you.

I have to kill him.

First things first—I was in no shape to go after Landon.

Should have asked Evan to do it.

No, that wasn't right. I needed to take care of Landon. I wanted him to know it was me. I didn't give a shit about Franks—I'd wanted him dead since that night I watched him torture and murder people, Raine's father included. I didn't care how it happened as long as he was gone. Landon was a whole other issue. I was going to get him out of my way once and for all, but I couldn't do that in my current condition. Even at full strength, Landon wouldn't be an easy man to eliminate, but that wasn't going to stop me. I still needed to get myself back into shape before I conquered him.

My plan would wait. At least for now, I'd let myself heal.

Chapter Seventeen

Getting back to normal was a long fucking road.

I spent two weeks in the hospital after I was transported back to Miami. Had it been any other tournament, I would have told the doctors to fuck off and left earlier, but Raine made me promise to do anything they said. Any time I tried to protest, she'd say something about how Alex was going to need me to be able to walk and run so I could teach him to play football or some such shit.

I couldn't really argue with her emotionally charged logic. In fact, I thought about it a lot while I was lying around in the private hospital room, going to physical therapy sessions twice a day, and trying to get around on crutches. I thought about how life just wasn't the same when you had a kid to think about. I loved Raine with every ounce of my being, but Alex…Alex made everything different.

Raine brought him to the hospital a lot while I was recovering. We stuck with the skiing accident story though the way he looked at both of us when we told him gave me the impression he didn't believe a word of it. The kid had been in a mob family for the first six years of his life, so he had probably seen more shit than he should have for a kid his age.

While he visited, he'd color pictures of the three of us or of the *Teenage Mutant Ninja Turtles*. He also kept drawing the same picture over and over again of a house with a big field of rolling hills behind it. He said it was the place we were all going to live someday. All of the pictures ended up taped to the walls of the hospital room so I could see them from the bed.

The more I watched him, the more I wanted to ensure he had the best fucking childhood anyone had ever given a kid. I wanted to make up for not being there when he was younger but also for what he had to go through living with Jillian and her husband. I didn't know the details, but Alex's reaction to his parents' death was so… *calm*. There had to be more to it than he was sharing, but I didn't know what. I just knew he didn't talk about them much at all.

I had no idea how to handle it. I'd never been a father and certainly didn't know shit about child psychology. My only experience was my own fucked up life, and I didn't want his to be anything like that. Everything about Alex's life needed to be the exact opposite of mine. That meant *I* had to change.

I had always been a selfish bastard.

Even when I considered everything I'd done to try to make Raine happy since we returned from our isolation on the island, I'd still been thinking more of myself than her. My focus was on how miserable I was and not on how I needed to be. I was supposed to be her partner in life, but I wasn't. I had been focused on pitying myself and ignoring what she wanted and needed from me. She had put up with it, but it also reminded me of how unworthy I was of her, not because of my past, but because of the present.

As I lay in the bed, I was still being that man from the past. I couldn't think of much of anything except how I was going to get rid of Landon. I also waited for news of Franks, but I was in the dark about everything that had happened after the tournament ended. By the time I was released, I presumed Evan hadn't managed to get off that island after all, or if he had, that he wasn't going to do the job. Thinking about it too much gave me a headache, and I just hoped Evan was waiting for the right time.

Maybe that was the concussion talking.

After I was released, Raine made me keep a huge-ass boot on my leg as it continued to heal. I had physical therapy three times a week until I could walk without it. I spent most of that time researching places to live and plotting Landon's demise.

I hadn't seen him since the hospital in Thompson.

John Paul had traded a few messages back and forth between Landon and me, but he wouldn't come clean as to what Landon or Franks was doing. When Raine headed off to the university, John Paul stopped by and gave me some updates on the outcome of the war in Chicago.

"The Russians have gone back to wherever the hell they came from," he said as he helped himself to a bottle of iced tea from the fridge.

He glared at the beverage, and I knew exactly what he was thinking, but I wasn't keeping beer in the house. He could go fuck himself.

"Get over it," I snapped.

"I didn't say anything," John Paul insisted.

"You were going to tell me about Chicago." I leaned back on the couch and put my leg up on the coffee table. I'd taken the boot off; the damn thing was uncomfortable and itchy. Raine wouldn't be back from meeting with her university advisor about taking online classes for at least another hour. I could put it back on then.

John Paul sat in the chair across from me.

"Greco's organization stepped back and dropped out of the caviar business altogether. They're still at odds with Moretti but in a relatively peaceful way."

"What about Franks?"

"Back in Seattle," John Paul said. "He's taking a big chunk of Moretti's profits from caviar sales, but there hasn't been much grumbling about it. That dude is pissed, though."

"Which dude?"

"The Chicago guy—Moretti."

"About what?"

"Arden."

"What, because he died?" My heart beat wildly in my chest. John Paul had known me way too long. If I showed any signs of hiding something, he was going to sense it and call me out. I had to be very careful about what I said.

"Yeah," John Paul said. He glanced down at his tea bottle and began to peel the label from the glass. "He was a favorite, I guess, like the guy's kid."

"Were they related?"

"I don't think so," John Paul said, "but you know how some of these guys are. Sometimes what they do for each other goes deeper than blood."

I swallowed and nodded. I knew exactly what he meant. The desire to both think and talk about Evan Arden was a dangerous one, so I changed the subject.

"Are you going to tell me where Landon is?"

John Paul shrugged.

"I don't know for sure," he said. "He was going back and forth between Seattle, New York, and Chicago, but I couldn't tell you where he is right now."

"What's his game?" I pressed. "Is he going to lay off me now?"

John Paul looked at me, and his expression turned serious. He thought for a moment before answering.

"For now."

"Bullshit," I muttered.

We didn't discuss the topic any longer, but I knew what I had to do.

"I don't like this," Raine said.

Her eyes were still red from crying. I hated to do things this way, but I didn't have much of a choice. It's not like I could tell her I was jaunting off to kill my father figure.

"I know, babe," I said. "I'm sorry. Hopefully, I won't be gone long."

"Landon is making you do something, isn't he?" she insisted—again.

"He's not," I said. "I'm not saying any more about it. It's just something I have to do."

"What about Alex?"

I reached over and touched the side of her face.

"I know he's in good hands." I bent down and pressed my lips against hers. They were warm and soft, and even if she was mad at me, she didn't push me away. She ran her hand down my arm and held onto my fingers as our lips separated. I stepped backwards slowly, keeping my eyes on hers, until our hands slipped apart.

I wasn't going to say goodbye.

With my backpack secured over my shoulders, I headed down the stairs to the parking garage. The bike was gassed up and ready to go. It was going to be a long ride, but I needed the time to keep my head clear and focused.

The motorcycle roared in the enclosed space, and I pulled out and onto the road. The highway loomed in front of me, and I took one last look back at the condo building before I kicked it up a notch and merged into traffic.

The research took a lot longer than I had hoped. Landon was a man on the move, and tracking him down hadn't been easy. I used disposable phones to talk to Raine and Alex every day but still kept the calls short and ditched the phones right after we were done. She continued to ask me where I was and what I was doing, but I wouldn't tell her.

She just didn't need to know this shit.

I ended my evening call with Raine and got up from the hotel bed. Pushing the curtain aside, I looked out the window with a pair of binoculars. There was another hotel directly opposite mine, and I focused on the window of an eighth floor room. The sheer curtains were drawn but not the blackout curtains. I could still see a figure inside. I'd spent more than enough time in my life watching Landon move, and I had no doubt he was the one on the other side.

If I were a sniper, I could take him out from here.

If I ever saw him again, maybe Evan Arden would teach me. I smirked to myself and shook my head a little. Raine would love that idea.

Focusing the binoculars on Landon's silhouette, I saw him sit down at the desk inside the hotel room. Now was as good a time as any, so I set the binoculars down on the table beside me and pulled a Beretta out of my backpack.

I bought it along the way through a contact I remembered from the games I was in years ago. He was a meth-head, and I was pretty certain he wouldn't remember our encounter five minutes after I left. As far as he was concerned, selling a gun meant more money for drugs, which was all he cared about.

Leaning away from the hotel window, I checked over the weapon, made sure there was a bullet in the chamber, and tucked it away inside a shoulder holster. I took the stairs down to the ground floor and made my way across the street. I waited until the valets were all occupied with customers before slipping inside the building and heading to the front desk.

"Can I help you?"

"Yeah, sorry," I told the clerk at the desk, "I'm an idiot. I lost my key."

"No problem at all, sir," she said. "Your name?"

"Landon Stark."

"Can I see a picture ID, please?"

I handed her a false driver's license that was far more perfectly forged than would ever be needed for a hotel clerk. She checked it briefly before handing me a new key card.

I smiled and thanked her before heading to the stairway. Once I arrived at his floor, I easily found Landon's room in the corner of the building. I took a deep breath, centered myself as much as I could, took the gun out of its holster, and swiped the card. It made a slight beeping sound, and Landon looked up as the door swung open.

Our eyes met, and there was no question in my mind that he knew exactly what I was there to do. He didn't even need to look at the weapon in my hand to understand. The door swung closed behind me, and Landon quickly stood up, reaching toward one of the drawers in the dresser.

"Don't even think about it," I said.

Landon paused and then slowly raised his hands up in the air.

"Whatever's going on in your head," he said, "we can work it out."

"I've already got it worked out," I responded.

"I don't think you've considered the consequences." Landon's voice was calm, and his face was expressionless. He was likely thinking I was acting on impulse as opposed to how much time I'd been thinking about how all this had to end.

"It's the only choice you guys left me with," I said. "I'm done with this—all of it. I want to move on. I want a different life. As long as you hold the past over my head, I can't do that, and you're always going to want me under your thumb. There's only one solution."

I slid my finger up against the trigger and held the Beretta level with Landon's head.

"You don't want to do that."

"The fuck I don't."

Landon's eyes didn't change but remained filled with their usual clear and focused determination. His chest rose and fell once with his breath.

"You want to kill me, yes, sure," he agreed, "but if you do, you'll never figure it out."

"Figure what out?"

"How to do it," he replied.

I raised an eyebrow and pulled the hammer back with a click. Landon responded with a smirk.

"You can't live like this. You want to go back to that deserted little island and play native, but she can't live like that. You have no fucking clue what to do about it, but I do."

I stared at him until I was sure he wasn't giving me a line of bullshit. It didn't take long—Landon wasn't one to make shit up just to save his life. Whatever he had in mind, it was something he'd thought about, weighed all of the pros and cons, and determined the best possible course.

"Spill it," I said. "If it makes sense, maybe I don't need to pull the trigger."

"I'm not stupid, Sebastian."

"But you are on the wrong end of the barrel this time."

For a moment, I saw a flash in his eyes. I wasn't sure if it was anger or fear, but it was a show of emotion. Weakness.

"Time's up," I told him.

"The Everglades," he said bluntly.

"What about them?" I asked as I narrowed my eyes.

"Lots of little hammocks where you could build a decent shelter," he responded with a shrug. "Plenty of birds and fish, lots of edible plants around. You gotta watch out for gators, but I think you can manage that. Twenty minutes to Miami, so she's got her civilization. Even if she doesn't want to live in a fucking tiki hut, I bet she'd be willing to stay there on the weekends. The rest of the time, she can hang out in that condo of yours."

As he talked, I could see it all forming in my head: a little shelter with a grass roof, a fire pit off to one side to cook and boil water, and Raine curled up next to me while the spring rain falls around us. I could teach Alex all about the plants and animals, and Raine would make sure he learned about conservation of the ecosystem. I could use a kayak or even an airboat to get to a place where a car could be parked, ready to take them both back to Miami any time they wanted to go there. I could even go with her as long as it wasn't for too long or anything. I could wait in the fucking car for all I cared.

Part of me wanted that. A lot.

Landon's vision made sense for the man he knew, for the man I used to be. This was just the sort of thing I would have desired. It would keep me away from people, which I didn't care for, but still let me have access to Raine and Alex whenever I wanted to see them.

But it wasn't about me. Not anymore.

Alex needed a father—someone who was there with him all the time—and not the shit kind of relationships I'd had as a kid with part-time foster parents and counselors in group homes. He needed me to be there for him every day.

Raine did, too.

I didn't need to isolate myself from the rest of the world. I just needed to be Alex's father and Raine's…Raine's…

Shit.

I knew what I needed to do.

It all clicked inside my head. The flash in my mind was as brilliant as the flash from the gun would have been had I decided to pull the trigger, but I didn't need to. Franks and Landon were completely irrelevant.

"Yeah," I said quietly. "I know what to do now."

"And I can keep everyone else away from you," Landon said.

I looked back to him. There was nervous sweat covering his forehead—something I'd never seen before.

"Don't bother," I said as I lowered the gun. "I don't need you to. I'm done with you and Franks. You're never going to contact me again—either of you. This isn't a request or a threat; it's simply the way it's going to be. Do we understand each other?"

Landon nodded as he lowered his hands.

"The two of you forget I ever existed," I said. "No one else gives a shit about me or what I do."

We stared at each other for a long time. He looked like he was going to say something else but just nodded again instead. As he did, I saw the one thing I never expected to see on his face—defeat.

It was…*satisfying.*

I kept the gun in my hand and my eyes on Landon as I backed up to the door and opened it. There was always the possibility he would shoot me in the back as I left though I didn't think he would.

Not at this point.

He spoke just before I maneuvered myself into the hallway.

"I still give a shit about you," Landon said in a gruff voice. "I always did."

I stared at him, refusing to alter my expression even though it felt like his words were ripping me up inside. I'd always known it, but he'd never said it before. It was too late now. I was no longer the lonely, fucked up, futureless kid he'd found in the streets and trained to be a killer. I had moved on.

"Goodbye, Landon."

He nodded once, and I walked out of the hotel room.

I never saw him again.

<hr />

Staring at a computer screen aggravated the hell out of my headache. I was actually considering getting some fucking reading glasses or something. I wasn't sure how Raine managed to do it all the time for school.

I glanced down at the list Raine and I had made with a little input from Alex of all the things we wanted in a house. I was anxious to get the whole process over and done with before I lost my fucking mind.

I needed everything to be just right before I did what I had to do next.

Focus.

Using an online app, I poked around at the houses brought up with the search criteria I had entered. There were a lot of nice ones, but nothing seemed exactly right. There was always something major missing from our list of "must haves" that made me pass over the listings.

I glanced up at Alex. He was kneeling next to the coffee table with crayons all over the place, drawing another picture of a house. It was always the same—a little cottage with two windows and a door in the front, and rolling hills behind it. This time, he was adding a bunch of trees to the picture and had even included a big, red bird sitting on a branch.

I looked back at the list of criteria I'd added to the paper and then to the computer screen.

Selfish bastard.

I deleted one of the items from the list, and a whole new group of houses popped up on the screen. Even though I felt like I was starting over, I did it with vigor. My mind was made up, and I wasn't going to let my own neuroses stop us from finding a place to live. I flipped through a couple dozen places that still didn't seem quite right, but I kept going. I was as determined as I had been to get down that frozen mountainside.

Then I saw it.

It was fucking perfect.

Rolling hills and everything.

It wasn't exactly like Alex's picture, of course, but the outside of the house I was staring at still had a cottage-like feel to it. The picture must have been taken in the spring because there were flowering trees in the front and daffodils all around in the flower beds. The website said it had four bedrooms and three bathrooms, which was more than enough for us. There was even a finished basement and a swing set in the back.

"Hey, Alex," I said.

"Hmm?" He didn't even look up from his picture.

"Take a look at this, and tell me what you think."

He let out a dramatic sigh but placed his crayon down and hauled himself up from the floor. He walked around the coffee table three times before I told him to cut it out, and he plopped down in my lap to look at the computer.

"What do you think of this house?" I asked.

Alex studied it for a minute and had me go through some of the pictures of the house's interior.

"That one," he said as the website displayed a picture of one of the bedrooms. It was painted light green and had a wide strip of wallpaper full of spaceships running around the top of the wall.

"That one what?" I asked.

"That's my room."

"It is?"

"Yep."

I smiled.

"Okay, then."

Alex rolled off my lap and went back to his crayons. He picked up a brown one and started adding a swing set to the drawing.

Raine returned an hour later with carry-out in her hands.

"I didn't feel like cooking," she said as she walked in.

"I could have made dinner," I said. The vast majority of what we could get for carry-out around here was full of fat and carbs. There were very few cuisines I would put up with except for…

"It's Thai," she replied with a wide grin and raised eyebrows.

"Did you get me a tofu tower?" Alex piped up.

"I did."

"With peanut sauce?"

"Yep."

"Sweet!" He jumped up from his spot on the floor and raced to the table.

"Hey, Raine?"

"Yes?" she asked as she started taking red and white containers out of a plastic bag. She arranged them on the table as Alex grabbed each box to open and sniff at it.

"This one's Dad's!" he announced as he wrinkled his nose and shoved the container to the other side of the table.

"Could you come take a look at something?" I asked.

"Just a sec," she replied. She grabbed some juice out of the refrigerator and poured Alex a glass before joining me on the couch.

Nervously, I handed the laptop over to Raine. She peered down at the screen, and creases appeared on her forehead.

"What do you think?" I asked. I didn't know why I was so nervous.

Raine flipped through the online pictures one at a time. I could practically hear her checking off little boxes in her head as she went through the details of the listing.

"What school district?" she asked.

I pointed to the screen where it was listed, and Raine nodded.

"That was my top choice for Alex."

"I know."

"What about public transportation?" she asked.

"There really isn't any," I said. "It's a small community—you can practically walk anywhere you want to go. The elementary school is just four blocks away. I figured I could walk Alex to and from school, and when he gets older, there's the school bus for the middle school and high school."

Raine nodded again and turned her eyes to me.

"But it's nowhere near a beach."

I swallowed.

"Yeah," I said, "I know."

"That is your number one item," she reminded me.

"No," I said softly, "it's not. You and Alex are number one."

Raine looked at me, set the laptop down on the coffee table next to Alex's drawing, and reached over to hug me.

"I love you," she whispered into my ear.

The choice was made. At least for now, we knew our direction.

Chapter Eighteen – Epilogue

"Did you hear?" John Paul said as he sat down. Before he could explain any further, the server asked him for his drink order.

"Hear what?" I asked after the server jotted down his request on her notepad and walked away.

"About Franks." John Paul shoved a handful of my chips into his mouth.

"What the fuck are you talking about?"

"He's dead," he said as bits of tortilla chips crumbled into his beard. He wiped them away and swallowed. "Somebody put a hit out on him, and he was taken out last night. Single bullet to the head."

"No shit?"

"No shit."

I looked down at the iced tea in my hand and tried to keep my expression blank. If there was anyone I could have confided in, it probably would have been John Paul, but I wasn't going to risk it. He would never say anything to the organization about me, but that wouldn't stop him from ratting out Evan, and I wasn't about to risk anyone finding out he was still alive.

I owed that guy. Big time.

"There's more," John Paul said. His eyes darkened as he leaned closer to me.

"What?" I asked.

"Hey there!" John Paul sat back quickly as Raine burst around the corner of the booth and slid in beside me. "Sorry I'm late. My professor wanted to chat after class, and I missed the early bus."

"I would have picked you up," I said.

"Aren't you on the bike?"

"You can ride bitch," I said with a grin.

"No, thanks," Raine replied. "You drive like a maniac."

John Paul laughed out loud and picked up the beer the server had delivered.

"You should see him ride when you aren't around," he said under his breath.

"Shut up, fucker," I snapped.

Raine turned toward me and raised an eyebrow.

"Sorry," I muttered. I'd been trying to keep the cursing to a minimum with Alex around all the time, but as soon as I got around John Paul, the cuss words just seemed to start flying.

"Everything packed?" she asked.

"Pretty much," I replied. "Lindsay was finishing the shit in the kitchen when I left. There are a few of Alex's toys still not in a box, but he claimed he was still playing with them. I figured we could just throw them in his backpack when it's time to go."

"What about your stuff?"

"All ready," I said. I really didn't have much, which was fine with me. It all fit in one suitcase and a box. I didn't count all the household stuff as mine. It always felt like Raine's to me.

Lindsay and Nick showed up right behind Raine.

"Alex hates the sitter," Lindsay announced immediately.

The hair on the back of my neck stood up, and I felt the muscles down my arms clench.

"Why?" I demanded.

Lindsay laughed.

"Just kidding!" she said. "I think he's in love. He was drawing pictures of her when I left."

I relaxed a little, but Lindsay's idea of a joke made me want to punch her in the face. Her little sister, Laura, was visiting from Ohio and had volunteered to babysit so we could all go out. I hadn't been happy about the idea of some chick I didn't know watching my kid, but Raine knew her from when they were kids, so I'd given in, but I wasn't happy about it.

"Don't goad him!" Raine snapped at her friend. "That was just rude, and you know it!"

"Stop that shit," Nick scolded his girlfriend under his breath. "What's wrong with you?"

John Paul snickered behind his beer bottle.

"Sorry," Lindsay said.

She seemed to mean it.

I took a deep breath and looked at Raine as she reached over to put her hand on my leg. Part of my trying to be civilized around her friends involved her sticking up for me a lot. I didn't like it, but it was probably better than having me react with any of my violent tendencies.

We ordered, and everyone started with the small talk as we waited for our food. I still sucked at small talk, but I was getting better at sitting back and pretending I was interested. I'd already lived through two evenings with Lindsay and Nick without biting their heads off. This would make it three, and I planned on surviving the encounter.

I made it all the way through the meal. I even talked to Nick a bit about his latest escapades as a flight instructor. I couldn't have cared less, but every time I talked nicely to him, it made Raine smile.

"So who's up for a club?" Lindsay asked as she looked over the dessert menu.

The last thing I wanted was to go to some bar, even if I was trying to prove that I could do all the things Raine wanted to do and still keep my cool. I did have my limits, but I didn't have to voice them.

"I really need to finish my packing," Raine stated. "I'm sure Laura would like to join you though."

Thank you, Raine.

We paid the bill and headed outside to part ways. Before we could, John Paul called me over for a cigarette. Raine rolled her eyes, but she was happy enough to chat with Lindsay and Nick a little longer before we headed back to the condo.

"We got interrupted."

"Yeah," I said as I lit my smoke, "what were you going to

say?"

"It's about Landon."

"What about him?"

"Well, he is basically the next logical dude in succession after Franks," John Paul said. "The thing is, they'd been arguing— arguing a *lot*. People knew about it, and now everyone's convinced he put out the hit on Franks."

"Fuck," I muttered under my breath. "What's he going to do?"

"It sounds like he's made a run for it," John Paul said. "No one's seen him since this morning when Moretti made the accusation."

I considered the information for a moment. Normally, I would have thought Landon was too difficult to track, and he'd never be found by anyone. However, I had found him, and I wasn't a bounty hunter. If I could trace him, maybe someone else could, too.

My thoughts shifted to Evan Arden. If anyone could find and locate Landon, it would be him, but he was dead as far as Moretti was concerned.

Wasn't he?

Would he have gone against everything he seemed to believe and contact Moretti to let him know he had survived? Had he even gone as far as to tell him about the hit on Franks and to plan to blame it on Landon the whole time? Just how devious was this guy?

I had no idea.

The whole line of thinking made me uncomfortable, and John Paul was giving me a bit of a look, so I swallowed and focused my thoughts elsewhere.

"Landon could be in trouble," I said.

"I know," John Paul agreed. "That's why I'm leaving. Tonight."

"I'm not getting involved," I stated. "No fucking way."

"Not asking you to, bro," he said. "I just wanted you to know."

"I appreciate it."

We shook hands, and John Paul walked off toward his car as I rejoined Raine and her friends.

<hr/>

Lindsay decided to stick around for a bit and keep Alex

occupied so Raine and I could finish the packing. The whole condo was a fucking disaster of boxes. I didn't know how we had managed to accumulate so much shit in the brief time we'd lived here, but I was sure it wasn't mine. I blamed Lindsay and the effect her addictive shopping habits had on Raine.

They had both bought a shit ton of stuff for Alex, too. The kid had more toys than he knew what to do with, and all he cared about was drawing and playing with any kind of blocks you put in front of him. He was either going to end up in art school or engineering school.

I made sure Alex and Lindsay were occupied with a movie on Disney before I snuck off to the bedroom. Raine's ass was sticking out of the closet and making me want to grab on to it for a little ride. I didn't though.

Focus.

I took a deep breath, but it didn't help. My hands were shaking a little, and I rubbed them against my thighs to try to make them stop. Maybe I wasn't ready for this. Maybe I should just wait until we were all moved in to the new place. Right now, it was too easy for her to grab her stuff and take off if I fucked this up.

She wouldn't do that.

I couldn't quite convince myself.

Just fucking do it, you pussy.

"Hey, Raine?" I called softly, almost wishing she wouldn't hear me at all.

"Yes?" She pulled her head out of the closet and looked at me expectantly. When I didn't answer right away, she narrowed her eyes a little. "What is it?"

"I was just...um..." I looked toward the balcony door and tried to come up with the right words.

"What, Bastian?" Raine dropped a couple items from the closet into her suitcase and came to my side.

I ran my hand over my face.

Just fucking say it.

"I was wondering if...if maybe...shit."

Raine placed her hand on my arm, and I realized it was shaking as much as my hands.

"Bastian, what's the matter?"

I closed my eyes again. I could do this. I was sure I could. I just needed my mouth to fucking work for once. I needed to say the right words in the right way, but all I did was babble.

"I just thought maybe with Alex and all and starting a new life in a new place…" I continued to stammer, trying to find something in my head that didn't make me sound like a total idiot. With another deep breath, I fell back to the only way I'd ever managed to express myself without getting into trouble.

The Bard's words were far better than my own.
"Might I not then say, 'Now I love you best,'
When I was certain o'er incertainty,
Crowning the present, doubting of the rest?
Love is a babe, then might I not say so,
To give full growth to that which still doth grow?"

I looked to the floor, took a deep breath, and then stared into her eyes. I pulled a little box from my pocket and laid it in my palm before I opened it. The shining, simple solitaire ring in the center of the velvet sparkled in the bursting Miami sun.

"Raine, will you marry me?"

Raine said nothing for the longest fucking time. There was sweat dripping between my shoulder blades, and the gleam from the ring was refracting rainbows all over the walls as my hand continued to shake. I realized I'd totally forgotten to get down on one knee, and mentally smacked myself for fucking up the easiest part of all of this.

I glanced from the ring to Raine's face. Her eyes brimmed with tears, and my heart stopped. For a brief moment, my world ended as I waited for her to deny me.

"Yes, Bastian," she whispered as the tears overflowed. "Yes, of course. Of course I'll marry you."

A huge breath escaped me, and I couldn't stop myself from grabbing her and picking her up to hold her to my chest. I buried my face in her hair and tried to pretend all the tears belonged to her alone.

"Thank you," I whispered against her ear. "Thank you so fucking much, Raine…thank you."

"Oh, Bastian." She tightened her arms around my neck and wrapped her legs around my waist. "I love you so much—so, so much!"

"I love you," I replied, "more than fucking anything."

I squeezed her to me again, and the shaking in my hands and arms finally stopped as I held her. Figuring I was probably keeping her from breathing, I relaxed my grip and set her down. I reached up and wiped the tears from her face.

"Do I get to put that on?" Raine asked with a smile. She pointed down at the ring still in my hand.

"Shit! Yeah...I forgot." I grabbed the ring out of the little box and took Raine's offered hand. With a deep breath, I slid it up and over the ring finger of her left hand.

It looked fucking perfect.

"What are you doing?" Alex asked as he came into the room. He narrowed his eyes at Raine's outstretched hand. "What's that?"

"An engagement ring," Raine said. "Your dad and I are going to be married."

Alex furrowed his brow and looked back and forth between us.

"Will you be my mom then?" he asked.

Raine smiled.

"If you want me to be."

Alex considered this for a moment.

"Okay," he said with a shrug. "Can we have macaroni and cheese for dinner? Lindsay said I had to ask first."

Raine bit her lip as she stifled a laugh.

"You know that stuff is nasty," I said.

"It's good!" Alex insisted.

Raine elbowed me in the ribs.

"Fine," I said, "but you have to have vegetables with it."

"Ugh!" Alex looked up at the ceiling and spread his arms out wide. "Why?"

"Because if you don't, no macaroni."

"Ugh!" he cried again. "Does it have to be green?"

"Yep," I replied with a half-smile.

"Not broccoli!"

"Green beans?" Raine suggested.

Alex slumped his shoulders and let out a ridiculously long sigh.

"Fine," he muttered as he turned and ran off to the kitchen, yelling at Lindsay. "Dad said yes!"

Raine was shaking with silent laughter.

"He's a lot like you," she said.

"I don't eat that shit."

"I mean the way he acts when he doesn't get what he wants."

"It's a good thing you said yes, then." I smiled and pressed my lips to hers.

Raine curled up beside me and kissed my shoulder as she trailed her fingers across my chest and down my abs, and my cock responded. Her eyes glanced up at me, and her tongue darted over her lips.

"Got something for me?" she asked with a sly smile before her hand dropped lower. She stroked slowly down my shaft to my balls and then made her way back up again. I turned my head and brought her face to mine, kissing her deeply as she kept running the tips of her fingers over my dick. I moaned into her mouth, and her tongue traced over my lips.

She pulled back, released my cock, and swung one leg over my hips. Placing her hands on my chest, she rubbed herself up and down my cock slowly.

"Oh fuck, baby," I groaned. "You're driving me crazy."

"Good," she replied. "That's exactly what I wanted."

"Anything you want," I said. "It's yours. Just keep doing that."

"Is that all you want?" she asked with a sly smile. "You are easy to please."

"Tease," I mumbled. I tilted my hips up and ground against her.

"I don't think you can call me that when I'm naked and on top of you," she said.

"I can when I'm not buried inside that quivering vagina of yours."

"Quivering vagina?" Raine started laughing, and I grinned up at her like the love-struck idiot I was.

"You know," I said, "the one hiding in your moist triangle of curls."

"Way to set the mood!" She rolled her eyes at me.

"Set the mood for my purple helmeted warrior? He's just dying to fight his way through your underbrush."

"That's it," she said as she started to get off of me.

I grabbed her wrists and held her in place. She laughed as she struggled, and I pulled her down to me and tickled her sides, which just made her laugh harder.

"Shhh," I whispered, "you'll wake Alex."

She covered her mouth with one hand as she tried to gain a bit of control.

"Where do you come up with that stuff?" she asked.

"I used to watch a lot of porn," I admitted. "Oh, and I got Penthouse—you know, for the articles."

More eye-rolling. I responded by pulling her back down on my cock. Raine groaned and moved her hips in time with mine. I found her throat with my mouth and tongue, tasting her flesh as my hand came up to cup her breast and pull at the nipple.

"Oh, God...Bastian..."

"Shh..."

She bit down on her lip and closed her eyes. I couldn't wait any longer, so I sat up and rolled her on her back. Stroking down her side, I stopped at her thigh and lifted it up over my hip before I slid into her.

Our sounds were rhythmic, like ocean surf rolling over smooth sands after a summer storm. We moved slowly, purposefully, completely calm in our love for each other. Raine's head tilted back and her mouth opened slightly. I counted every breath she took, timing them with my own.

With an increased pace, I moved inside of her. Raine twisted her legs around mine and gripped my arms tightly. She lifted her hips as her face contorted, and she gritted her teeth to keep from crying out loud. The sight was more than I could stand, and I followed her lead with a blissful groan.

My heart continued to race as I held myself deep inside of her and tried to make mental contact with any part of my body. It all seemed to be in some sort of post orgasmic shock, though, and kept insisting my legs were no longer attached to the rest of me.

With a final shudder, I kissed her lightly on the temple and rolled onto my back, exhausted. My leg throbbed, which it often did after overuse, but I ignored it. It was my final tournament injury—the last scar to leave its mark on my body and soul.

"I love you," Raine said softly as she curled up against me and planted kisses on my shoulder.

I turned my head to look at her. Her hair was a mess all over her head and around her shoulders, and her makeup was smeared under her eyes. There were splotchy red marks all over her face from our tryst—the most beautiful sight in the world.

She was my drink—the only one I would ever want again.

I touched the tip of my finger to her cheek and stroked slowly downward.

"And on that cheek, and o'er that brow,
So soft, so calm, yet eloquent,
The smiles that win, the tints that glow,
But tell of days in goodness spent,
A mind at peace with all below,
A heart whose love is innocent!"

I took her face between my palms and stared into her beautiful eyes. I emphasized every word I said so she would know how much I meant it.

"You are my world."

"You are incredible," Raine responded. "You are everything I have ever wanted."

For the first time since we met, I truly believed her.

My life was balanced. From this point forward, I'd be the man she always believed I could be.

The End

POETRY CREDITS

Othello —William Shakespeare

"Sonnet 115"—William Shakespeare

She Walks in Beauty—Lord Byron

OTHER TITLES BY SHAY SAVAGE

THE EVAN ARDEN TRILOGY

OTHERWISE ALONE - EVAN ARDEN #1
OTHERWISE OCCUPIED - EVAN ARDEN #2
UNCOCKBLOCKABLE - EVAN ARDEN #2.5
OTHERWISE UNHARMED - EVAN ARDEN #3

SURVIVING RAINE SERIES

SURVIVING RAINE - #1
BASTIAN'S STORM #2

STANDALONE TITLES

WORTH
TRANSCENDENCE

ABOUT THE AUTHOR

Always looking for a storyline and characters who fall outside the norm, Shay Savage's tales have a habit of evoking some extreme emotions from fans. She prides herself on plots that are unpredictable and loves to hear it when a story doesn't take the path assumed by her readers. With a strong interest in psychology, Shay loves to delve into the dark recesses of her character's brains–and there is definitely some darkness to be found! Though the journey is often bumpy, if you can hang on long enough you won't regret the ride. You may not always like the characters or the things they do, but you'll certainly understand them.

Shay Savage lives in Ohio with her husband and two children. She's an avid soccer fan, loves vacationing near the ocean, enjoys science fiction in all forms, and absolutely adores all of the encouragement she has received from those who have enjoyed her work.

Made in the USA
Charleston, SC
07 June 2014